S0-ACV-485

Praise for
UP JUMPED THE DEVIL

"A KEEPER AND AN INSPIRATION."
San Antonio Express-News

"A VERY GOOD READ . . .
A mystery written with wry humor and a sense of
social awareness. Walker's style brings to mind
the works of Chester Himes."
Louisville Courier-Journal

"WITH A DISTINCT AND SOULFUL VOICE,
Blair Walker has woven an intricate web of
drama, conspiracy and homeboy humor
into this gem of a book."
Keith T. Clinkscales, President & CEO, *Vibe* Magazine

"FULL OF RAUCOUS GOOD HUMOR,
TRAGEDY, SUSPENSE,
flashy bad guys and flashier ladies,
and one brave, big-hearted, upstanding,
larger-than-life hero, Walker's debut mystery
makes fine entertainment."
Booklist

"HUMOR . . . EXCITEMENT . . .
A debut that promises more good things to come."
Washington Times

"BLAIR WALKER HAS CREATED A CHARACTER
WORTHY OF A LONG SECOND CAREER."
David Simon, author of *Homicide*

Other Books by
Blair S. Walker
Coming Soon from Avon Twilight

Hidden in Plain View

UP JUMPED THE DEVIL

A MYSTERY

BLAIR S. WALKER

AVON
TWILIGHT

AVON BOOKS, INC.
1350 Avenue of the Americas
New York, New York 10019

Copyright © 1997 by Blair S. Walker
Excerpt from *Hidden in Plain View* copyright © 1999 by Blair S. Walker
Author photo by Hillery Smith
Visit our website at **http://www.AvonBooks.com/Twilight**
Library of Congress Catalog Card Number: 97-3155
ISBN: 0-380-79025-4

First Avon Twilight Printing: February 1999
First Avon Books Hardcover Printing: October 1997

AVON TWILIGHT TRADEMARK REG. U.S. PAT. OFF. AND IN OTHER COUNTRIES, MARCA REGISTRADA, HECHO EN U.S.A.

Printed in the U.S.A.

WCD   10 9 8 7 6 5 4 3 2

This book is dedicated to
Robert F. Blair and Samuel C. Walker,
my grandfathers.
Men who invariably stood tall.

ACKNOWLEDGMENTS

Time for a reality check. This novel isn't "all about Blair," even though my name and likeness are on this bad boy. A good many individuals, living and departed, helped me get this project over the finish line.

Long before I had a pot to . . . my wife Felicia was in my corner. Thank you for your love and support, which includes dealing with that zombie who occasionally logs on to my computer and writes the night away (who is that guy, anyway?).

Before Darryl Billups made it into print, you gave homeboy a thorough going over, as did my parents, Dolores Pierre and James Walker, my sisters, Rhonda Walker and Angela Walker-Campbell, and dear friends Kim and Deborah Moir, Juanita James and Jessica Kaye. Thank you all.

To my agent, Faith Childs, what can I say? If there's ever a war where the combatants get to choose comrades, I want your foxhole beside mine. You're tough, smart, funny, and into nurturing authors' careers.

To Lou Aronica and Carrie Feron at Avon Books, thank you for believing in me.

Up Jumped the Devil came about because I was able to stand on the shoulders of giants with names like Langston Hughes, Zora Neale Hurston, and Richard Wright.

But ultimately it was made possible by the Creator, from whom all blessings flow.

UP JUMPED THE DEVIL

A MYSTERY

ONE

THE DUMBSTRUCK FACES OF THE BLACK MEN AND WOMEN trapped in the disintegrating NAACP building were what Mark Dillard recalled most vividly about *the dream*. That and the voluptuous woman in the tattered green dress whose breasts jiggled like Jell-O as she fell slow-motion to her death.

"Serves you right, stupid nigger bitch. Serves you right," Dillard muttered.

Groping under his bed for a smoke, he brushed his callused hand against a gritty work boot, a size 32B WonderBra and a rubber whose ninety seconds of glory had come and gone.

"Shit."

Dillard snapped the bedsheet off and sat upright in one athletic movement. His woman, under the influence of a marijuana/scotch sedative, never altered her light, rhythmic snoring.

A pastel Baltimore dawn gleamed faintly through the bedroom window as Dillard got down on all fours. Naked as a jaybird, straining to see in the semidarkness, he could barely make out the outline of a cigarette pack.

Last night marked the third time in a week the dream had rattled around inside Dillard's head. It never varied in detail, from the shock wave of superheated gases peeling away the

1

front of the NAACP's national headquarters, to Dillard's dispassionate gawking.

Judging from his cool reaction, he knew he would be up to the task. D-Day was inexorably approaching, in fact, although not fast enough for Dillard.

It never occurred to him that the dream always unfolded silently, without the cataclysmic thunderclap of the bomb or the otherworldly groans of the wounded and dying.

All that mattered was that he was locked on the target.

Placing a Camel between his lips, Dillard struck a match and sat motionless, mesmerized by the quivering flame. Yellowish white at the top, indigo at the bottom, it danced a lively minuet dictated by the subtlest change in air currents. It amazed Dillard that something so small and seemingly benign could unleash such incredible destructive power.

Thank God for little miracles.

Two

Chomping an antacid into what must be microscopic flecks, Sergeant Roland Stevens is wearing that constipated-looking scowl again. His full lips are downturned and his narrow-set eyes are unblinking black lasers set between ridges of blubbery, perspiring flesh.

Warning signs I need to limit contact, because Stevens is obviously having a day dipped in shit. On days when he acts like an ornery, menopausal bastard, that needlessly complicates my task at Baltimore police headquarters.

Which is to banter briefly with the desk sergeant, leaf through the police reports for stories to put in the *Baltimore Herald*, then leave.

My name is Darryl Billups and I've been the *Herald*'s cop reporter for the past five years. Visits to police headquarters are a pain, an unavoidable one.

"How about them Os last night? Check out the game on the tube?"

Stevens emits a porcine grunt and rudely shoves a stack of reports across his desk. Obviously the excrement has been rolling downhill prior to my arrival and thoroughly buried one of Baltimore's finest.

Not particularly anxious to make small talk anyway, I scoop up the reports from Stevens's paper-strewn work area. A half-eaten cheese steak sandwich wrapped in oily deli paper serves as a paperweight. Like a fearsome Rottweiler, a picture of Stevens's butt-ugly, no-neck wife guards the telephone. And scattered everywhere are white antacid crumbs. Must really be a day from hell.

For some inexplicable reason I feel a pang of sympathy for Stevens. He, on the other hand, is probably visualizing me in a holding cell, doing the lambada with Bubba. I make up my mind to get a smile out of Stevens. Desk sergeants can sometimes steer you toward little gems.

"Looks like you're having a rough one. Need me to go upstairs and straighten out the commish?"

Stevens sighs and straightens in his chair slightly, the boulderlike chip on his shoulder beginning to crumble. The hardness leaves his face and he shoots me a wan smile containing more resignation than mirth. I'll bet it's the first time today anyone's shown a personal interest.

"Just the usual B.S.," Stevens says. "Just the usual B.S. If you hang around about fifteen minutes, we're finishing a report you might find interesting."

Bingo.

Mama always said it pays to be nice to people.

"You're sure you don't want me to tighten up the commish, now?" I say, putting on my most menacing expression. "I'll put his sorry ass on the front page—you just say the word."

Stevens laughs out loud, this time with genuine humor. "I got it under control, Darryl. Just a lieutenant with a wild hair up his butt."

"Huummppph. I'll stack him up against an editor with a wild hair any day."

People think graceful writing and a nose for news are what make good reporters. They do, but so does knowing when to be confrontational and when to stroke. I've got those skills down, in my humble estimation.

"What the hell you starin' at?" Stevens growls at someone behind me, back in mean mode that fast. I turn to see a petite white woman in her early twenties who looks like she's struggling to recall my name. Wearing suggestively tight black satin pants and a frilly blue blouse, she holds a pair of black high heels. The woman is wobbling so precariously that if a mouse farted she'd go sprawling.

Taking a few teetering steps in my direction, she crooks her index finger. She looks me dead in the eye and makes an exaggerated come-hither gesture. I could just die.

Stevens's colleagues, slow-moving cadavers up to that point, instantly come to life. They fill the air with whistles, taunts and catcalls. "It's the *Herald* Whoremonger," some wit yells out.

Arching my eyebrows, I turn and look at Stevens.

"Get your narrow ass outta here, missy, 'less you wanna go back to the lockup," he booms. "You're out on recognizance, so git!"

Unfazed, the woman gives me one last gaze, then flicks her medium-length mouse-brown hair over her shoulder. Moving with a slowness born of intoxication or defiance—or both—she takes her pigeon-toed time strolling to the lobby. Flinging open a set of double doors and causing everyone in the lobby to stop in his tracks, she wobbles out. She sure knows how to make an exit, that's for sure.

I turn to face Stevens, who wears a leering smirk.

"Been hangin' out on The Block, huh, Darryl?"

"Cut me some slack, Sarge. I've never seen that woman in my life—I don't have a clue what that was all about."

"Heh, heh, heh. Uh-huh. Banging poor-white-trash hookers these days?"

That last comment has a mean, goading edge to it I don't appreciate. Even if that preposterous notion were true, it's none of his goddamn business. Anyway, it's my job to ask the questions.

"You see right through me, don't you, Sarge?" I say, masking my irritation. "Where's that Pulitzer-winning story?"

On cue, a sad-sack patrolman shuffles up to Stevens's desk and lays down a tan manila folder as though it were fragile china. The patrolman shuffles away, eyes locked on a black-and-white wall clock.

Stevens casually scans a two-page report inside the folder before handing it to me with a flourish.

It's not that big a deal, not from a news standpoint anyway. Phil Curry, the owner of Curry BMW, was charged with assault during an argument with his wife. Definitely not Pulitzer material. But the *Herald*'s editors are hot for spouse-abuse stuff, this being the post-O.J. era. Anyway, it's a cut above the robberies, homicides and auto accidents I usually dredge out of police headquarters.

"Thanks for the tip, Sarge."

Writing hurriedly in my scribble-scrabble, makeshift shorthand, I jot the information in my notepad.

Skimming the rest of the police reports, I see where the general manager of a black AM station got busted frolicking with a prostitute. I copy that info, lay the reports back on Stevens's desk and head toward the door.

"Look out, Baltimore, the *Herald* Whoremonger is about to hit the streets," a voice sings out, followed by uproarious laughter. I smile, aware the teasing means I'm well regarded.

She's waiting for me as soon as I walk out the door, into a humid summer night that smells of creosote. Smiling like we're long-lost lovers, the hooker still holds one of her high heels and is crouched over the sidewalk in a baseball catcher's squat. She leans at a ridiculous angle against a brick wall. Her eyes appear unfocused, although she sure doesn't have a problem recognizing me. Her unlined face exudes youthfulness and is free of scars or bruises, making it a safe bet she's new to the world's oldest profession.

As was the case inside, she starts crooking that damn index finger again. That's always been a pet peeve of mine—you waggle your fingers at small children. And dogs. But definitely not at me. And why does she assume I'm interested in anything she has to say?

Anticipating a bum's rush, or an offer to contract every venereal disease known to man, I'm all set to rebuff her and keep moving. I couldn't be more off target.

"You a reporter, right, hon?"

Why did that catch me off guard? I'm lugging around a

notepad and a microcassette recorder plain as day. Maybe because she seems barely cognitive.

"Yes, ma'am, you got it. What's up?"

"You ain't gonna stick me in the paper, is you?" She lurches in my direction and stumbles, scraping her head on the wall and tumbling on her elbows and knees. I wince, curious why Miss Thang is damn near killing herself. Plus, I'm concerned some chivalrous cop will come bounding upon the scene and automatically assume a dastardly black pimp needs to be taught a lesson.

"Don't hurt yourself, Miss . . ."

"Vicky. Don't put me in no newspaper, pleeease," she wails, the words slurred and vicious. "My man don't know nuthin' and he'll kill me if he finds out I been with a black man."

Instead of being offended, I struggle not to burst out laughing. Which is worse: her man discovering his squeeze is a two-bit ho', or that his swatch of heaven is berthing big black *Polaris* subs? Dive, dive! Mr. Charlie's chocolate nightmare come to horrifying life.

"Seriously, what do you want from me?" I ask, chuckling and flipping through my notes on the black radio-station executive. A quick glance shows the prostitute arrested in his car was Victoria Ambrose.

"Your last name isn't Ambrose, is it?"

Her face blanches, followed a millisecond later by hysterical—and horrifyingly loud—wailing. Passersby and motorists on Baltimore Street turn toward the commotion. Clamping onto my arm like it's a falconer's glove, Ambrose sinks to her knees.

"Get up!" I hiss, shaking free and quickly walking away from police headquarters. "You're making a scene."

If one of my boys rolled up on me now, I'd never live this shit down.

Miss Vicky's face is shiny with tears and her shoulders shake convulsively as she follows me. I walk rapidly to the corner and make a quick left on Gay Street, doing a risk/benefit analysis in my head.

I'm not that keen on putting her in the paper anyway—
not so much to protect her, but because I know the *Herald*'s
editors would blow the black radio-station executive's mis-
deed out of proportion, no pun intended. My editors would
deny this vehemently, but when African-Americans appear in
the *Herald* they're generally handcuffed, dribbling a basketball or gazing out from the obituary page.

"Tell you what," I say to Ambrose, who has calmed down
somewhat. "This story ain't gonna make or break my career, okay?"

She looks at me uncomprehendingly. But once her drug-
addled synapses finally register what I've said, she smiles,
exposing surprisingly perfect teeth.

"You ain't gonna write about me?"   •

"That's right."

I cringe inside, wondering what the *Herald*'s sanctimo-
nious metro editor, Tom Merriwether, would do if he saw
me ceding journalistic control to the whims of a street walker.
A young Ed Bradley or Bob Woodward probably would have
snapped up the story and run with it. Maybe I'm too soft to
ever join that pantheon.

Regardless, I'm a huge hit with Victoria Ambrose, who's
overjoyed her submarine berthing sessions will remain on the
q.t. Her hot hand grabs mine and pumps vigorously—at one
point she actually splooshes a big wet kiss on it. Yuck!

Along with nonstop expressions of thanks and gratitude,
she keeps asking me to repeat my name. I say it three times,
even spell it once, but quickly fail to see the sense in that
exercise. In five minutes she probably won't even recall having met me.

I drive the handful of blocks back to the *Herald,* flash my
ID at the lobby guard and make a beeline for the first-floor
men's room. Turning the water on full blast, I squirt a small
sea of green soap into my right palm and lather up, filling
the sink with soap bubbles. Who knows what exotic microbes
were lurking on and around Ambrose's tonsils?

Yanking a sandpapery brown paper towel from the metal
dispenser on the wall, I dry my hands and say a silent prayer:

Lord, please don't let Ambrose and the radio exec appear in the *Tribune,* the *Herald*'s arch-rival, tomorrow morning. Because if they do, my ass is grass.

With that I stride out of the bathroom and wait for an elevator. The huge printing presses in the basement make the lobby floor vibrate slightly, as they always do this time of night.

As soon as the elevator door creaks open on the fifth floor, I hear night editor Russell Tillman's devilish guffaws bouncing through the empty newsroom.

It's 10:30 P.M., Tillman has only thirty minutes to get out the final edition of the paper and here he is yukking it up like it's poker night with the fellas. Impervious to deadline pressure and a walking Baltimore encyclopedia, Tillman consistently outshines the power-hungry editors who work the day shift. They're more adept at currying favor and backstabbing everyone within a hundred-foot radius than improving stories or directing news coverage.

But Tillman's congenital bluntness and refusal to kiss heinie guarantee he'll never rise beyond night editor at the *Herald.*

I hustle over to my desk, smiling as I wait for his trademark greeting.

"Lay it on me, chief, so we can put this puppy to bed."

Call-and-response time. Tillman asks what I have and I tell him. He gives me a story length in inches and asks if I can fill it.

Phil Curry beating his wife merits six inches and the coveted front page of the metro section. As I start typing, I wonder what Ambrose's story would have gotten. I haven't written two inches when pistachio-stained fingers creep into my vision, interrupting my train of thought. The fingers belong to Tillman, who looks agitated.

"We're killing Curry. You can go ahead and cut out," he says curtly.

"Why? What's up?"

"Curry and the publisher are golf buddies. Plus . . ." He unfolds the *Herald*'s sports section to page 6D. At least a third of the page is occupied by a Curry BMW ad. I say nothing for a moment.

"Lemme get this straight. Because Curry and the publisher play in the same sandbox, and because we run Curry's ads, he gets to clock his wife and we have to look the other way? Is that right?"

Tillman's lips are pursed as though sucking lemons. "You catch on quick, chief. I just got off the horn with the publisher if you'd like to call him back."

"I'd like to call him, all right, but what I'd call him wouldn't do much for my job security."

Tillman snorts, pats my shoulder and hurries back toward his desk. "If it's any consolation, you could probably get a helluva deal down at Curry BMW."

"I wouldn't drive one of those overpriced shit boxes even if I *could* afford one."

"Know what you mean," Tillman calls over his shoulder.

I slam my notepad down in disgust, thinking about Journalism 101 and all that crap about objectivity and the public's right to know. But I can't get too self-righteous, since I'm wallowing in the same ethical dung heap as the publisher. Ambrose, you know.

When I get back to my apartment and finally go to bed, I have a harder time drifting off than usual. I'm usually wired after touring Baltimore's sordid underbelly, then writing about it on deadline, but tonight Curry and Ambrose are tap-dancing all over my brain.

The next day, I arrive at work to find that someone has conveniently placed the latest *Tribune* on my desk. Circled in red ink is a story on WQQD-AM executive Harold Dawson. There's even a picture of Dawson being led to police headquarters in handcuffs. Under the story someone has scrawled a huge question mark, as in "How the hell did we miss this?"

It looks to be the handiwork of Tom Merriwether, whose primary responsibility is to demoralize and dis me whenever possible. Editing is a distant second. Very distant.

Obviously this is not going to be one of my more memorable days. It doesn't get any better a few minutes later when some crackpot calls up with a cryptic warning about a conspiracy to bomb the NAACP.

Slumping in my chair, wondering if anyone else can hear my stomach's tortured moaning, I rummage through my desk drawer in search of antacid tablets.

I feel your pain, Sergeant Stevens. I feel your pain.

THREE

Little puffs of dust marked Mark Dillard's progress as he loped along the right shoulder of the Baltimore-Washington Parkway, wearing a light gray suit and cradling a red plastic gasoline container.

Sweat had already formed dark semicircles under the armpits of his suit jacket, even though Dillard had run only a quarter mile and was probably in the best shape of his life. Better than when he'd been an Army Ranger. He could have folded his jacket and left it on the front seat of his green Chevy pickup. But Dillard didn't have a second to waste—he couldn't chance some nosy cop poking around under the tarpaulin covering the Chevy's flatbed while he was fetching gas. It would be damn hard to explain why the flatbed contained a stack of neo-Nazi propaganda, ten blasting caps and twelve sticks of dynamite in a brown, watertight plastic pouch.

Dillard had another reason for wearing his suit jacket: It covered the nine-millimeter Beretta he'd pulled from under the passenger seat and tucked into his pants.

As he ran, a thought flashed through Dillard's brain that made him smile grimly.

What if he'd forgotten to put the safety on the Beretta and managed to wound himself while running beside the parkway? His comrades would really know then that they'd chosen the right man to lead their assault on the NAACP. Some leader—here he was doing an impromptu 8 A.M. marathon because he'd gotten too blitzed the night before to remember to gas up.

Real bright, Mark.

A lapse in discipline had needlessly jeopardized the mission. Not only should he have stopped at a service station last night, but the dynamite should have been removed from his truck and squirreled away in a hiding place.

Jogging double time, listening to the crunch, crunch, crunch of his black dress shoes hitting gravel, Dillard swore that from then on he would be the strongest, most dependable link, not the weakest, stupidest one.

He began to run a little faster.

Dillard knew his rapid pace was probably attracting attention, since motorists who run out of gas tend to take their time going to and from the gas station. But every second his truck sat unattended brought him a second closer to his plan derailing.

Sticking out his thumb and veering a little closer to the rush-hour traffic zooming past on his left, Dillard began to chant an old Army ditty sung during physical-training runs:

Two old ladies sittin' in bed,
One looked over at the other and said:
Am I right or wrong?
You're right.
Are we weak or strong?
We're strong.
Sound off—

His reverie was interrupted by the sound of tires scooping up gravel and flinging it into a car's wheel wells. Dillard snapped around to see a white U.S. Park Police cruiser slowing to a crawl behind him, its lights flashing. It was driven by an officer whose square jaw and thick neck were the stuff of recruiting posters. The dark hue of his aviator glasses nearly matched that of his skin. The set of his mouth carried the slightest hint of a sneer.

Dillard veered to the right, allowing the cruiser to pull up beside him. The officer sat ramrod-straight as the passenger window slowly glided into the door.

"Run out of gas, buddy?" came a warm voice belying the stern visage.

"Yeah, brother, I have a job interview and wouldn't you know that I'd pick today to run out of gas." Dillard grinned, shaking his head self-deprecatingly. Other than sexual performance, few things bruise a male ego like running out of gas. Or getting lost.

"Hop in. There's a gas station about a mile down the road, past the Greenbelt exit."

Dillard opened the passenger door and plunked down on the seat. He gently placed the gas container between his feet and glanced at the officer to size him up. He was heavily muscled, clearly someone who knew his way around a weight room. But he would be easy to take out because his open, friendly manner indicated his guard was down.

No cop should ever let his guard down with a total stranger, Dillard mused disapprovingly.

The burly officer pushed a button on his dashboard to turn off his emergency lights, then eased back onto the highway. His appearance magically transformed other drivers into law-abiding citizens who maddeningly slowed to fifty miles per hour, five below the speed limit.

"That your green pickup parked back on the side of the road?"

"Yeah, that's my baby," Dillard said, keeping his response short so the cop would move to another subject. Stealing another sideways glance, Dillard took in a gold, rectangular name tag embossed with "J. Burke."

"I was about to put an abandoned-vehicle tag on it when I saw you flying down the road," Burke said as he passed a car doing forty-eight miles per hour. Traffic bunched into a knot behind the cruiser, since no one wanted to risk passing it.

"Maybe you should get on the radio and tell your partners not to tag it," Dillard said, forcing a short, nervous laugh and instantly wishing he hadn't said a word. Sure enough, he immediately felt the officer's eyes on him and could sense an unspoken question in the air. The rock-hard Beretta poked him in the back reassuringly.

A millennium seemed to pass before the officer spoke again.

"The next police car is further south, near the Washington-Maryland line, so I don't think you have anything to worry about."

Dillard relaxed a little. That meant that not only would the truck be safe but back-up assistance was at least fifteen minutes away if he had to deal with Burke.

"Hope I haven't blown this interview, 'cause I need this job bad," Dillard said, looking around the interior of the police vehicle. A yellow traffic citation book was on the front seat, right behind a shotgun rack holding a twelve-gauge pump action. An orange wet-weather slicker was spread across the backseat, partially obscuring a copy of *Bodybuilder* magazine.

Taking a close look at Burke for the first time, Dillard guessed he was in his mid-thirties and could more than hold his own in a straight fistfight. He had a little gut to go along with his heavily muscled arms and thick chest, too.

"Maybe I should go on that interview with you," Burke said with a bitter laugh. "This cops-and-robbers stuff is gettin' old after eight years." The cruiser pulled off at the Beltsville exit and made a right turn at the first light. Burke drove about three hundred yards down a two-lane road and made a left into a convenience store that had several gas pumps situated under a metal overhang.

Bleary-eyed commuters craving java had taken all the parking spaces, so the police cruiser eased to the side of a gas pump and stopped.

"I'm gonna use the can while you get gas," Burke said, grabbing the shotgun rack with a bearlike paw and shaking it to make sure it was secured. Then he exited the police cruiser, waited for Dillard to get out and locked the doors.

Customers in line inside the convenience store looked at Dillard oddly when he entered. It was an unusually cool June morning, too cool for Dillard's suit jacket to be covered with sweat stains. A crater-faced teenager wearing a backward baseball cap nudged his friend when Dillard walked by and they both started snickering loudly.

Taking his place at the end of the line, Dillard kept his eyes fixed on a brunette beehive adorning the head of a plump woman in front of him. She held a half gallon of French vanilla ice cream and idly flipped through a soap opera magazine.

Looking neither left nor right, Dillard just stared at the beehive, committing each strand of hair to memory. The towering creation appeared to be hardened and bolstered with bobby pins, shellac and reinforced concrete. Nothing short of a two-megaton nuke would displace a hair on this woman's head, Dillard thought as he silently tried to will the line forward.

An elderly gentleman in faded denim overalls near the front of the line must have heard Dillard's unspoken plea.

"Young man, you can come on up and get in front of me," he said, waving his arm like a traffic cop. "You look like you're in a bigger hurry."

Dillard could have kissed the old-timer.

The teenagers sniggered even louder as he ambled past, cradling his gas container.

"Thank you very much, sir, I really appreciate it," Dillard said, patting the older man on the shoulder. "I'm definitely about to be late."

Dillard handed the cashier a tattered $10 bill for $2.50 worth of gas. He quickly pocketed his change and walked outside. Burke's police cruiser was nowhere to be seen.

Looking from side to side, Dillard saw Burke about thirty feet away. He was seated inside the cruiser, which was parked near two pay phones. Burke nodded casually when he saw

Dillard, then raised his police radio to his lips and started talking.

Fear rippled through Dillard's body.

"Stay calm," he mumbled under his breath. "There's no reason for him to be talking about you."

Dillard activated a gas pump, squatted over the gas container and began unscrewing the cap. Inserting the pump nozzle, he let the gas flow slowly, causing it to lap gently against the sides of the red plastic container. It was time to slow things down. Time to think and act deliberately.

He felt the same tenseness, the same tight gut he'd experienced in that armored personnel carrier during the Gulf War. He'd kept his head, relied on his mother wit and come through unscathed. No reason to alter that modus operandi now.

After about half a gallon trickled into the gas container, Dillard raised his head and looked directly at Burke, who by now had replaced his microphone and was staring back with an expressionless gaze.

Dillard couldn't wait to be rid of Burke and be on his way.

When Dillard was finished pumping, Burke glided the cruiser over and unlocked the passenger door. Dillard studied his face intently, looking for a sign anything was amiss. But the officer's already inscrutable face was made impossible to read by his dark shades.

Dillard figured that if Burke suspected anything, he would have done something by now. So Dillard set the gas container on the floor of the vehicle and got inside. He immediately spotted something he'd overlooked before: Burke was wearing a bulletproof vest.

"Got enough gas to square you away?" Burke asked, putting the car into gear and pulling way from the convenience store.

"Yeah, I should be in pretty good shape. I can't thank you enough—you're a godsend."

"No problem, partner. No problem at all."

Neither man said anything as Burke turned at the north-bound Baltimore–Washington Parkway entry ramp and accelerated onto the highway. Traffic was lighter going north toward Baltimore, since most motorists were headed south to jobs in Washington.

As before, motorists slowed dramatically when they saw the marked cruiser. Some abruptly pulled out of the passing lane into the slow lane, then stared straight ahead, as if glancing at Burke and Dillard would bring an automatic citation.

Dillard drank in the show, secretly enjoying having other drivers clear a path for him as though he were a dignitary. Which, to his way of thinking, he definitely was.

When the car approached an unpaved emergency road running through a thicket of trees between the northbound and southbound sides of the parkway, Burke gently applied the brakes. The cruiser slowed to forty miles per hour, with the northbound motorists obediently following suit, before Burke pulled onto the left shoulder.

When they reached the other side of the thicket, Dillard saw a sight that made his heart flutter in his chest. Behind his green pickup truck, three-quarters of a mile down the road, was a police vehicle that had its lights flashing. An officer stood beside the pickup's flatbed.

"Thought your partners were near the D.C. line," Dillard said, slowly reaching under his suit jacket.

"Probably Maryland State Police," Burke said casually, looking past Dillard at oncoming traffic. "Their guys patrol the parkway, too."

Creeping along the left-hand shoulder, Burke slowly picked up speed and pulled onto the highway. Now Dillard could clearly see that the state trooper had one corner of the tarpaulin drawn back and was peering under it with a flashlight.

"Don't stop and don't try anything funny," Dillard said quietly, sticking his gun directly into Burke's groin. No sense aiming at Burke's chest, because of his bulletproof vest. Anyway, hard steel against his testicles would definitely get his attention and make Burke less likely to try something stupid and heroic.

"You don't want to do this, man," Burke said in a calm,

firm voice as Dillard eased the lawman's service handgun from its holster. "Why don't we pull over and talk—"

"Shut the fuck up. You think you talkin' to some dumb hillbilly peckerwood, don't you?" Dillard screamed. "Wave at your friend when we go past, but don't slow down. I don't want to shoot you, but I'll fire your friggin' ass up if I have to."

Burke said nothing and for a fleeting second Dillard wondered if he was going to play the hero anyway.

The state trooper motioned as though he wanted them to pull over. But Burke kept going, giving a wave so wooden that a five-year-old would have understood he was in trouble.

Dillard saw the puzzled look on the trooper's face as they cruised by. He might be on his police radio within a matter of seconds.

"Real cute, motherfucker," Dillard yelled, whacking Burke in the Adam's apple with his service revolver. "Speed up. Now!"

The cruiser accelerated to seventy as a wheezing Burke drove with one hand and vigorously massaged his throat with the other. "What's this all about?" he managed to croak between labored breaths, his evil expression making it clear that if he got his gun back, Dillard would be dead meat.

"I could tell you, boy," a poker-faced Dillard answered, "but then I'd have to kill you. Drive faster—and put your emergency lights on."

The speedometer was reading eighty-five in no time, bringing about the rapid approach of the Beltsville exit again.

"Pull off. Do it!"

Dillard could feel the car skidding ever so slightly, its tires quivering at the limit of adhesion as Burke made a quick right and braked heavily to avoid crashing on the thirty-five-miles-per-hour exit ramp. The car barely screeched to a stop at the light, a cloud of blue tire smoke overtaking it.

"Run the goddamn light and get back on the parkway going north. And turn off your emergency lights."

Dillard was worried the state trooper might have followed

them to see if something was amiss. Doubling back toward Baltimore would buy him a little time if that turned out to be the case.

"Hurry up and get back on the entrance ramp," Dillard barked, waving his Beretta at a green-and-white road sign reading B/W PARKWAY NORTH, BALTIMORE. He shot a glance at the side mirror to see if they were being followed.

Suddenly the pungent, overpowering odor of gasoline was inside the car. In his haste Dillard had forgotten to replace the gas container's vent cap, and some of the fuel had trickled onto the floor. The smell would make Dillard easy to track if he got it on his clothes.

"Pull over!"

Burke viciously slammed the brake pedal with every ounce of strength he could channel into his right leg. The rear end of the car skidded around to the left and pushed Dillard unexpectedly against his seat belt. The service revolver flew from his left hand, hit the dashboard and clattered to the floor. Before the vehicle came to a complete stop, Burke was already coming out of his seat belt and grappling with Dillard for the Beretta.

Dillard managed to get off a single shot that sounded like a howitzer detonating inside the closed car. The bullet slammed into Burke's chest directly over his breastbone, knocking the wind out of him and throwing him against the door. He began to claw desperately at his door handle, as did Dillard.

Burke managed to exit first and ran, doubled over, in the direction of a thick expanse of forest near the right side of the road. Dillard half leapt, half tumbled out of the car just as the officer started to disappear inside a canopy of green. Dillard got off one more shot that kicked up a divot of black earth where Burke had been a split second earlier.

He started to follow Burke to finish him off, like he'd done to those two badly wounded Iraqi soldiers he'd encountered during Desert Storm. It had been like shooting fish in a barrel. In both instances he'd felt no more exhilaration or remorse than when he'd shot deer during boyhood hunting trips in nearby Pennsylvania.

But Dillard reminded himself the fire burning within him wasn't about some nigger police officer. It was about much, much more than that.

Listening to Burke crash through the forest like an enraged bull elephant, Dillard sprinted back to the police cruiser and slammed the passenger door shut. Then he ran to the other side and jumped behind the wheel of the car, which was still running. Flinging his Beretta on the seat and frantically poking at the button activating the emergency lights, Dillard flicked the transmission from park to drive and headed toward the parkway and Baltimore. The big engine emitted a throaty roar as he slammed the accelerator.

He was quickly parting traffic like Moses in the Red Sea, particularly once he'd figured out how to turn on the mammoth car's siren. Maintaining a steady ninety, Dillard tried to calm his roiled mind and plot his next move.

As the cruiser came flying around one bend, sitting on the left-hand side of the road and partially hidden by an earthen berm was an unmarked police car with a radar unit hanging out its right window.

Dillard peered anxiously at his rearview mirror to see if the car pursued him. But it remained in its ambush spot, shrinking rapidly into the distance. Only then did Dillard begin to entertain thoughts that maybe it really *was* his day and that he might not wind up getting incarcerated or killed after all.

Why had he doubted for one second that the dream was anything less than preordained?

It took about ten minutes for Dillard to motor from the Beltsville turnoff to the Baltimore-Washington International Airport exit. Leaving the parkway, he shut off the police cruiser's siren and lights and slowed to sixty-five.

Before reaching the airport, Dillard exited at the sign for the BWI Rail Station. Commuter and Amtrak trains stopped there, allowing him to formulate a strategy: He would ditch the car, catch an airport shuttle bus to the train station and grab the next thing headed for Baltimore's Pennsylvania Station.

The plan worked to perfection. Driving into a commuter parking lot about a half mile from the rail station, Dillard parked the U.S. Park Police cruiser at a distant corner of the crowded lot, leaving the gas container inside the vehicle. Then he exited the parking lot and walked toward a Plexiglas-and-metal bus stop shelter. It was for passengers awaiting a shuttle that made a continual loop between the airport, the parking lot and the rail station.

Taking out a black comb, Dillard casually pulled it through his reddish, neatly cropped hair. He fashioned the slightest hint of a cowlick, as was his custom. The sun was shining and a slight easterly wind was stirring, drying the sweat on Dillard's suit and transforming him into another nondescript commuter.

A creaky red-and-tan shuttle bus appeared in the distance, leaving tendrils of black diesel smoke in its wake. The driver said nothing as Dillard boarded and took a seat near the rear exit, the better to facilitate a quick departure if necessary. It couldn't have taken more than a minute for him to reach the rail station, an unremarkable, small concrete building nestled beside the railroad tracks.

Dillard got off through the bus's rear door and breathed a deep lungful of summer air. It smelled of freedom. Another, more worrisome odor materialized once Dillard was inside the train station—the faint smell of gasoline, emanating from his shoes and lingering wherever he traveled.

That's easily enough explained, Dillard thought as he waited in line at the ticket counter. When his turn came, he paid $4.50 for a one-way trip to Baltimore via a commuter train arriving at 9:05 A.M.

But Dillard had one more pressing matter to take care of before getting on the train. Stopping at one of three pay phones, he began fishing through his pockets for a quarter. Finding two dimes and a nickel, he guided them into the coin slot and hurriedly dialed.

"Good morning, Chesapeake Brewing Company," a pleasant female voice answered.

"Can I speak to Rick Allen, please?"

"Please hold." There was about a fifteen-second pause. "I'm sorry, I'm not showing Mr. Allen on my phone list."

"He's new there and he works in Maintenance. I'm his brother and this is an emergency." Actually, they weren't related at all, but it was imperative that Dillard talk to the younger man.

"I'll page him. Please hold."

Nearly a minute went by, prompting Dillard to look at his watch. It was 9:03, giving him two minutes.

"Yeah," Allen finally answered, sounding out of breath and somewhat annoyed at having been summoned at work.

"Rick, it's Mark," Dillard said. "You've got to leave work *now,* because the cops are going to be looking for you. What are you driving?"

"I rode my bike to work this morning. Why, what's up? What's going on?"

"No time to explain now, Rick," Dillard said in a tone someone might use on a younger sibling. "Leave work now and ride over to my house. I should be there in about half an hour."

"But, Mark—"

"And by the way, Rick," Dillard said, cutting the younger man off, "don't mention this conversation to anyone. Do you understand? No one!"

Dillard hung up the phone and walked toward the train tracks.

He arrived about half a minute before the commuter train, its electric engine humming loudly as it glided to a stop. He handed the conductor his ticket and looked for an isolated seat. Walking past his bored-looking fellow riders, Dillard mused that it wasn't even noon yet and he'd already had a bigger adrenaline rush than these pampered, complacent suburbanites would probably ever experience in their entire lives.

It had taken months of meticulous planning to steal twelve

measly sticks of dynamite from the construction company where Dillard worked. That small amount of explosive was nowhere near what Dillard needed for the NAACP bombing. Now it was gone, sitting in a truck no doubt surrounded by an army of law enforcement officers.

The pickup belonged to Rick Allen, the youngest—and most impressionable and impulsive—of Dillard's small band of neo-Nazi cohorts. Every law enforcement officer in Maryland would be looking for Allen soon, in light of the fact one of their brethren had been fired on.

Dillard would have to deal with that. There was also the possibility his standing as the unofficial leader of his loose-knit confederation might be undermined.

But for the moment, Dillard was filled with relief he wasn't headed for a morgue slab or a jail cell. For that he was grateful.

When the commuter train coasted into Baltimore's Penn Station, Dillard luxuriated for a few extra moments in the air-conditioned car. Then he stepped out onto the train platform and walked two steps at a time up the concrete stairway leading to the station. Strolling calmly across the marble floor, he passed through the building and went outside. Spotting several cabs waiting in line, Dillard climbed into the first one. He exhaled softly and closed the door.

"Take me to 4503 Baker Street, please."

Eyeing a foot patrolman hectoring a black panhandler near the entrance to Pennsylvania Station, Dillard looked the other way and laughed as the cab cruised up Charles Street.

FOUR

WHATEVER TOM MERRIWETHER IS DRONING ON AND ON ABOUT, it must be pretty important.

I know, because I'm gazing at the *Herald*'s metro editor and he's wearing one of those omniscient/stern expressions usually seen on traffic cops and parents of wayward toddlers.

I've got one of my masks on, too, the one showing respectful attentiveness. In reality my mind is a thousand miles away. Because Merriwether has nothing to say I want to hear. Unless I see his pinched lips mouth the word "raise" or the words "more money." And the chances of that happening are slim and none.

Whenever he summons me to his office it's usually to berate. And the criticism is never constructive. Consequently I don't respect Merriwether much as a person or a journalist. And I have a sneaking suspicion the feeling is mutual.

So little snippets of his conversation register on my consciousness, like an AM radio that fades in and out after picking up a distant station late at night.

Blah, blah, blah "inexcusable for us to have missed this," blah, blah blah, "I've seen better news judgment in interns . . ." Etc, etc.

I focus on the window behind Merriwether's desk, half watching two scrawny pigeons execute a herky-jerky mating dance on the ledge. I wouldn't mind being one of them for however long it takes Merriwether to castigate me, then show me the door. Animal, vegetable, mineral—it really doesn't matter. I'd rather be anything but Darryl Billups listening to a stream of nonstop blather whose underlying message is: You're inferior, have no business being here and don't carry your weight.

Blah, blah, blah, blah, blah.

Every ten seconds or so I make fleeting eye contact and nod, giving the impression I'm hanging onto every sage word.

Meanwhile, in my head I'm listening to a voice far more compelling, one that's oddly androgynous and menacing. It belongs to whoever called ten minutes before Merriwether summoned me into his office. Crank callers are always dialing up newspapers: It's an occupational hazard. Whenever the phone rings, chances are it will be a PR person peddling some goofy story idea. Or some lonely soul demanding we investigate the Trilateral Commission's links to Satan.

But what am I supposed to make of a caller warning that a tan Dodge van will blow up the NAACP's national headquarters in downtown Baltimore? On or around July 11, about three weeks from now?

Weirdos seldom deal in that kind of detail. Naturally, when I pressed for more information, I got a click in my ear for my trouble.

I'm sitting in Merriwether's office, staring at an autographed picture of Ronald Reagan. And wondering why a purported terrorist has singled me out. Is it just some twisted cretin messing with one of the paper's few black reporters?

The call was definitely unanticipated and unappreciated. Truth be told, it intimidated me a little, too.

I'm nobody's cream puff, but there are definitely some crazies out there. Witness the burnings of all those black Southern churches.

"Did you hear what I said? Apparently that doesn't faze you?" Merriwether's mean-sounding voice drones, breaking into my thoughts.

I'd managed to totally tune him out, but now he's back,

large and in charge and colored a brilliant vermilion. Unfortunately, I have no idea what he's just said.

"I heard exactly what you said," I tell him in a neutral tone, bluffing for all I'm worth. "I'm just surprised you would say that."

"Damn right, and it's about time someone did," Merriwether replies, giving me that look victors reserve for the vanquished. "The next time we get whipped like we did on the WQQD story, I'm yanking your butt out of here and shipping you to the Howard County bureau."

Howard County! I catch myself, struggling to make sure my expression registers neither surprise nor consternation. Merriwether has just yanked my chain hard, hard enough to make me gasp, but he'll never get the satisfaction of knowing.

Howard County! That's where green reporters are assigned to cover county government meetings and write puff-piece human interest stories. Howard County is the home of Caravanland, my nickname for Columbia, a white-bread, bedroom community twenty miles to the south where every other resident seems to have a Dodge Caravan for shuttling pampered brats to soccer practice.

Any *Herald* reporter worth his or her salt wants to be in the main office in downtown Baltimore, where the action is. Where I am now. Where I fully deserve to be.

"You're the boss," I tell Merriwether with a noncommittal shrug. That never fails to get a rise out of him when he's attempting to push my buttons. Actually, he's succeeded magnificently—I hope he can't hear my stomach gurgling like an out-of-control Crock-Pot.

It probably would make sense to be more deferential around Merriwether, and on a few occasions I really have made an honest effort. But with me, what you see is pretty much what you get. No airs, no complicated backstabbing schemes, no insincere smiles if I know you're not in my corner. If I don't like you, it's hard for me to be phony and pretend otherwise.

Which worries me. I want to go far in this business, but sometimes I wonder if I have the personality for it.

Don't get me wrong—I get along famously with most people. Tom Merriwether is just one sucker I don't like. A close second is Cornelius Lawrence, a handkerchief-head *Herald* reporter who rues the day he left the womb any darker than alabaster.

"This may come as a shock to you, Darryl, but we work for a *newspaper*." The word is enunciated precisely and is practically hurled across Merriwether's desk. "That means our job is to cover news, not let it slip through our fingers. You can leave."

Is that a fact? Tell me, is Phil Curry kicking his wife's ass news? I wisely keep that little bon mot inside my head.

Three days ago I mailed my résumé and writing samples to *The Washington Post,* the *Philadelphia Inquirer* and *USA Today.* We'll see who laughs last.

Merriwether's office is a small, glass-enclosed fishbowl just off the main newsroom. So I'm sure my nosy colleagues are furiously debating my fate and gossiping with a blizzard of e-mail messages. In fact, one awaits when I return to my desk.

> Don't let Ichabod Crane get you down, yo.
> You still the man!
> <MURDOCK>, 27-JUNE, 14:23

I chuckle as I delete the message from John "Mad Dawg" Murdoch, a six-foot-four dreadlock-wearing, ebony brother who writes like a dream and covers the Baltimore Orioles. Mad Dawg is my boy, my port in a storm, my confidant and all that good stuff. Hell, I'd elevate him to sainthood if the Negro would just repay a loan without having to be chased to the ends of the earth.

He worked for Merriwether before switching over to sports three years ago, so Mad Dawg knows what I'm going through. I send him a quick message before making phone calls to different police and fire departments in the Baltimore area.

Damn right I'm THE MAN. Just had to remind that
punk of that . . . any openings in sports?
<BILLUPS>, 27-JUNE, 14:35

I push the SEND button and log off. I know Mad Dawg
will have something suitably ignorant and totally hilarious to
write in response. If I start trading messages with that fool,
he'll have me sitting here laughing and acting unprofessional.
Before you know it, a half hour will have gone by and I
won't have gotten a thing done.

I begin calling around to see who has an interesting story.
The state police have a damn good one. Seems a U.S. Park
Police officer had his cruiser stolen by a motorist who also
fired a shot into the officer's bulletproof vest. Plus, the motorist's pickup was filled with explosives and neo-Nazi hate
literature. This story has "front page" written all over it.
After I alert my editors, sure enough they decide to stick it
on 1A. Yes!

If you've never seen your byline plastered across the front
page of a major metropolitan newspaper, it's pretty intoxicat-
ing. Hell, getting on 1A almost makes up for the substandard
pay print journalists get.

I arrange for Photo to shoot the pickup truck and the recovered police cruiser, then start working the phones. I make
calls to the U.S. Park Police, a city police bomb-squad expert,
the NAACP, B'nai B'rith and a local group that monitors
hate organizations. All this while halfway listening to a police
scanner on my desk that has the volume turned down.

In the midst of all the excitement, the Androgynous One
calls.

"Did you warn anyone about July eleventh?" the caller
asks in a tone simultaneously unctuous and insistent. As the
hairs on the back of my neck stand at attention, I try to get
a fix on whether the caller is male or female. Plus I listen
for background noise that might help identify the caller or
the caller's location.

I look around suspiciously to see if anyone is hunched
over his phone, playing a practical joke. But everyone is

busily chatting away or staring at a computer screen, poker-faced and intent on making deadline.

If this is somebody's idea of a prank, I don't find this shit amusing.

Prankster or not, the caller is a patient soul, because the line remains dead silent as my response is awaited. There's not even the sound of breathing. I sense that the person on the other end is getting off on this game of cat and mouse.

"Where are you calling from?" I finally ask.

The answer is a startling burst of laughter, a high-pitched warble that could belong to a fey-sounding man or a husky-voiced woman. Fumbling furiously in my desk drawer, I find my microcassette recorder and Radio Shack phone-tapping device. I hurriedly connect both and begin secretly taping the call.

"You might as well go ahead and ask me who I am," the caller finally says after enjoying a hearty laugh at my expense.

"Fine. Who are you? Because I really don't have time for foolishness. Why are you calling me?"

"It's not important for you to know who I am," the Androgynous One replies mildly. "What is important is for you to know that everything I say is true. You'll be a believer in a couple of days."

Click.

Right before the phone was hung up, the caller's voice had taken on a furtive quality, as though he or she didn't want to be caught using the telephone. And what does "You'll be a believer in a couple of days" mean? How can that be the case when the bombing is supposed to be on July 11 and today is June 27?

I turn off my tape recorder, remove the microcassette and print BOMBER on it.

Forgetting momentarily about the task at hand, I replay the call in my head, pondering the significance of it. About the only thing I'm reasonably sure of is that the caller sounds white. That hardly narrows down the field.

Without realizing it, I gently tug at my mustache, a habit

when I'm deep in thought. A flashing e-mail prompt on my computer yanks my mind back to the present.

> How's that state police story coming? .
> P.S. I need to talk to you later.
> <TILLMAN>, 27-JUNE, 17:11

I don't ever recall Russell Tillman asking me about a story as early as 5:11 P.M. And what could he possibly want to talk to me about? Unlike most of the white editors at the *Herald*, Tillman continues to make eye contact even when white reporters and editors are present. Also, he doesn't snatch high-profile stories from me to feed to the *Herald*'s prima donnas and he consistently goes out of his way to teach me the tricks of the trade.

Tillman's cool in my book.

I'm guessing that whatever he wants to talk to me about might have to do with my Merriwether tête-à-tête.

Messaging Tillman that I should be finished in another half hour or so, I get back to work, laughing gently to myself. I must be crazy to tape some looney-tune crackpot obviously fixated on Oklahoma City.

The deadline for the first edition of the *Herald*, which is distributed primarily on Maryland's Eastern Shore and in neighboring Pennsylvania and Virginia, is six-thirty. I beat that with fifty minutes to spare and my story "sings," newspaper parlance for a well-written piece.

By the time Tillman edits my story and I make some minor modifications, then make more police calls, it's after eight o'clock. Five hours inside the *Herald* is more than enough, so I'm relieved when a call comes across the police scanner about a double shooting. That's my cue to hit the bricks.

As I quickly gather up my notebook, a walkie-talkie for communicating with Tillman and a portable police scanner, I'm feeling pretty pleased with myself. Yeah, Merriwether dissed me and I probably humored that terrorist wannabe longer than I should have.

But when all's said and done, I'm going to be on 1A

tomorrow, a prime piece of real estate coveted by any reporter worth a damn. And no one has to tell me I did a helluva job.

"I'm headed to the eleven-hundred block of McClure Street," I yell across the newsroom to Tillman. "Cops are reporting a double shooting."

"Okay," a bored-sounding Tillman replies. "Keep me posted."

The crimson puddle on the sidewalk is just starting to crust over by the time I roll up to the crime scene.

An inquisitive evening crowd of about fifty black men, women and children wearing summer garb rings the shooting victim, who lies near a Korean mom-and-pop grocery. Some of the young folks seem as accustomed to sprawled corpses as many of the grown-ups, I observe sadly as I back the *Baltimore Herald* press car into a parking spot.

There's that familiar tingly feeling again, voltage flowing into my spine and chest. I'm embarrassed by the rush of excitement. What does *that* mean—some hapless soul's demise is as much a diversion for me as for the milling throng?

Messenger boy of the white press corps at your service, y'all, I muse as I roll up the passenger window and lock the door. As if on cue, a few onlookers—their faces shaded a ghoulish blue from blinking police lights—glare in my direction.

It's damn difficult to be unobtrusive in an ivory-colored sedan with THE BALTIMORE HERALD—THE TRUTH IS THE LIGHT splashed across both sides in large red script. Within the white community, the *Herald* is a venerable institution with a rich journalist legacy. Within the black community, the *Herald* has a richly documented history of marginalizing and humiliating African-Americans.

As soon as I open the car door, a high-pitched, feral wail punishes my eardrums. The plaintive cry of a mother brutally deprived of her child.

At one point in my career the sound would have put Himalayan-sized goose bumps on my arms. Now, five years into the business, I feel nothing. I learned long ago to tuck my emotions away in an inaccessible spot, to be retrieved later.

This may sound cold, but at the moment, I'm concentrating on my lead. How many ways can you tell people that some mad-at-the-world sonofabitch blasted yet another black male to kingdom come?

Bounding out of the car, I make my way down the narrow, one-way street, past the brick-and-sandstone row houses with their glistening marble front steps. Quintessential East Baltimore. Suburbanites have row houses, too. They just call them town houses and pay $80,000 more for them.

Not that anyone would ever mistake this neighborhood for some antiseptic suburban enclave. Veteran cops refer to it as "The Pit." Roughly eight square city blocks and home to only forty-five hundred or so people, The Pit usually accounts for ten percent of the homicides in a city with more than four hundred thousand citizens. That never fails to amaze and sadden me.

If not for The Pit, I might not even be working for the *Herald.* The paper never had a black reporter prior to 1968, when urban unrest turned the night sky over The Pit a hellish orange. The then lily-white *Herald* was forced to press black file clerks and mailroom workers into emergency reporter duty.

Since then, plenty of black *Herald* reporters have served as the paper's eyes and ears in urban war zones, but not in the tranquil state capital bureau located in picturesque Annapolis. Or the prestigious Washington bureau forty-five miles to the south.

At least my reporting from The Pit will never be challenged or second-guessed. I'd be shocked if any of the *Herald*'s editors have ever been within five blocks of this rough-and-tumble neighborhood.

The evening air has a soothing, almost palliative quality. The temperature is in the mid-seventies and there's none of the stifling humidity that usually creeps off Chesapeake Bay to mug the city. Whatever led to tonight's homicide, heat wasn't a factor.

It's too pretty an evening to die.

Seemingly oblivious to the grisly tragedy a few yards away, two teenage girls wearing Daisy Dukes bob to the beat of a blasting boom box. Backup singers to the Grim Reaper, the Reapettes gently undulate, laughing and joking whenever they spot a familiar face. The Reapettes have obviously peeped this gruesome scene before and are thoroughly unfazed by it.

Wiry at five feet ten and one hundred forty-five pounds, I weave my way through the crowd, which smells of cologne, bubblegum and the pungent aroma of malt liquor.

"Heard that fool got smoked goin' after the cash register, yo," a boy who looks to be about ten mumbles in his best tough-guy voice. His partner, who's the same age, nods. Both boys try hard to pass themselves off as hard, unfeeling gangstas unimpressed by human slaughter. But they can't disguise their awe and wonder at seeing a homicide victim up close and personal.

There's hope for them yet.

I'm so busy looking at the boys that I literally bump into an attractive, heavyset black woman in her late forties. She's clad in white shorts, pink plastic sandals and a screaming-pink halter top; her mahogany face is a quivering mask of horror and revulsion. The woman's curiously mannish hands are being wrung so forcefully the color has been squeezed from them.

"Lawd, Jesus, Lawd, Jesus," she quietly drones, a mantra for resurrecting the dead.

A relative or friend of the homicide victim.

A few feet away, a muscular white-uniformed cop rocks back on his haunches, struggling to restrain the victim's mother, a petite, light-skinned woman with a short Afro. She looks to be in her early thirties and wears the grayish-blue uniform of a city bus driver. Hysterical with grief, she flails away at the grim-looking young officer, staining his white uniform shirt with her tears. A pas de deux of death.

Tsunami waves of raw emotion pour directly from anguished soul to vocal cords as the woman strains to get beyond the policeman to her only child, who is about ten yards away.

"Ooooweeeee," she screeches. "No, God, oh, noooooo."

A number of bystanders look at the victim's body and his distraught mom, their heads swiveling as though watching a tennis match. A few women fan themselves, more to release tension than to stay cool.

"Please, ma'am, I really don't think you want to see your boy right now," the cop says, a look of helplessness and frustration on his face as the inconsolable woman bucks and writhes in his embrace.

Out of nowhere a smallish, angry-looking black man wearing a red jogging suit pushes his way through the crowd. The cop instinctively releases his grip, allowing the victim's mother to bolt toward either her husband or her boyfriend.

The instant she touches him it's as though a switch has been pushed, shutting down the incredible energy boiling inside her. The woman's body goes limp and she slumps onto her diminutive companion, who locks his arms under hers and gently drags her to the front steps of a house near the mom-and-pop grocery.

He put his arms around his woman and embraces her tightly. Rocking slightly, they both emit high-pitched moans.

I look away, feeling I'm intruding on the most intimate moment this couple will ever share outside a bedroom.

Suddenly someone roughly grabs my left shoulder, making me instinctively jerk away. "Did you hear me tell everybody to move back?" a beefy black cop snarls at me, his comment more challenge than question.

A protruding gut gives him the appearance of being seven to eight months pregnant. I start to volunteer this observation but think better of it after one look at the menacing nightstick swinging from his thick leather belt.

"Don't put your hands on me," I growl back, glaring and shoving my press pass in his face. I then make a show of craning my neck toward the officer's badge. Embossed on the shiny tin slab, just below the detailed city seal, is "No. 5644."

The change in the lawman's demeanor is dramatic and instantaneous. "Sorry about that." He grins at his newfound best friend. Receding gums making his bottom teeth look like inverted, yellow garden hoes jammed into red clay.

"Just having a little trouble keeping folks out of the crime scene, chief. If you need any help getting info, lemme know, awright?"

Yeah, right. If I'd been just another nigger, I know damn well this encounter wouldn't be going nearly so smoothly. Bastard.

A short, unexceptional-looking black man with neatly cropped salt-and-pepper hair walks out of the grocery store, pen and pad in hand. His rumpled tan rayon slacks and dark green cotton shirt are as unkempt as if he'd slept in them. Even the brown leather gun holster on his left side appears wrinkled. Detective Philip Gardner looks at me and smiles.

"Still chasing ambulances, I see." Gardner chuckles, stepping gingerly—almost prissily—around the dead boy. The victim is a teenager with a freshly barbered fade haircut. The boy's white-and-blue University of North Carolina T-shirt glistens red from a single shotgun blast under the left breastbone.

"How've you been?" Gardner asks with genuine concern.

"Not bad, not bad, thanks. Why did this come across the radio as a double homicide?"

"You know we embellish everything we do," Gardner responds with a lopsided grin. "Sort of like the press."

Gardner is a rare cop in that he has a great sense of humor. I'll bet it would dry up real fast if I misquoted him or second-guessed him in print, though.

"Okay, you got me. What went down?"

By this point Gardner is busily scanning the crowd, a bird of prey in search of quarry. I know his mind is racing two to three moves ahead of whatever he'll eventually disclose.

"Kid's name is Antoine Moore," Gardner says finally, zeroing in on a sullen-looking young man staring coldly at the victim. When he spots the detective measuring him, the man smirks and straightens up slightly, his stance a tad self-conscious and defiant.

"He was sixteen and lived on the next street over, 523 York Avenue. Turned sixteen two weeks ago."

"Drug-related?" I asked reflexively.

"Naw, kid was an honor student at Dunbar High," Gardner answers, still trying to engage Stone Face, who refuses to make eye contact. Embarrassed to have asked such a stereotypical question, I feel my face flush. At the *Herald,* I would have given a white reporter hell for making the same dumb assumption.

"His mom sent him to the store to fetch a pack of smokes and some scuzzball sticks a sawed-off shotgun in his face. Kid gives up his wallet and takes a hit in the chest anyway."

"Got a suspect or murder weapon?"

"Nope."

"Description of the perp?" I ask, flipping my notebook shut.

"Come on, Darryl! You know these streets as well as I do," Gardner teases, arching his eyebrows comically. "Nobody ever sees a goddamned thing out here. Don't you know that?"

I nod. "I'm outta here."

At one with his thoughts, jaws pumping like pistons, Gardner gives a barely perceptible nod and grunts.

The Reapettes are still going through their paces, waiting for the Grim Reaper to take the stage as I half walk, half jog back toward the car.

As I open the door to the *Herald*mobile, I flinch at the sound of a booming basso profundo voice.

"Where my newspaper at, bitch?" some ignorant, intoxicated old fool bellows, triggering riotous laughter. Certain every eyeball is boring into my skull, I feign deafness and slink into the car.

It cranks on the first try and I flick it into drive and mash the accelerator, making the *Herald*mobile emit a wheezing laugh. Once I'm headed in the direction of the *Herald*'s downtown office, I reach toward the passenger seat for my walkie-talkie.

"I'm on my way back in, Russell. Got a sixteen-year-old gunned down in an apparent robbery in East Baltimore, instead of the double homicide the cops advertised."

"Gotcha. See you when you get here."

Not before I take care of some pressing business.

In the distance, roughly half a block ahead, I spot a dimly lit alley running between several row houses. Jerking the *Herald*mobile toward the curb, I brush the right front tire against the curb and skid to a stop. A maelstrom of chewing gum wrappers, Popsickle sticks and empty crack vials boils in my wake.

Switching off the ignition and snatching my walkie-talkie from the passenger seat, I open the driver's door and sprint about ten yards into the deserted alley. Only some dented trash cans will bear witness to my actions. Because my mama definitely taught me better.

Seeking cover between a telephone pole and a dilapidated wooden garage, I unzip my pants and begin emptying a bladder shrieking for relief.

"Oh, God!"

Funny, how passionate sex and a timely piss make people invoke His name.

Two figures suddenly materialize at the far end of the alley. Walking fast in my direction. Young men with medium frames and troubling swaggers. In the dim light they appear to be either white or Hispanic. One thing is certain—both are converging on yours truly.

Shit, I'm about to get jacked. Or worse!

They *would* show up when both of my hands are occupied, and not with anything to deter young toughs bent on violence.

Damn, damn, damn! Stay composed. Keep your wits.

"Baltimore City Police Department," I bark, surprising myself. I hold my black walkie-talkie high over my head where both men can see it. "Can I help you, gentlemen?"

One of them jerks his head in the direction of the *Her-*

*ald*mobile. They both smile and continue their silent approach. Street smarts have told them I'm no cop.

As they move closer I can see that my antagonists appear to be light-skinned blacks in their late teens or early twenties. Wearing baggy jeans and untucked athletic jersey shirts.

Meaning guns, bazookas, F-16s—anything could be stashed in their pants.

I bring my walkie-talkie slowly to my side, squeezing it tightly. They may gun me down, but at least I can crack one of my assailants upside the head.

With the thugs almost on top of me, I whirl and swing the walkie-talkie in a violent arc, intent on fracturing a skull. But the intended victim adroitly sidesteps. Instead of a busted head, he escapes with an angry red scrape on his face.

Simultaneously a torrent of warm liquid scores a direct hit on the pants of one of the hooligans, leaving a dark splotch. In the excitement, I'd forgotten what I was doing.

"That's yo' ass, punk muthafucka!"

A fist slams into my jaw, jamming my teeth against my tongue and dislodging a grunt from my throat. The other attacker runs behind me, black object in hand.

A sickening crunch radiates from the base of my skull, followed by a bluish-white flash. From that point on, everything looks like a VCR playing at half speed. Feeling myself falling, I try to extend my arms to cushion the impact.

The ground rises slowly to meet me, but my arms won't budge.

So this is what it feels like to die.

The concrete continues inexorably toward my face and I seem to hover briefly over a cracked section that looks like the Grand Canyon from thirty-eight thousand feet.

A kaleidoscopic burst of color is followed by blackness.

FIVE

Wherever I am, I'm bathed in a brilliant light filling me with warmth and tranquility.

"I am in heaven?" I mumble.

The angels must be having fun, because I can hear their laughter.

The "angels" are Ida B. Wells Hospital emergency room workers amused at my disorientation.

"Naw, kid, this ain't heaven by a long shot," attending physician Fredi Norment replies. "Sometimes we tend to think of it as hell on earth, actually."

Seeing me tense, Dr. Norment quickly reassures me.

"Relax, Darryl, relax. Just a little joke. My name is Dr. Norment and you're in the emergency room at Ida B. Wells. Seems you were conked on the head and knocked unconscious. "Me, Dr. Hess and Nurses Chisholm and Bailey are checking you over and are going to run some tests. Open your eyes for me, please."

Lying on an examining table with a circular examining light suspended over it, I do as I'm told. When I open my eyes, light with the intensity of the midday sun streams violently into my head.

"Ooohhhhh. Man!"

"Pupils look normal," Dr. Norment says, suddenly clinical and detached. "Can you tell me where it hurts?"

40

"Yeah, my head. Feels like I've been drinking Richards," I answer, scrunching my eyelids shut and folding my arms over my face.

As I lie on the table I can feel nerve endings in different parts of my body powering up, getting on-line with pain central. My right knee adds its contribution to the jangling cacophony, followed by my back and an aching jaw. But the biggest hurt is in my head, which feels like it's expanding and contracting with pain.

"What day is it, Darryl?" Dr. Norment asks. I must be groggy or hallucinating, because the antiseptic smell inside the emergency room gets stronger every time I hear her voice. And her voice sounds like it's coming from the bottom of a syrup-filled vat.

I pause to ponder her question.

"Monday?"

Dr. Norment's face registers no reaction as she scribbles something on her medical chart.

"When is your birthday?"

I have to think about that, too. Nothing is coming easily. "July . . ."

"Yes?"

"Uh, June the . . . the twenty-seventh. June twenty-seventh, 1965."

Dr. Norment glances at the other members of the emergency team, then scribbles some more.

"Darryl, you may be interested to know that today is Thursday—Thursday at two forty-five in the morning, to be exact. We want to take some X-rays of your head. We also want to do an EEG and give you a CT scan."

I nod and stretch out on the examining table.

"Doc, wake me when you're finished, okay?" I yawn.

"No—DON'T go to sleep!"

Her stern tone makes my eyes fly open. The unforgiving light makes me pay.

Dr. Norment switches the light off and orders me to turn onto my side.

"You experienced a blow to the head and were knocked

unconscious," she explains, roughly probing my cranium. "If we let you go to sleep right now, you might not wake up. You wouldn't want that, would you?"

Before I can answer, a burst of pain that makes me go rigid flashes through my head. Dr. Norment is poking the spot where one of the thugs whacked me.

"Dr. Hess, would you take a look at this, please?"

I feel gloved fingers timidly palming my head, as though it might shatter like an egg if handled roughly.

"How would you proceed, Dr. Hess?" Dr. Norment asks. Her tone makes it clear she knows the answer.

"I'd put some sutures in that head wound," the young physician says hopefully. "Might as well put them in now, since a suture kit is right here."

"Really?" Dr. Norment answers dryly. "And what if he has subdural hematoma? It would be a shame to waste time sewing up his head if there's bleeding on his brain. "We wouldn't want that to appear on the front page of the *Herald,* would we?" Dr. Norment says, grasping my arm with a strong hand.

How does she know where I work?

When I open my eyes, a full-figured black woman dressed in sterile green hospital garb fills my field of vision. Her stethoscope bobs on an ample chest. I wonder how many times a day she's mistakenly approached as a nurse or a nurse's aide.

"Because we're dealing with head trauma here, I'm holding you for observation," Dr. Norment declares, her tone indicating the decision is non-negotiable.

That's the last thing I want to hear. I'd rather be jabbed with a stick than visit a hospital, much less stay in one. From the stomach-turning, disinfectant odor to the legions of infirm people hobbling and wheezing all over the place, hospitals are to be avoided. They're glorified germ repositories. Exotic, incurable diseases lie in ambush in every ventilation duct.

"I'm starting to feel pretty good now. Much better," I tell Dr. Norment. "Why don't you just sign me out of here?"

For my trouble I receive a just-try-it look. Dr. Norment

takes a piece of paper from her clipboard and hands it to one of the nurses.

"Take this down to Admitting." She turns on her heel and strides out of the examining area, her behind gyrating like two beach balls going to war.

Great.

I try to sit up on the examining table, but experience a horrible surge of nausea. Maybe the good doctor knows what she's talking about. Easing myself back down, I close my eyes and hear a familiar voice bubbling in the syrup vat.

"Howya doing, big guy?"

There's Russell Tillman, who'd been standing in the examining area all along.

"What are you doing here?"

"When you didn't come back to the office with that homicide, I knew something must be up," Russell says, looking at me with that curious sideways gaze of his. A rangy man with a pronounced five o'clock shadow, Russell looks like he could use a shave and a shower.

"I figured you probably drove down Frank Robinson Way, so I had the cops look for you in that area. They found your car about six blocks west of Frank Robinson. They located you about an hour later, in an alley, with no wallet. I gave the cops your description."

"Thanks, Russell," I say slowly. I like Russell and am extremely grateful. But at the moment, I wish he would leave, because I'm really not up to talking.

Dr. Hess comes to my rescue. "If you could wrap up your conversation, we'd appreciate it," the young physician says officiously. "We have some tests to run, plus Mr. Billups really shouldn't be talking."

I must have gotten pushed through every floor of the hospital for a succession of tests. When the ordeal finally ends, I'm assisted from a gurney by two orderlies who bird-dog my every move. They walk me into an in-patient room and help me get into bed.

A dowdy nurse who's a dead ringer for Huckleberry Hound

carefully hooks me to a machine that will monitor my vital functions through the night.

"Is this really necessary?" I grouse, not bothering to camouflage my irritation. I've been assaulted, robbed, poked and prodded. Now all I want to do is sleep.

"Doctor's orders," the nurse answers cheerfully, fiddling with a piece of electronic equipment.

"Can I have some aspirin?"

"I think we can manage that."

I'm sound asleep before the nurse returns to my room ten minutes later with a cup of water and two pain pills. My guardian angel is undoubtedly off somewhere collecting overtime pay.

A few hours later I awaken to five pairs of eyes arrayed around my hospital bed and peering at me intensely. They belong to Dr. Norment and four solemn-looking doctors-in-training, each with a clipboard and an expression suitable for the Last Supper.

"How are you feeling?" Dr. Norment asks, glancing first at me, then at some medical charts.

What am I supposed to say—that I feel like death on a soda cracker? At least the unbearable pain in my head is just a dull ache now.

"I feel great." Thanks to my cheery tone, the lie sounds convincing.

"And can you tell me what day it is?"

"Thursday. All day long."

"Excellent, excellent."

Dr. Norment smiles at me. Her face is attractive and her chocolate skin is free of blemishes. I'm guessing she's in her late thirties or early forties.

"You suffered a minor concussion," Dr. Norment informs me. "You also have a small puncture wound on your head. We want to watch you for twenty-four hours. Since you were admitted early this morning, you should be out around noon tomorrow."

"As long as I'm here with you, I'll be fine," I say in my best Barry White voice, prompting a high-pitched giggle.

"You're a mess, aren't you? I see your ability to flirt came through intact." She winks at me, then scoots down the hall with her entourage.

It's 7:30 A.M.

My parents show up about half an hour later.

Dolores Billups makes quite a show of fussing over her second oldest son and I secretly luxuriate in the attention. Despite occasional bluster and bravado, I'm still a mama's boy at heart. She's been doting over me shamelessly since 1970, the year my older brother, James Jr., died in Vietnam. I was only five, but I remember being told of Jimmy's death like it happened yesterday.

James Billups, my father, is more low-key, preferring to talk about the weather, the Orioles, everything but the hospital and why I'm here. The familiar, impenetrable wall of stoicism I long ago stopped trying to breach is firmly in place.

But just before he leaves the hospital room, Dad squeezes my hand for the briefest of moments. The gesture conveys everything his banal chitchat sought to avoid.

I must have dozed off after my parents left, because the sound of silverware jangles me awake. And since I'm lying in a hospital bed with my face bruised, lip swollen and ass exposed to the world in a silly hospital gown, the last thing on my mind is beautiful women.

So who should sashay into the hospital room, pushing a tray of multicolored, gelatinous glop that passes for hospital food? Just Yolanda Winslow, the most exquisite sister I've ever seen. Period.

And there isn't a wedding band in sight. Lawd, have mercy.

Willowy at what I'm guessing is five feet eight, she wears what appears to be a pink nurse's uniform. Yolanda is free of jewelry, save for a watch and an enormous pair of gold hoop earrings. Her reddish-brown hair is short and styled in an undulating, cold wave perm.

In addition to my germ fetish, my other major thing is a weakness for women with slightly flared nostrils. Maybe it's a coincidence, but every woman I've ever dated with flared nostrils was a demon in bed.

Yolanda's skin is bronze and she has a pointed chin with the slightest hint of a cleft. Her only concession to makeup is gold-colored lipstick that would be big-time tacky on anyone else. But the truly remarkable thing about Yolanda is her eyes: They blaze defiantly and are framed by thick, unruly eyebrows.

Say something suave. Something memorable. Something to let this woman know she's encountered a man of substance.

"Uh, I'm glad they put me on your floor—got any corn flakes?" Smooth, Darryl. Real smooth.

Acting as though the wind just blew through the room, Yolanda pauses for a beat or two before acknowledging my comment.

"There aren't any on your tray, but I can get you some if you like," she says in a flat voice. She comes toward me and bends over my bed to lower my food tray. God, the woman makes Pond's Cleansing Cream smell like Paris's most expensive perfume.

After adjusting the tray, Yolanda walks out of my room with long, fluid strides.

Say something, quick.

"Thanks in advance for the cereal."

She glances over her shoulder at me and keeps right on moving. Her face contains not a hint of a smile.

I make a silent vow to get one before the day is over.

I sure would appreciate one, because my love life ain't much to speak of these days.

There are two women in my life right now. One is an attractive television reporter I accompany to the movies, concerts and restaurants on occasion. I'm at a loss to explain how, but somewhere along the line we fell into a dumb brother/sister routine. Strictly platonic stuff.

The other is a shapely thirty-eight-year-old who typically calls when she's pissed at her husband and ready to do a Lorena Bobbit on him. Instead she drives to my apartment, wearing the flimsiest of negligees under her clothing. I eagerly await her visits because she invariably screws my brains out in a multiorgasmic frenzy before hopping back into her red convertible and driving home like a bat out of hell.

The·major problem I have with her is that she doesn't fly into a murderous rage often enough.

Most of my friends are on their first marriage or second, but I've never gotten around to jumping the broom. And frankly, I ain't pressed, if you know what I mean. And I suspect a lot of sisters do.

Eyeballing the so-called food on my tray, I instead pick up the *Baltimore Herald* the hospital considerately sent to my room.

Touching only the orange juice, which is in a sealed container and impervious to the treacherous microbes whizzing out of the ventilation system, I open up the paper.

It contains all the Baltimore news the *Herald*'s white editors deemed fit to print. Which is ironic, since Baltimore is predominantly black.

On the paper's coveted front page, the lead story is by none other than King Handkerchief Head himself, Cornelius G. Lawrence. He's written a piece about Cecil Rivers, a black city councilman running for city comptroller, and how, twenty years earlier, Rivers had filed for personal bankruptcy following an acrimonious divorce. The story is sprinkled with digs from Baltimore's power elite, who question how someone with a Chapter 11 in his background can possibly be entrusted with millions of hard-earned, taxpayer dollars.

The fact that Rivers has since opened two prosperous inner-city hardware stores is buried way down on page A-17—where the story jumps from the front page.

Far more prominent play is given to when Rivers fell asleep during a council meeting three years ago after taking medication for a sinus infection. A large color picture of that embarrassing episode—which is thirty-eight months in the past—graces the front page!

Much is also made over the fact that Rivers has had six traffic violations in the past five years, and that his restaurateur brother is in the state penitentiary for state income tax evasion.

In other words, the story is just another Cornelius Lawrence hatchet job on a prominent member of the black community.

Not to put too fine a point on it, I despise Cornelius Lawrence. And Cornelius ain't fond of me.

I close the paper, not wanting to see anything else, including my police stories from the previous day.

Yolanda glides back into the room, carrying a carton of milk and a sealed container of cereal. She places them on my tray and flits toward the door.

"Aren't you the friendly one!" Damn, I hadn't meant to blurt that out. Must be the blow to the head.

Yolanda turns slowly, her eyes singeing into mine. Hers is a classic put-upon look, a fine woman weary of being howled at.

"Do you practice acting snooty, or does it come naturally?" I ask quietly. That crack over the noggin must have given me Tourette's syndrome. Or is Yolanda having this effect on me?

I never was one to fawn over attractive women and have little patience for men who sing choruses of "Oh, baby" when one walks into a room.

"The least you could say is good morning."

Yolanda stands frozen in her tracks, incredulity and indignation flaring inside her. "Excuse me," she says, hands anchored on hips. "I just *know* you're not talking to me."

Yolanda turns and stalks out of the room.

The woman is starting to look less attractive by the second.

Three *Herald* reporters visit at various times during the day, which is dragging on interminably.

I'm relieved when night finally comes, bringing sleep and a merciful end to the tedium.

Then something incredible happens. Around two or three in the morning, I'm not sure which, Yolanda comes into my room and quietly stands near my bed. She doesn't bother turning on the light.

"Darryl. Hello, are you awake? Darryl?"

"Uh, what are you doing here?" I answer drowsily, shaking my head is disbelief. Yolanda is beautiful even in the dim light streaming under the door. She has on a pair of blue jeans that accentuate her curvaceous hips and a red cotton T-shirt that follows the shape of her smallish, firm breasts. I can see the outline of her nipples, as well as freshly applied gold lipstick.

"I'm about to start work in a few minutes and I, um, just wanted to apologize for yesterday. I've been under a lot of stress lately, but that's no excuse."

"Well, I owe you an apology, too," I say, sitting up in bed and propping the pillow behind my back. "I was way out of line talking to you the way I did. But when I get out of here, I'd like to take you to dinner or something. That okay by you?"

"Sure," Yolanda said shyly. "I'd love that."

"Since you're here, do you mind if I get your phone number? I think there's a pen on the nightstand."

"I have one," Yolanda said, reaching into a pocket and pulling out a pen and a scrap of paper. Smiling the entire time, she scribbles her name and number, then gives it to me.

"Please allow me to apologize again," I say, extending my hand.

Yolanda's hand feels soft against mine. I pull her toward me with the intention of kissing her hand, but she continues moving forward until she's in my face.

Before I realize what's happening, Yolanda is kissing me passionately and pushing me hard against my pillow. Her breathing quickens as I put my arms around her back.

Hopping effortlessly onto the bed, she straddles my midsection with her strong, lithe legs. Our clothes are strewn on the floor in no time and my African manroot is pressing insistently against Yolanda's flat stomach.

"Do you have any rubbers?" I whisper.

Yolanda responds by pressing her forefinger against her lips, a call for action, not talk.

Flipping Yolanda onto her back, I rub my hand lightly

between her legs. Surprisingly hairy and very wet, Yolanda starts moaning loudly as soon as I touch her.

"Hurry, Darryl," she says suddenly, arching her back. "Please hurry."

I slide in easily and it can't be more than ten seconds before I feel Yolanda contracting rhythmically as she thrusts her hips in unison with mine. Her ecstasy is so complete, so infectious, that I start moaning, too, not giving a damn about macho conventions.

I awaken to find a rapidly spreading wet spot on the front of my hospital gown and on my bedsheet. No one is in the bed. Except me, that is.

"Dammit, I can't believe this. A friggin' wet dream!"

The door to my room opens and the overhead fluorescent light flicks on. I reflexively twist toward the wall, leaving my back to the door. My embarrassment is total.

"Is everything okay in here?" a nurse asks cheerfully. Thinking back on it, I'm positive I heard laughter in her voice.

"Everything's fine," I answer sheepishly. "Good night."

Six

W<small>HENEVER</small> M<small>ARK</small> D<small>ILLARD</small> <small>LOOKED AT</small> R<small>ICK</small> A<small>LLEN</small>, <small>IT WAS</small> like peering back into time at a younger version of himself.

It wasn't all that long ago that Dillard was twenty-two, like the wiry, pimple-faced man in front of him. He was familiar with Allen's cynical, tough-guy facade, and appreciated how an uncertain, scared man-child could hide just beneath it.

Like Allen, in his younger days Dillard came across as cocky and something of a know-it-all, a persona anchored in inferiority and insecurity. Easily punctured by the most casual remark or slight. For example, merely alluding to Allen's dropping out of Patterson High was a surefire way to provoke a spluttering confrontation.

Dillard was willing to bet that Allen was spectacularly ill at ease around women, despite his constant hints of being a swordsman. Naturally his purported conquests were of the "love 'em and leave 'em" variety, because no one ever saw them.

"Sorry to call you from work," Dillard said with a nonchalance he didn't feel, given what had transpired that morning. Gesturing casually for the younger man to follow, Dillard walked into the tiny kitchen of his sparsely furnished two-story row house and swung open the refrigerator door.

"Wanna beer?"

"Naw, man, I don't want no beer. What's going on—why did you call me?" Dillard detected an edge in a voice that had displayed only deference and admiration up till then. The scowl etched across Allen's features and the hands on his narrow hips signaled unmistakable annoyance.

"Obviously it has somethin' to do with *the cause*. But if you're too busy—"

"Naw, man, ain't nothing like that," Allen said, instantly backing down, his tone more appropriate for a protégé addressing a mentor. In no time he'd reverted back to the son trying hard to please his exacting, emotionally distant father.

Sweat rolled down his scraggly brown hair and onto a gray-and-orange Orioles tank shirt that made its youthful owner look like a sixteen-year-old truant.

He'd had to pedal a ten-speed bike from his job three miles away in east Baltimore to Dillard's house in the southwest section of the city. The reason Allen had no car? Several weeks earlier, Dillard had called Allen about three o'clock in the morning and mysteriously stated he needed Allen's pickup immediately. Something about mission preparedness. Allen had rolled out of bed and driven over the same night, no questions asked.

That was the kind of relationship they had. The kind of dominion Dillard enjoyed over Allen. At the moment, it was critical for Dillard to reestablish control in his life. His dealings with Allen were an excellent place to start.

Allen reminded Dillard of a cartoon he used to see in the Army. It featured two vultures perched on a tree limb, with one telling the other, "Patience, hell—I want to kill something!"

That was Allen: Mr. Impatience. Act now and think later.

He was the one constantly pressing to do something impetuous and dramatic—strategy and planning be damned. Allen would make a kamikaze charge on the NAACP building this second if he could get his hot hands on a couple of hand grenades and a handgun, Dillard mused.

Ripping two paper towels from the wooden wall dispenser

in his kitchen, he handed them to Allen, who mumbled and started dabbing at his glistening brow.

Dillard watched him, still wondering how he would explain the confiscation of the pickup and its payload of dynamite without losing face. And, more important, control. Striding a few paces, he stood directly in front of Allen and unexpectedly grabbed the younger man's shoulder.

"Look," he said, mussing Allen's damp hair, "we need to head over to your house ASAP. If you need anything inside—money, guns, whatever—now is the time to get it. In a little while the cops will be on your house like stink on shit, if they're not already. I'll explain on the way over."

Ignoring Allen's bewildered expression, Dillard tilted back his head and raised his sixteen-ounce beer bottle to the ceiling. Delicious coolness radiated throughout his throat and midsection. Then Dillard wiped his mouth with the back of his hand and slipped out of his suit jacket.

The nine-millimeter tucked in his waistband popped into view.

Yanking open a kitchen drawer, he rummaged for a gun lock, inserted it in the handgun's trigger mechanism and locked it. Standing on tiptoe, feeling a slight pull in his left calf muscle, Dillard shoved the Beretta out of sight on the top shelf of his kitchen cabinet.

He knew Allen was on the verge of exploding from so many unasked questions. Gently grabbing the younger man's elbow, he ushered him toward the front door.

"Wait for me right here. Gotta find my car keys."

The keys were sitting on a wooden handyman's bench in Dillard's basement. He'd left them there while trying to fashion a detonation device out of electrical wire and household switches.

Gliding back up his basement steps two at a time, Dillard avoided Allen's unwavering gaze. Letting the younger man out first, Dillard locked the front door and they walked toward a 1988 red-and-black Camaro Z28 that had been sitting for a week.

The sun had transformed the car's black leather interior

into a bun-roasting mobile oven. When Dillard opened the driver's door, a hurricane of musty, hot air gushed out.

Ordinarily, he would have lowered both windows and waited outside for the interior to cool off. But this was no ordinary morning, so he unlocked Allen's door and turned the ignition key. The Z28 rumbled to life on the first try, despite a week of idleness.

Dillard unexpectedly switched off the engine and hopped out.

"Wait here."

Jogging back to his front door, Dillard opened both locks. The door opened easily and tiny geysers of dust sprang from the frame when the door was slammed shut. A fine layer of gray dust covered everything in the house, which was crying for a thorough dusting and a vigorous vacuuming.

Dillard could sit for hours cleaning and oiling the assault rifle and shotgun he stored in the basement. Housework was another matter. He'd loathed it ever since he was eight years old and his mother designated him the official floor scrubber and bathroom cleaner. She'd always worked two, sometimes three jobs to support a fatherless household with three children, so the lion's share of the housework fell to Dillard and his younger brothers.

The trend continued after Dillard joined the Army, where he'd cleaned many a latrine and folded bedsheets with military precision during his twelve-year tour. He liked to joke that now he was on strike after years of being forced to work as a domestic.

But in truth, his dusty house wasn't about rebellion. It was really about Jenny.

Dillard had met Jennifer Langston when he was stationed at Fort Bragg, North Carolina. She had been a cocktail waitress at The Warrior Bar & Grill, a stone's throw from the main gate. Six years younger than Dillard, Jenny was from a tiny, one-stoplight town about twelve miles west of Fayetteville, where Fort Bragg is located.

If Dillard lived to be one hundred, he'd never meet another woman as funny, smart, optimistic or courageous as Jenny.

They'd gotten hitched in Fort Bragg's chapel eight months after their first date. The union was never blessed with children, because Dillard had always known that he never wanted kids and had a doctor do the appropriate snipping long before his marriage.

So he and Jenny lavished the attention that would have gone to offspring on each other. She had a way of gazing up at him with loving, admiring eyes that convinced Dillard he was the most capable, virile man on earth.

Jenny exposed a facet of him he'd never known existed, the side that laughed at silly jokes and enjoyed holding hands at the movies. And that viewed people as something other than interchangeable pawns for waging war.

Sweet, beautiful Jenny.

Dillard loved the way she embraced him, warts and all, and chose to accentuate and nurture the good things about him, rather than dwell on the negatives. Sure, sometimes she teased him about being obsessed with warfare and about being a bigger bigot than Archie Bunker.

When it took him two attempts to get promoted from sergeant to sergeant first class, Jenny always had an encouraging word or a supportive smile, never ridicule or second-guessing. And when he got average, and often below-average, performance evaluations, Jenny always commiserated with him and empathized with his version of things.

Not that she always agreed with him. When her dander was really up, the assertive tomboy from rural North Carolina would come roaring out, cussing and fussing during tirades that could last an hour. Once her piece had been spoken and her bile vented, Jenny never carried a grudge and invariably returned to her old, sweet self.

At her urging, he'd actually started going to church on Sundays and memorizing Bible passages!

It had been twenty-two months since cervical cancer had snatched Dillard's angel from him. They'd been married four years, and her death had been some kind of cruel message from God, a wicked joke that innumerable drunken nights hadn't helped Dillard understand. One thing was crystal clear. Namely, He would never be forgiven. Never.

That same God allowed unwed, black welfare mothers to live forever, pumping out baby after baby like breed sows. Dillard and his wife hadn't been a burden to society and had lived as husband and wife. Like the Bible taught.

Why had his Jenny been taken? Where was Jesus when she'd been reduced to a seventy-nine-pound morphine-dependent, breathing cadaver? Where was the justice?

Their home was still pretty much as it had been when Jenny passed on. Dillard would attack the dust and vacuum when things got totally outrageous, but otherwise 4503 Baker Street was an undisturbed shrine to the memory of Jennifer L. Dillard.

Her clothes still hung in the bedroom closet. Her depilatory, feminine hygiene spray and hypertension medicine were still in the medicine cabinet, ready in case she walked through the door tomorrow. Jenny's sewing machine sat in a corner of the small bedroom, its needle stopped in mid-stitch over a simple white dress she had been making when the cancer rendered her too weak to finish.

The only thing different was that Dillard had bought a new bed and donated their old one to Goodwill. The thought of screwing another woman in the bed where he and Jenny had woven magic bordered on sacrilege. One silly tramp had asked about the framed picture of Jenny still displayed on the living room wall. Although three sheets to the wind, Dillard sobered up instantly. The question was answered with a withering glare and an angry request to leave.

Sometimes when he stood near Jenny's portrait, Dillard swore he could feel her presence, could almost hear the laughter that reminded him of tinkling wind chimes. It was a calming, albeit immensely sad, sensation he'd felt on several occasions since her death.

"I'll always love you with all my heart, babe," he called out mournfully. "Why'd you hafta go? Why?"

Dillard knew his late wife would have objected to his NAACP mission. Jenny wouldn't have stood for it. Sometimes he talked to her until the wee hours 'of the morning, explaining how, if the white race didn't make a stand at some point, the window of opportunity might bang shut forever.

"Five or ten years from now, it'll make perfect sense to you, babe," Dillard cooed in a low, soothing voice as he yanked off his tie and began to take off his white shirt. "You'll see why I had to do this."

He was interrupted by three thunderous knocks on the front door that echoed like sonic booms inside the still house. When Dillard flung open the door, Allen was standing there, sweating and disheveled.

"Who you talkin' to, man?" Allen asked, peeking around Dillard suspiciously.

"Didn't I ask you to wait for me in the car?"

"It's hot as shit in there, man," a truculent Allen shot back. Behind him, Dillard could see the passenger door to the Camaro wide open, the key still in the ignition. Nothing would have given Dillard greater satisfaction than to put his foot up Allen's ass and send him sprawling down the steps.

The heat waves shimmying from the asphalt street mirrored the anger Dillard felt inside. He looked down at his shoes, trying to reign in rage building like a fast-moving summer storm. No sense alienating the one member of the group who would unhesitatingly run through a brick wall if asked to.

But then again, Allen was going to be of limited usefulness if he couldn't follow simple directions. Like, "Wait outside in the car."

When some of his heat had dissipated, Dillard crossed his arms and simply stared at Allen, an exasperated parent tempted to spank his hardheaded child with a belt.

"Rick, where are my keys?" Dillard hissed through clenched teeth.

Patting at both pants pockets and feeling nothing, Allen gave an embarrassed shrug. He slowly walked back to the car, got in and closed the door, a chastened dog just yelled at by its master.

Dillard shook his head and forcefully slammed his front door, rattling silverware in the kitchen and nearly causing

Allen to jump out of his skin. Dillard gathered up his tie and shirt from the floor, jogged upstairs to the bedroom and took off the rest of his clothes.

In a little while, local television and radio would be inundated with reports of how a U.S. Park Police officer's vehicle had been hijacked on the Baltimore-Washington Parkway by a suit-wearing white male. One a little over six feet in height. With neatly trimmed reddish hair.

I should have had my suit off and jeans and a T-shirt on before I even let Allen in, Dillard thought, smacking his forehead with his palm. *Oh, well, too late now.* Throwing his rumpled suit across the bed, he put on a pair of faded blue jeans, a Budweiser T-shirt and running shoes.

Allen was slouched down, sweating profusely and sulking like a petulant child when Dillard returned. *What had gotten into the boy? Maybe it was the weather. Whatever the malfunction was, it needed to get fixed quick, fast and in a hurry.*

"Any particular reason why you're acting like a goddamn bitch today?"

Allen's mouth formed a perfectly round O, as if he'd been unexpectedly punched. He recovered quickly, replacing his startled expression with a belligerent sneer. Rolling his eyes evilly, but taking care not to look at Dillard, Allen turned his head toward the sidewalk.

His gaze took in Dillard's next-door neighbor, a chunky welfare mom who sat on her marble front steps wearing a yellow blouse and funky-looking blue pants two sizes too small. She clutched a glass of lemonade while fanning herself languidly, turning pinker by the second under the broiling midday sun.

Not a glint of acknowledgment flickered across her face as she stared dully at Allen and the neighbor who'd forgotten how to speak ever since his wife died.

Not that Dillard, who was ensconced in his self-absorbed little universe, even noticed. He was thinking about how he couldn't control his boss, the Army, the cancer that took Jenny, the U.S. Park Police, his very destiny. Now he couldn't exert enough control over Allen to get the respect he deserved—no, craved.

If he lost his temper, the loss of control would be total. He couldn't afford that.

Hunched forward slightly and gripping the steering wheel, Dillard sat in the unrelenting sunshine for a good minute. His rage filled the car with a nearly palpable presence that crowded Allen against the door. Allen sat perfectly still, fearing that if he moved, the presence in the car would devour him.

Pursing his lips and exhaling slowly, Dillard started the car, pushed in the clutch and pulled off smartly. He ignored the little voice suggesting he spin his wheels to demonstrate his vexation.

Driving purposefully, but not quickly enough to draw police attention, Dillard set out toward Allen's neck of the woods, a mostly white, blue-collar enclave south of Baltimore known as Dundalk.

Dillard was surprised at Mr. Impatience's restraint thus far. Where was the barrage of questions about why he'd pulled Allen away from work and why he'd had a handgun in his waistband?

No explanations were offered by the time they reached a stoplight four blocks from Dillard's house. In fact, not a word was exchanged. The only sound was the din from the Z28's engine as it merrily slurped high-octane.

By the time they had traveled a mile and a half, Allen could stand it no longer. He waited until they were behind a blue-and-white city transit bus taking on passengers. Staring at a huge green cartoon roach in a bug spray ad on the rear of the bus, Allen took a deep breath.

"You said you would clue me," he said gingerly, anxious not to appear pushy. "What's going on?"

With all the coldness he could muster, Dillard locked his eyes onto Allen's for several seconds, then turned away. When he finally spoke, it was in the quiet, low voice of someone at home with murder and mayhem.

"Someone in this group has a big fucking mouth. Know anything about it?"

"W-w-whatcha talkin' about, Mark?" Allen stammered. "You accusin' me of something?"

The bus pulled away from the stop, spewing dark smoke that floated through the Camaro's open windows. The car's air conditioner worked perfectly, but Dillard seldom used it—air-conditioning was one of the creature comforts making the white race soft, complacent and ripe for overthrow.

Dillard glanced briefly at Allen and kept driving. Three minutes dragged by, which seemed like three centuries to a baffled and increasingly apprehensive Allen.

Then a fearful thought flew into his head—maybe Dillard was driving him somewhere to make sure his lips stayed sealed. Permanently. None of the group members doubted Dillard was capable of cold-blooded savagery, having listened in awe to his tales of vanquishing platoons of Iraqis. But Allen never dreamed that Dillard would unleash his prowess against one of the brethren. Now he wasn't so sure.

"I ain't said shit to nobody, man," Allen shouted, looking wild-eyed and feeling a burst of energy as his body's fight-or-flight responses kicked in.

The desperate quality in Allen's voice sent a narcoticlike rush of satisfaction through Dillard. The sensation was fleeting and couldn't have lasted more than a second, but it was the high point of his morning.

You've got it back, he thought. The *power*. Naw, fuck that. Never lost it in the first place. His bosses in the Army had been too stupid to recognize the obvious: Mark Dillard was a born leader. The Pentagon had been too intent on promoting affirmative action jigs who'd cut and run the first time they were fired on.

They wouldn't know how to command someone like Allen, a tough little knot of sinew and bluster who intimidated most people, regardless of skin color. And here he was eating out of Dillard's hand like a meek kitten. Feeling self-congratulatory and even a little smug, Dillard looked at Allen with a suspicious expression.

"Something went down this morning," he began slowly, "that makes me think we have a traitor in the group."

Allen inadvertently shifted his eyes, even though he'd had no hand in Dillard's problems. When he looked up, Dillard's jaw muscles were pulsating and he wore a wistful expression.

"What happened?" Allen asked softly. He and the other members of the ragtag confederation were used to walking on eggshells around Dillard.

"The reason I needed your pickup was to transport dynamite and blasting caps I stole from construction sites I've been working on." The words were regretted as soon as they left Dillard's lips. Allen didn't need to know that. Plus, the admission linked Dillard to the pickup's contraband cargo.

He paused for a moment, mentally previewing what he would say next and how. If there was a chink in his leadership armor, it was the inability to talk off-the-cuff without committing gaffes. Even as a little boy he'd had a knack for saying the wrong thing at the wrong time. Unfortunately, the little boy had a habit of materializing unexpectedly.

Dillard grimaced and shielded his eyes, battling reflected sunlight from a passing vehicle.

"When I was driving your pickup to work this morning, a coupla guys with guns stopped me at Martin Luther King and Pennsylvania Avenue. I was stuck in traffic at a light, so I couldn't move." He sneaked a peek at Allen, gauging his yarn's impact. "Some burly nigger and a white guy about six feet two with short, reddish hair. Damnedest thing was, the white guy was wearing a suit!"

Aware he'd pretty much described himself, Dillard awaited Allen's reaction. Might as well disclose it now, because the media would be hammering away at that description shortly. Hell, there'd probably even be composite drawings on TV and in the newspapers.

Allen just grunted and swiveled around in his seat toward Dillard, who looked oddly tentative instead of cocksure.

"You call the cops?"

Dillard snorted. "Hell, naw. Why would I call 'em when your truck was carrying explosives?"

"You're right . . . heeeeeyyyy, the cops are going to be looking for *me!* Hey, man, this shit is fucked up." Allen's voice was whiny. All pretense of being a tough guy had evaporated.

Dillard knew Allen wanted some soothing reassurances that would magically make things right. But he was stumped regarding what to say. He hoped his voice wouldn't reflect uncertainty and confusion. He felt under pressure to perform and on the spot.

"Don't worry about it, kid; we'll figure something out." Dillard frowned, angry his mouth had let him down once again. Would Patton or MacArthur have been so inelegant when inspiration was called for?

Some men cross the divide between words and deeds with enviable ease. Even Martin Luther King had been able to whip his people into a frenzy at will, Dillard thought dejectedly.

He felt a coldness in his chest, a dulling sense of being impotent and insignificant despite his dreams and efforts to the contrary.

When she was around, Jenny's warm, sunny disposition kept the icicles from tearing at his soul. But since her death, he was frequently filled with despair, self-loathing and hostility no amount of Jack Daniels could thaw. God knows he'd tried.

After thirty-four years, his life wasn't much to write about. He ignored that nagging little voice insisting the brass ring was well beyond his reach and always had been.

It wasn't his fault the counselors in Baltimore's schools were too incompetent to assess his true worth. Ditto the Army. The cycle would not repeat itself. It was going to stop and there was no better time than now.

Dillard glanced at Allen, who looked puzzled.

He's not going to be the hard sell—he already thinks I walk on water, Dillard thought. The old heads, Harold Boyles and Robert Simmes, would be the ones who would need convincing. Forty-one and thirty-seven, respectively, they would listen to Dillard's tale a lot more skeptically than Allen. But they could be managed.

Dillard laid a strong hand on the scruff of Allen's neck, a gesture that could be construed as reassuring or threatening. There was no question how Allen took it. He flinched and appeared ready to bolt from the moving car.

"Boy, I love you like a brother. But I will blow you away in a heartbeat if you jeopardize what we're about. We clear on that?"

"You ain't gotta worry about me," Allen replied in a near whisper. "And if you find the bastard who ratted us out, I'll take care of him."

Dillard allowed himself a grin that didn't reveal his full elation.

One down, two to go.

But first he had an unbreakable date at the Flock of Good Shepherd nursing home.

SEVEN

THE BEIGE PHONE BESIDE MY HOSPITAL BED SURPRISES ME WHEN it starts ringing a little before eight in the morning.

I don't remember asking for a phone. Anyway, you'd think a hospital would refuse to patch through early calls to poor souls trying to convalesce.

Rolling over, I notice the throbbing headache that dogged me yesterday is gone. But my back, shoulder and jaw ache like they've been in a train wreck. I'll take that trade-off.

This had better be Halle Berry or Bill Clinton, I think as I reach over to pick up the phone, which rings with a soothing, muted warble.

"Yeah?"

"Is that Darryl Billups, the *Herald* reporter?" That husky-sounding, oddly androgynous voice again. This time the Bawlimer accent displays the slightest hint of urgency.

"Don't tell me, lemme guess. You're going to blow up the NAACP *and* B-nai B'rith now, right?" For some reason, probably boredom, I stay on the line instead of hanging up.

It's momentarily quiet, save for the soft rustling of bedsheets as I squirm to find a comfortable position for my back. "Look, slim, get a life. Go play your game—"

"I ain't playing games." The firm, calm reply contains neither aggression nor hostility, just concern. Whoever uttered it has deftly snagged my attention with a velvet glove. "A

64

lot of people are going to get hurt and I thought you might be able to do something about it."

At that moment inside my room in Ida B. Wells Hospital, I realize that whoever is on the line is a true believer. He or she sounds too lucid, too sincere to be a wacko or a prankster.

It dawns on me that possibly, just possibly, I might really be in a position to save innocent lives and get a hell of a story, too.

"Why are you calling me?" I ask, slowly propping my back against the pillow. I glance at the little table next to my bed, hoping to find a pen or some paper. No luck. "Why not call the police?"

"I did. They can't do nothin', 'cause they say nothin' ain't happened yet."

"If what you're saying is true, tell me what your name is. Who are you?"

The request elicits a quiet chuckle, but not one that's mean-spirited or derisive. *Exasperated* is more like it.

"Lookit, it's not important you know who I am. What is important is you know what I say is true and that you do something about it. Anyway, I could get hurt if they find out I'm talking to you."

"Who is 'they'?" Over the phone I hear a door creaking loudly on its hinges.

"Gotta go," the caller whispers furtively; then I hear a click, followed by light static before the dial tone starts.

Easy come, easy go.

This time I don't feel spooked by the encounter, like I did in the *Herald*'s newsroom. I'm reasonably sure I'm dealing with a gentle soul, albeit one a little misguided.

Next door, phlegm gurgles in the throat of some tortured being whose concussive hacking kicks in like clockwork every eight to ten seconds.

I climb gently from my bed and, with an old man's choppy steps, walk to the door and close it. Whatever the guy next door is spewing, I don't want it.

That just strikes me as being sensible, but Mama jokes I'm the black Howard Hughes. I can see laugh lines crinkling her smooth face when she says, "Mr. Clean, I hope there's a Miss Clean out there; otherwise I don't see you getting hitched."

My thoughts drift from my mother to the unpredictable nature of life. You can feel great one minute and be in a hospital the next because of some fool's random act. As I'm pondering this, Yolanda comes sashaying into the room after tapping lightly on the closed door.

Her performance yesterday was strictly ill-mannered yo girl bullshit, if you ask me. Still, you gotta give the devil her due—girlfriend is fine as wine. One side of me wants to snub her, the other wants to go trolling.

She looks me dead in the eye as she walks toward my bed, her athletic body bringing a ballerina's grace to the simple act of carrying a plate of food. As was the case yesterday, I find her penetrating, unblinking gaze slightly unsettling.

The wonderful scent of her moisturizing cream outpaces her, caressing my nostrils when she's still five feet away. I shudder inwardly, partially because I wonder if anyone told her about my little nocturnal misfire. And because she tugs at the section of my heart where the crush-prone little boy hides.

The woman is dangerous.

"I was having a bad day yesterday," she says quietly. I notice she's wearing an inexpensive-looking gold necklace as she balances my breakfast in one hand and adjusts my food tray with the other. "Sorry if I was rude."

"No, I'm the one who needs to apologize," I say in my best Denzel Washington voice. I see surprise flicker across her beautiful face ever so briefly; then it's gone.

It dawns on me that I want to know everything about this women. Which is silly, because I haven't spent a good sixty seconds with her yet.

Unfortunately for me, the interest isn't mutual. Yolanda's focus is on getting her duties finished quickly so she can leave work, then stop by the hairdresser. I don't interest her in the least. Unbeknownst to me she's already cataloged me with a dismissive snap judgment.

I've been tossed on the refuse pile reserved for middle-class Negroes who work downtown, then flee to suburbia before the sun goes down.

Like a lot of sisters who bemoan the dearth of decent brothers, then unerringly gravitate to narcissistic pretty boys or doggish jocks, Yolanda probably craves men with an "edge." Not good men looking to do right by her and treat her with respect. Brothers like those—like me—are too boring. Predictable. Safe.

Yolanda gently lays my breakfast down and turns to walk out the door.

I have other ideas.

"Not so fast," I nearly shout. "How about putting the hospitality in hospital?" Ugghh, that was corny.

Still facing the door, Yolanda rolls her eyes back in her head. I've really hit the jackpot in Room 1107, she says to herself sarcastically.

"Don't make a sick man shout," I say casually. "Come closer so I won't have to scream." My tone is confident, borderline arrogant.

Feeling guilty about having been so abrupt the day before, Yolanda decides to humor me. Her cart sits outside the door, sending the aroma of Canadian bacon wafting through the hallway.

"I owe you an apology, too," I say coolly. "Two, in fact. First of all, I was a little rude yesterday myself, so I hope you'll accept my apology in that regard."

Yolanda takes note of my diction and the ease with which I handle English. She's not impressed.

"Second, I hope you don't take offense with what I'm about to say, but you are a very striking young lady and I would love to have dinner with you after I get out of here." I hadn't meant to move that fast, but hell—why dilly-dally?

Yolanda crosses her arms across her chest. Bad sign. "Hey, we all have our days," she says in a deflatingly blasé voice. "Yesterday was a bad one for me. Like I said, I'm sorry. I've got three more floors after yours, so you take it easy."

"I'll definitely do that," I assure her. "But I'd sure heal

faster if I could see you after I get out. What's your name, anyway?''

"Yolanda. Yolanda Winslow. Take care, Mr. Billups." The sound of my name rolling off her tongue is music.

Time for a bold gambit.

"When I get back to work, I'm going to write a story about a dedicated hospital worker I met named Yolanda Winslow."

Yolanda looks at me curiously at first, then starts smiling.

"You're a reporter?" she asks excitedly. "Do you work for the *Black Chronicle?* I've always had an interest in journalism." Once Yolanda stops acting like a she-devil, she has an engaging, girlish quality.

"Nope, I work for the *Herald*. What kept you out of journalism?"

"I, uh, just got sidetracked I guess," Yolanda says, a sad look crossing her face. "Maybe it was just never meant to be. I do write poetry, though."

"Well, I would love to take you to the *Herald* and show you around one day. And I love poetry—maybe you could share it with me if it's not too private."

That's a damned lie. I've never particularly cared for poetry. But having discovered one of Yolanda's hot buttons, I'd be a fool not to mash the hell out of it. "How do I get in touch with you in case an interesting poetry reading comes up?"

That question brings Yolanda's guarded reserve crashing back down. "I'm not in the habit of giving my number to strange men," she responds coolly.

"There's only one Darryl Billups, B-I-L-L-U-P-S, in the phone book. My address is listed, too. Okay?"

"It was nice meeting you, Darryl. Good luck with your career. I'd better go now." She gives a little smile, one surprisingly warm. Yeeessss!

"You're crazy about me," I mutter as she glides away. "I'm the Mac Daddy and you know it."

I'm sure of two things about Yolanda. First, she's probably not in a superserious relationship, based on the fact she stayed in my room as long as she did. Number two, I have got to see this woman again. Don't know where, don't know when, but I definitely gotta. Even if I have to drop back by the hospital.

Smiling, I lift the plastic lid off my food. Not finding the breakfast particularly appealing, I pick up the *Herald.* Incredibly, there's a second part to Cornelius Lawrence's hatchet job on Councilman Rivers. This time the emphasis is on Rivers's city council voting record and how he usually votes in favor of community-based special interest groups, rather than Baltimore's business elite.

The story goes on to surmise that if Rivers wins the comptroller's race, his presence might scare businesses away from Baltimore at a time when the city's tax base is shrinking.

Incredible.

I shake my head sadly. Cornelius is so intent on doing massuh's bidding, it's scary.

After the front page, the rest of the paper—from the features section to sports to business—is equally uninspired. Readers sure didn't get their fifty cents' worth today.

At quarter to ten Dr. Norment shows up, trailed by her entourage of young physicians. I'm pleased to see her because she seems pleasant and positive. And because she has the power to spring me out of here.

She's all business this morning. "Let's take a look at you." She immediately starts examining my eyes, her face hovering inches from mine. It always makes me feel like a lab rat when doctors invade my space to poke and prod.

Dr. Norment writes something on her chart, then sticks a scope into my left ear. I can feel her body warmth, smell peppermint on her breath.

"Dr. Stanley, could you look at this for a moment?" A young male doctor takes the scope from Dr. Norment. A coffee aroma seems to ooze through his every pore.

"Does the external meatus show hemorrhaging Dr. Stanley?"

There's a pause. "No, looks clear to me."

"And what about the tympanic membrane?"

"It looks perfectly normal," Dr. Stanley quickly answers.

"Good, good." Dr. Norment gently grabs the scope from her youthful charge and performs a quick check of my right ear.

"You're free to leave," she says. "Unless you want to stick around for the wonderful food here, of course."

The neophyte physicians all laugh at Dr. Norment's joke a little too hard. I scrunch up my nose and make a face at Dr. Norment. We both smile.

I'm out of bed in a flash, forgetting my aches and the hospital gown exposing my behind to the world. Unfazed, Dr. Norment heads toward the door, trailed by her eager-beaver entourage.

"Thanks, Doc," I call.

"Be careful out there, Clark Kent," she says as she walks out of my room.

I'm totally unprepared for what's in the small clothes closet. Dried blood is all over my blue denim shirt. One of my pants pockets, the one where I keep my wallet, is ripped. There's also a hole in one knee.

Fortunately, the keys to my car and my apartment are still in a front pants pocket. Did I mention that my pants are grimy and reek of dried urine?

To fetch my car from the *Herald*'s employee parking lot, I have to slip on these disgusting threads. Then walk five blocks to the *Herald*, since I have no cash.

My clothes feel repugnant against my skin when I slip them on. And in no time flat, my room is smelling like a New York subway station.

Hoping not to see Yolanda, I stick my head into the hallway. It's empty except for two nurses laughing and talking at a nurse's station. Good.

Slinking into the hallway, I head toward a red exit sign that seems like it's miles away.

"Hey! What are you doing up here?"

I turn to see one of the nurses walking tentatively in my direction while the other picks up a phone.

"I'm a patient here," I explain sheepishly. Maybe if my inquisitor gets a snoutful, she'll send me on my way. The nurse, a middle-aged white woman, continues to advance cautiously. Fortunately, Dr. Norment and her entourage walk out of a patient's room behind the nurse.

"Could you please tell her who I am?" I ask with a frown.

Dr. Norment engages my eyes for a split second. That sliver of time is all she needs to read my indignation and nod understandingly.

"He just got released," Dr. Norment says curtly. "He had a slight mishap and his clothes didn't fare very well."

"I'm terribly sorry, sir," the nurse says apologetically. "Do you have everything you need to check out?"

My response is to lope down the hall and open an exit door that opens into a quiet, humid stairwell. Not sure if it leads to the lobby and not really caring, I descend the stairs as quickly as my aching back will allow.

When I reach the first floor, several people in the lobby stare rudely as I scoot by. Ordinarily I wash my hands when leaving a hospital, but liberty outweighs cleanliness today.

A soft rain is falling when I get outside, and the pungent smell of damp earth hangs in the air. After more than twenty-four hours of breathing hospital odors, I've never smelled anything as wonderful.

Following the walkway to the sidewalk, I turn right and walk with my head to the sky. Warm raindrops massage my face and rinse my skin. In lieu of jumping into a tub of hot, soapy water, this is the next best thing.

Pedestrians give me a wide berth, and several women—black and white—clutch their purses. Everyone is wary of the homeless black man grinning like a giddy fool as raindrops trickle down his face.

I'm oblivious to them all. So much so that I nearly overlook a familiar figure heading my way. Squinting, I recognize Evelyn Stewart, an old girlfriend.

The daughter of one of Baltimore's more prominent black lawyers, Evelyn just turned thirty-one and is an executive with a local nonprofit organization. Petite, pretty and a skilled pianist, she and I dated seriously two years ago and contemplated tying the knot.

That is, until she determined my print-journalist salary would never support the lifestyle she aspires to. Her decision to break things off caused both of us a lot of pain.

Evelyn's pea-green designer raincoat flaps in the breeze as she races to greet me. Her right hand clutches a green-and-black designer umbrella.

"Darryl! What in the world happened to you? Are you all right?"

I just grin. "You know how it is scraping by on a reporter's salary," I say with a laugh. "Say a prayer for me, Evelyn. Say a prayer."

I peck her on a rouge-covered cheek, making her recoil involuntarily. Then I nonchalantly stroll away without a backward glance, leaving Evelyn standing on the sidewalk, mouth agape, as raindrops splatter down.

That should give her highfalutin friends something to talk about.

As I saunter along, thoroughly enjoying my unplanned shower, the brick *Herald* building suddenly looms. Dripping water and feeling dangerously liberated, I stand near the front door, debating whether to enter.

"Boy, you blew it this time," I murmur to myself as I stroll self-consciously into the *Baltimore Herald*'s newsroom. "What was I thinking?"

It takes about 3.5 seconds for a mortifying hush to herald my arrival. Conversations are abandoned in mid-sentence—fingers abruptly levitate from keyboards. Editors, reporters and editorial assistants stop what they're doing. Everyone turns to marvel at the unexpected apparition.

"Brother, what happened to you?" the guard at the front desk had asked, rising from his chair when I entered the building. "You look like five miles of bad road!"

"Man, I've got to go to the newsroom," I'd told him brusquely, circumventing the usual small talk. "I don't have my ID because I got mugged."

"Sorry to hear that, podna—go right on up." The guard

was solicitous, almost pitying, as he gestured toward the elevators.

My wet, thick-soled work shoes announced every step on the way to the elevators: *squeak, squawk, squeak, squawk.*

Now I'm in the newsroom, wishing I'd never entered the building. Too late. I'm here now. Bigger than life. How the hell do I extricate myself from this one?

As if hearing my query, four angels flutter to the rescue. Three reporters and an editorial assistant, all female, with worry lines on their cherubic faces. They'll never know the full measure of my gratitude.

"We heard what happened. Are you okay? Did the police catch the bad guys? Why aren't you home?" Every man loves being fussed over by women, whether he admits it or not.

I unconsciously straighten up and stick out my chest. It feels good to know someone cares about Darryl the man, as opposed to Darryl the story-writing machine.

With a minimum of prodding, I relate what getting mugged in a Baltimore alley was like. My audience is so enthralled that no one thinks to ask why I was in the alley in the first place. To my relief.

Yes, my head and lip hurt and so does my back.

Yes, I was pretty sure I got whacked with a gun, but I didn't get a good look at it.

No, I'm not afraid to return to the streets now.

No, I'm not coming to work today, because I'm tired and need some rest.

By now several other *Herald* employees, male and female, encircle me, vicariously experiencing the urban violence they're forever writing about but seldom encounter.

Remembering that I'm supposed to be under the weather, I tone down a bit, making my voice softer, my gestures less animated.

"I just came up here to get a spare set of car keys out of my desk," I say, lying facilely. "My doctor thought it would be a good idea to go home and rest—head injury, you know."

"Oh, is that a fact? I was hoping to pencil in your name in

the lineup today,'' Tom Merriwether says cheerfully, moving toward the center of the circle as reporters part to let him through.

"No, Tom, I'm just here to get my car keys," I reply blandly. "I took a nasty shot to the head and I really don't feel up to working today." The seething animus I'd felt toward Merriwether moments earlier is totally gone.

He, on the other hand, is sure I'm trying to show him up. Merriwether deeply resents being dictated to by reporters. Particularly in front of other reporters and editors. Particularly in the middle of the newsroom. Particularly by Darryl Billups.

"I see," he says smoothly, even managing a forced smile. "That shouldn't be a problem. I'm sure you brought medical documentation?" Merriwether reaches out and woodenly places a hand on my shoulder. The gesture comes off as stiff and insincere, which it is.

Everyone stands around quietly, waiting for my response. For a split second Merriwether and I look into each other's eyes, mongoose and cobra searching for an opening. To our credit, our faces remain neutral. The silence is dragging on too long—some of my co-workers stare at the floor and clear their throats uncomfortably.

"What happened, young man—you go twelve rounds with Mike Tyson?" someone bellows. It's managing editor Walter Watkins, an unlit Louisville Slugger stogie clamped between his tobacco-stained teeth. "I was really sorry to hear about what happened to you, but I'm glad you're out of the hospital," Watkins says, slinging a beefy arm around my neck and sending a jolt of pain arcing through my back.

"Thanks a lot, Mr. Watkins, I really appreciate that," I say, shooting Merriwether a faint smirk.

"Boy, you look like hell," Watkins says innocently, making me wince at his noun selection. "Go on home and take a hot bath. I think we can manage to get the paper out."

"Yes, that shouldn't pose an insurmountable problem," Merriwether says, his voice snide and cutting. Some people deliver put-downs with such finesse and wit, you don't realize you've been mortally wounded until later. Not ham-handed

Tom Merriwether. He's just blundered by hacking me in front of Watkins, who has a soft spot for reporters injured in the course of duty.

Naturally, all this is escaping Merriwether. To his warped way of thinking, I've just grandstanded him with an assist from Watkins.

The three of us stand there, Watkins reflectively stroking his chin and daydreaming about his reporting days and Merriwether displaying a closedmouthed grimace he's sure passes for a smile.

Across the newsroom, Cornelius Lawrence catches my eye. He hasn't bothered to get up from his desk, even though every other black *Herald* reporter in the building has checked on me.

His expression is one of bored indifference, but could just as easily be scornful by changing a facial muscle or two. Having seen enough of Cornelius, I turn and face Watkins.

I have no appetite for confrontation at the moment. A potentially disastrous situation has unexpectedly turned into a public relations bonanza. It's time to get while the getting is good.

"Thank you for your consideration, Mr. Watkins," I say in a voice conveying just the right mixture of deference and relief. "I'm not quite one hundred percent just yet, so a day's rest should do me good."

"By all means," Watkins replies placidly.

My newfound celebrity is amusing. But what I crave is peer recognition for my journalistic talent.

Finally alone inside my gray cubicle, I log onto my computer terminal, a two-step process that requires me to type my last name, then a secret pass code. Fourteen messages await.

I read them quickly, log off and make a beeline for the door.

Outside, my trusty steed awaits in a far corner of the newspaper's employee parking lot, water beads giving it a coat of sparkling sequins. The sight of my black, Japanese economy car brings a smile to my lips. Not only do I lovingly massage it twice a month with expensive paste wax, but I'm always pampering it in some way or another.

Mama claims me and Daddy dote on cars so much because we relate to machines better than people. There's no denying cars never let you down like people do, I muse as I open the door. But love machines more than people? Daddy, maybe, but definitely not me.

Driving slowly because my driver's license is missing, I head for the Ridgely's Delight section of the city, not far from Orioles Park at Camden Yards. My cautious pace makes a ten-minute trip fifteen.

As I ease into a parking space in front of my apartment, I see nosy old Mr. Vaughan, the neighborhood watchdog, outside enjoying the sun as it singes the rain clouds out of the sky.

"Hiya doin', young buck?" Mr. Vaughan grins, not the least self-conscious about having three teeth in his wizened head. If he notices my tattered, bloody clothing, he doesn't let on. "Haven't seen you in a couple of days. Everything all right?"

"I'm fine, sir," I answer, bending down to pick up a supermarket circular on the sidewalk.

"Real pretty girl came by here about twenty minutes ago asking for you," Mr. Vaughan says coyly. He clearly relishes having a juicy conversational tidbit to bait me with. "Real foxy mama. Had a little boy with her, too."

"Must be a mistake. We both know she was really here to see you."

Delighted, Mr. Vaughan throws back his gray head and guffaws with devilish delight.

"I started to steal her from you, young buck, but I didn't want to hurt your feelings," he says, capping his sentence with a burlesque wink.

"What did she look like?"

"Long, tall drink of water, with short brown hair and gold lipstick. Looked like she had a nurse's uniform on."

Uh-uh, no way . . . it couldn't be!

"Thanks for keeping an eye on things for me, Mr. Vaughan. I appreciate it."

"No problem keeping an eye on sumpin' like that. Filly was easy on the eyes."

I feel like somersaulting up the walkway. If it's not Yolanda, she must have a twin. But how did she know where I lived? And who's the boy?

Unlocking the wood-and-glass door leading to the vestibule, I stop by a row of tarnished brass mailboxes built into the wall. Maybe Yolanda dropped in a note?

There's no note, just a couple of bills, a letter from one of those sweepstakes nobody ever wins, and a postcard. It features two seals lazily sunning themselves at the National Aquarium in Baltimore.

On the back, scrawled in extra-fine red ink are the words:

YOU STILL DON'T BELIEVE ME, DO YOU?

The message is printed in large, childlike block letters. The postcard was mailed yesterday, in Baltimore, according to the postmark.

Exhaling slowly, I stand in the humid, sun-drenched vestibule and stare at the postcard. Isn't my life complicated enough without riddles or cryptic messages? I can't wait to switch on the window-mounted air conditioner in my loft, unplug the phone and collapse into bed.

The dead-bolt lock in the steel inner door turns easily, revealing an impressive foyer dominated by a white marble staircase set off by a black-and-white marble floor. The staircase ends on the second landing with three cobalt-blue doors, each an entrance for separate two-story loft apartments. I enter the door on the left, grateful to be home.

Instead of the rat warren that passes for most bachelor pads, Chez Billups is a model of order and neatness. The mahogany work desk and word processor atop it are dust-free, as is a red, '50s-vintage Coca-Cola vending machine in the living room. The polished hardwood floor glows a warm gold/amber in the sunlight—the black spiral staircase leading to the loft is unsullied by dirt.

I believe that wielding control over one's life begins at home.

Hoping to hear Yolanda on my message machine, I flip it on and plop down on a brown beanbag chair. My mother's voice wafts out, asking if I've left the hospital yet. My younger sister, Camille, sounding unusually upbeat and giddy, invites me to a gathering at her house tonight. My boy, Mad Dawg Murdoch, fills me in on the goings-on at the *Herald*.

But I only half listen to these messages, my mind locked on one that preceded them. To my chagrin, the Androgynous One knows not only where I live, but my phone number, too.

Muffled traffic noise can be heard in the background, along with a sporadic *huhwheeee, huhwheeee*. Sounds like an automotive air wrench.

"T'day or t'morrow, Sheldon Blumberg is gonna get shot," the Androgynous One warns breathlessly. "They could be bluffing, but I don't think so. They say Blumberg is a nigger-lovin' kike who deserves to be executed."

There's the sudden sound of gasping, the rapid hyperventilating of someone having trouble breathing. After a couple of seconds I recognize it as weeping. The voice that follows is disjointed, like that of someone who's had a drink too many.

"I don't know why I'm bothering you with this . . ." More fast breathing, as well as a couple of barely audible sobs. "I'm sorry. Maybe there ain't nothin' nobody can do. Oh, God, how did I git myself into this?"

That question is followed by loud bawling, and I can hear whoever it is trying desperately to regain control. I can almost feel the underlying frustration and remorse. "I'm so sorry, Darryl, I'm so, so sorry. God, I hope I'm wrong."

More crying, then the sound of the phone gently being hung up.

The combination of the message and the postcard unnerve me so badly that I jump off the beanbag chair and scurry through my apartment, peering under the bed and into closets.

If the Androgynous One is involved with crazies who want to blow up black people and shoot Jews, CALL THE COPS! Riding herd on murder and mayhem is not my bag. I just write about that shit.

Sheldon Blumberg is a prominent Baltimore businessman who made a fortune by parlaying one well-run pharmacy into a chain of drugstores and supermarkets throughout the Baltimore-Washington corridor. Now in his late seventies, Blumberg ceded day-to-day control of his businesses to a daughter about a decade ago, and devotes much of his time to running The Blumberg Foundation.

Fortunately, or unfortunately, depending on one's point of view, one of the foundation's biggest beneficiaries over the years has been the NAACP. That fact is a source of much eye rolling and sighing in some black circles, where the sense is that African-American institutions ought to be able to depend more on blacks and less on white largesse.

Another faction of the community maintains that after centuries of white oppression and subjugation, no amount of money from white charities and institutions could repay the towering debt this country owes African-Americans.

Blumberg also gives tons of money to Baltimore's artsy set and bankrolls a number of well-known, liberal Maryland politicians on the state and national levels. So a Blumberg execution would pretty well turn Baltimore on its ear. Not to mention the *Herald*.

Picking up the phone and feeling more than a little foolish, I dial the number for Phil Gardner, the homicide detective I ran into before I got cracked over the head. What am I going to tell him? That I have a sneaking suspicion Blumberg may be in danger of bodily harm? A strong hunch?

"Gardner, Homicide," his recorded message spits out. "Leave a message after the tone." BEEP.

"This is Darryl, Darryl Billups with the *Herald*," I say, opening my refrigerator door in search of a cool drink. "Sorry to bother you with this, but I got an anonymous call at home warning that somebody's gonna off Sheldon Blumberg today or tomorrow. It may turn out that I'm just wasting your time. The same caller also says somebody's gonna bomb the NAACP. It may turn out that I'm wasting your time with this, too, but I figured better safe than sorry." I give him my home number.

I call the *Herald* next and get assistant metro editor Barbara Rubenstein.

"Hey, Barbara, this is Darryl Billups. I'm a little embarrassed to bother you with this, but I'm getting anonymous calls from somebody who claims Sheldon Blumberg is going to get shot."

"Yeah, okay, hold on a sec, Darryl," she responds, sounding preoccupied. I can hear voices in the background. Nearly a minute passes before Barbara gets back on the line again.

"Darryl, lemme call you back, okay? It's a little crazy around here right now."

"Okay, but you heard what I said about Blumberg, right?"

"Uh-huh, sure. Call you back—at home, right?"

"Yes."

"Okay. Bye."

Brushing at the goose bumps on my arms, I walk to the door and set the burglar alarm to go off if a door or window opens. Then I shed my dilapidated clothing, ball it up and aim it at the trash can with a Jabbar skyhook. On my way to the bathroom I indulge my one narcissistic habit. Namely, I stop in front of the full-length mirror and admire the lightly muscled physique that's the result of several workouts a week.

Something else comes into view. A lump roughly the size of an acorn is under the right side of my jaw, and an ugly, blotchy bruise has staked a claim on my right shoulder. All in all, a small price to pay.

The wood floor feels cool and soothing under my bare feet as I pivot in front of the mirror, studying for signs of the thugs' handiwork. Satisfied that I'm still in one piece, and a well-toned one at that, I head for the bathroom. The price tag from my denim shirt is still on the floor where I dropped it, rushing to work two days ago.

With sunlight streaming through the bathroom skylight, I

scoop up the price tag from the floor, then turn on the shower, making the water a little warmer than usual. Ordinarily I would close the door to confine the heat and humidity to the bathroom. Today I not only leave the door open, but part the shower curtain a little, too.

When I step into the tub, the torrent of hot water takes up where the raindrops left off. The shower cascades soothingly over my aching back and shoulder, gradually loosening tightly coiled muscles. The water massages and caresses, even titillates when I face it and strategically position the shower nozzle.

But I can't stay in here all day, as much as that would please me. I reluctantly turn off the shower, then just stand in the tub, feeling totally relaxed as the water runs down my body. When I towel off, I can feel each individual tuft of terry cloth sliding across my skin. The scene in the alley flashes through my mind and I silently promise God not to take life for granted anymore.

Until the next time.

Unfortunately, my zone of well-being and tranquility extends no farther than the edge of the bathtub. The minute my feet touch the cool tile floor, my thoughts drift to mysterious phone messages and postcards and death threats aimed at Jewish philanthropists and black civil rights organizations.

I think I'll throw on some clean clothes, then head down to the Motor Vehicles office and get a new license. My original plan was to stay here and cop some zees, but that option grows less appealing by the second.

In light of the strange developments crashing down around me the past couple of days, right now my apartment gives me the creeps.

EIGHT

R. CHARLES COVINGTON III STOOD IN THE MIDDLE OF THE *Baltimore Herald's* busy newsroom quietly throwing a hissy fit.

On the R. Charles Whining Scale, it was a mild 3.4 magnitude outburst, with 8.0 being a profanity-spewing, trash-can-kicking R. Charles Blowout.

There was no way that he, the paper's City Hall reporter and ace of aces, was going to fill in on the cop beat for a day in light of Darryl Billups's misfortune.

R. Charles was genuinely insulted that Tom Merriwether had even asked. Plus, he knew that Merriwether hated confrontations and that if he held his ground long enough, R. Charles would prevail. As usual.

"Let's be reasonable about this," Merriwether said as firmly as an invertebrate can. "I have five reporters on vacation and three out sick—including Darryl. I'm not asking you to run around the city. All I need you to do is go to police headquarters from time to time, Charles. Police headquarters is only one block away from City Hall, after all!"

R. Charles wasn't having any of it.

Dressed as always in an expensive, double-breasted suit—which would make him stand out at any newspaper—he made an expansive gesture that took in the entire newsroom.

"Look around you," he said grandly. "Nothing but dead

wood. I see at this very moment at least four reporters who haven't had a byline all week, and it's Friday.''

R. Charles raised his voice slightly, and briefly kicked the Whinometer up to 4.0. "I have already done three stories this week, two of which have been on the front page. Mayor Shaw's reelection campaign is in trouble and I simply think my time would be better spent at City Hall than covering a beat you could give to any intern.''

His point made, R. Charles continued to loom over Merriwether's desk, crossing his arms and looking for all the world like a petulant child.

No one in the newsroom took notice of the encounter—R. Charles was always schmoozing or crying about something.

Editorial assistants scurried about doing gofer work for reporters and editors. Editors busily prepared for the daily 11 A.M. meeting, which was twenty minutes away.

The reporters were either on their phones or staring at computer screens, planting seeds that hopefully would sprout into finished stories by the 6:30 P.M. deadline.

"You're really making this difficult for me," Merriwether said, pretending to look through the top drawer of his desk for something. Merriwether had long ago crossed the line between being a supervisor and a friend to R. Charles, and now it was coming back to bite him.

"Look," R. Charles said, momentarily lowering his voice to a conspiratorial whisper, "I am forty-three years old and have been in this business for twenty-one years—eleven of them with the *Herald*. We both know that I've paid my dues. Do you want to humiliate someone with my credentials—and at this point in my career?''

There.

The ball was firmly in Merriwether's court, where R. Charles knew return of service was unlikely.

His mention of "credentials" had to do with attending Yale, a fact of which he was inordinately proud. The Ivy League connection played a large part in his ascension to the most golden of Merriwether's golden boys.

A graduate of local Towson State University, Merriwether

always had to stifle an urge to genuflect in the presence of Ivy Leaguers.

Quite adept at making lower-tier reporters bend to his will, he routinely kowtowed to a handful of prima donnas. And the prima donna king was R. Charles Covington, with his Italian-made loafers and slicked-back blond hair.

"Let me see what I can do," Merriwether said without looking up. Translation: "You win, so let's bring this uncomfortable episode to an immediate end, okay?"

"Thanks, big guy," R. Charles said, smiling triumphantly. Walking quickly, he left the newsroom, a drab village of gray cubicles that each had a tiny bookshelf area, file cabinet and about a square foot for tacking up notes or family pictures. Sickly white fluorescent lighting overpowered whatever sunlight sneaked through the windows.

Each cubicle afforded the reporter or editor caged within little privacy. Conversations were easily overheard, including those with sources, spats with significant others and furtive whispers to psychoanalysts. Journalists are unusually inquisitive—some say nosy—people whose job it is to snoop and pry.

So newsrooms have no secrets.

But it was the only workplace Cornelius Lawrence had ever known. Sitting inside his cubicle, rereading the front-page article he'd written the day before, he couldn't imagine pursuing any other line of work. Or why anyone would want to.

His reverie was interrupted by his desk phone. Cornelius let it ring three times, then picked it up. It was his wife, Stephanie, sounding like a sweet schoolgirl.

"Hey, baby."

"Hey, Stef, what's up?"

"Nothing going on," Stephanie replied, giggling. "Just wanted to say I love you."

"I love you, too."

"Bye."

"See you tonight, baby."

This was going to be a good day.

When Cornelius reached to pick up the paper again, he noticed an e-mail prompt flashing on his computer. It was a message from Merriwether, asking Cornelius to stop by at the first opportunity.

He allowed himself a small, self-satisfied smile. *Merriwether is probably just getting around to congratulating me on nailing that front-page story,* he thought.

Folding his newspaper carefully and placing it in a file where he kept his old stories, Cornelius straightened his tie and walked toward the metro editor's desk.

"You wanted to see me?"

"Yeah. I have a little problem I was hoping you could help me tackle."

"Sure, you name it."

"Let's go over to my office," Merriwether said unctuously.

Cornelius's curiosity was really piqued at this point: *I wonder if I'm about to get a raise. Something good is about to happen—I can feel it. Dedication and hard work do pay off.*

"As I told the staff an hour ago, Darryl had a little bad luck earlier this week," Merriwether began after they had sat down. "I would appreciate it tremendously if you could fill in for him today."

Cornelius's first reaction was disappointment. He was already looking forward to surprising Stephanie with news of his unexpected raise. It would have been sweet vindication for the long hours he routinely put in at the *Herald.*

Disappointment slowly gave way to anger. He was playing by the rules—was he just being a gullible fool?

After seven years as a *Herald* reporter, two on the cop beat, Cornelius was just a general assignment reporter without a specific beat or area of expertise.

He had been quietly, consistently paying his dues without complaint, rancor or fanfare. Unlike most reporters, who are continually bitching about something and in constant need of hand-holding, Cornelius was a low-maintenance model.

So what was up with the police-beat request?

"Hey, Tom, no problem," he heard himself saying. Not

only did Cornelius show no emotion, but his expression remained cheerful and upbeat.

"You're a saint, Corny," Merriwether said, looking away.

He had been spared obnoxious whining about time spent in the profession and dues-paying, nor had there been any other crybaby antics.

"I really hate to ask you this, but as you know, Darryl also covers cops tomorrow. In case he's not up to snuff by then, could you possibly come in on your off day and do the Sunday shift, too? Of course, if you have plans with the family, I'll understand."

Merriwether already knew Cornelius would say yes, but at least he could come off as humane and caring by throwing in the family stuff.

Feeling on top of the world a few seconds ago, Cornelius was now thoroughly bummed out.

"Hey, don't worry about it," he said in his best team-player voice. "My home phone number is in the computer."

"I really appreciate your getting me out of this jam," Merriwether said. "And if you do have to come in tomorrow, I'll give you a choice of overtime or comp time, okay?"

"Not a problem, Tom. Not to worry."

Cornelius gave a stiff, beauty-contestant smile, slowly left Merriwether's office and walked back to his desk.

Be patient and everything will work out in the end.

And call Stephanie now, so she won't still be pissed if you have to miss that party she was looking forward to tonight.

NINE

MUNCHING ON SAUTÉED SHRIMP AND SIPPING CHAMPAGNE, I stand transfixed, marveling at the shenanigans of Baltimore's black bourgeoisie.

Wonderful theater of the absurd unfolds all around me, set entirely in fast-moving, one-act plays. Whoever wanders by unwittingly takes center stage. The greater the actor's self-importance and affectation, the greater his or her entertainment value. Depending on the role being played, I'm whipsawed between the urge to cry or laugh until my stomach hurts.

This evening of comic relief is courtesy of my sister, Camille, the High Priestess of Booshie. This is her little soirée, which she has thrown for no other reason than to celebrate being young, gifted, black—and affluent—in the 1990s.

The gathering is as good an excuse as any for me to avoid spending time in my loft.

A Harvard Law School grad, Camille practices corporate law with Broadnax, Preston & Coulter, a white-shoe, WASP law firm considered Baltimore's best.

Camille works her tail off at Broadnax, Preston & Coulter, typically putting in twelve- to fourteen-hour days and most Saturdays. She works with most of the region's black businesses of note. Her legal skills and knack for attracting business got her promoted from associate to partner in only four years.

While I'm proud of my little sister, her success stings a side of me that I'm embarrassed to acknowledge—the petty side that can't rise above sibling rivalry. It galls me that the nappy-headed gnome I used to beat up now commands one hundred forty gees a year—more than four times my *Herald* salary. And it doesn't help that Camille occasionally points this out in subtle and not-so-subtle ways.

It's not done maliciously, I don't think. That's just the way Camille is. She needs nonstop competition the way other people need oxygen. I suspect that's why, at twenty-nine, she has no steady boyfriend and no prospect of marriage, even though she's an attractive woman. But I also admire the way she never gnashes her teeth about being single, or moans about ticking biological clocks.

Camille is married to her job, and until something better comes along, she finds that union satisfying. Other than Broadnax, Preston & Coulter, she's accountable only to Camille. So when the urge hits to escape to Brazil for a week, or Senegal or Martinique or Bermuda, she simply breaks out the plastic and scratches the itch. Without explanations for coddling some threatened brother's fragile ego.

And it annoys me that Camille probably suspects I'll be out of my depth at her affair. I know I got an invite because she was on a guilt trip over not visiting me in the hospital. That hurt my feelings, even though I played it off. Work on a corporate merger kept her away.

"What's up, Bro'? Got a proposition for you," was how Camille got around to inviting me, her voice charged with that familiar undercurrent of urgency. Whatever she's doing at a given moment is the most important matter in the universe, bar none. Camille could ask the time and make it sound as though the fate of the Western world depended on her getting an immediate answer.

"I've got a few people coming by tonight. There'll be some impressive women here. One thing could lead to another—who knows—Mama might even get that grandchild she's always complaining about not having.''

I had to laugh despite myself. Camille always could charm the birds out of the trees. We both know her last-minute invitation was an apology for not making it to the hospital.

So a few minutes earlier, I found myself driving to Camille's tiny downtown high-rise, with its security-patrolled parking garage, TV intercom system, hyperpolite front-desk personnel and tasteful lobby decor.

Three inches shorter than I am, Camille gives me a big bear hug when I enter her twentieth-floor apartment. Her arm strength indicates her health club membership is still active and being put to good use.

''How do I look?'' she asks, modeling an unremarkable, turquoise dress with puffed sleeves and a laughably ugly black bow in front. The outfit looks like a cross between something Shirley Temple and an antebellum Southern belle might wear.

Naturally I lie and tell her that she looks wonderful, momentarily avoiding eye contact. ''What's that perfume you're wearing? I like it.''

''Issey Miyake,'' Camille answers, vainly teasing her hair with a comb. ''Thanks for noticing.''

Thinking that it might make a good present, I start to ask how much it cost, but stop myself. Why bother? Camille has absolutely no interest in things inexpensive.

''So where's the party?'' I glance around Camille's deserted apartment, hoping that I haven't made a fool of myself by appearing on the wrong night.

''Honey, do you think people are going to be tramping through here, knocking over my nice things and soiling my carpet? Please! They can go to the reception room—that's what it's there for. In fact, I need to go down there for a minute. I'll be right back.''

She leaves me sitting on a supple, beige leather sofa. This is the first time I've been alone in Camille's apartment and I take full advantage. I case the joint room by room, saving the living room for the grand finale. I sweep it with my eyes, drinking in every Ethan Allen-inspired detail. The place is definitely hooked, and in a way that exudes casual elegant. Whoever lives here clearly makes good money, but is comfortable enough with it not to be lured into cheesy ostentation.

An entire wall of the living room has been turned into a seven-tier bookshelf stretching from floor to ceiling. A rolling librarian's ladder, made of mahogany, no less, leans against the bookshelf.

The living room walls are a peach color and the parquet floor is covered with a tan rug featuring a blue crisscross design. Above the fake fireplace, which is trimmed with white marble, hangs a colorful Romare Bearden print of a jazz band.

The sand-colored wood coffee table is dominated by a thick bound book titled *Henry Moore: Sculpture and Environment*. There is also a thin volume with black-and-white pictures, *I Dream a World: Portraits of Black Women Who Changed America*. And, of course, a bound *Cartier* book.

As I survey all this, I try to guess how much everything costs. I also wonder if Camille has ever given one red cent to a charity of any kind. Knowing my status-conscious, self-absorbed sibling, I kinda doubt it. If the woman ever had an altruistic thought, it probably died of loneliness.

One thing that I admire about Camille, though, is that she makes no bones about being a social-climbing, acquisition-minded, Aspen-vacationing elitist. None of that high-minded clucking about the plight of the black underclass, the stuff buppies drone on and on about over Chardonnay, then wind up doing absolutely nothing. Camille never does a damn thing either, but at least there's none of that dinner-party hypocrisy about pretending she wants to.

Tour time ends with the sound of a key turning in Camille's door.

She enters looking preoccupied, trailed by a tall, lean brother with a thin mustache so perfectly trimmed it appears to be drawn on. His light gray Giorgio Armani is clearly custom-tailored, with creases sharp enough to slice bread. Mr.

Armani has the practiced smoothness of someone hopelessly in love with himself. A pretty boy.

"I forgot my cellular phone," Camille says casually, walking over to the fireplace, where the phone sits on the mantel. I notice her demeanor is basically unchanged despite the presence of Mr. Armani. Camille never was one for putting on airs. If anyone's supposed to be impressed, it's definitely him.

"Oh, Darryl, this is Jeff Danielson, a guard for the Washington Bullets," Camille says offhandedly, bending to rearrange some yellow and violet flowers in a glass vase. I thought Mr. Armani looked familiar. I smile, guessing Camille failed to mention her brother was back at the apartment.

Danielson offers a manicured hand redolent of Lagerfeld cologne.

"Nice to meet you, brother," I tell him easily, mildly surprised an NBA player would have lacquered nails and soft hands.

Camille has accomplished her mission, which ostensibly was to get her phone, but probably centered around showing off her digs to Mr. Armani. She suggests that we grab an elevator to the fourteenth floor, where the reception room is.

In the elevator, Camille makes small talk about Mayor Clifford Shaw and how his upcoming mayoral race is too close to call. I volunteer that he'll probably win, which would be a good thing since Shaw's basically a decent man. Danielson says nothing.

My guess is he's sulking after having been surprised by Camille's cock-blocking brother.

As soon as we enter the spacious reception room, Camille plunges headlong into a sea of Calvin Kleins, Ralph Laurens and Liz Claibornes. About sixty of Baltimore's most influential black heavy hitters are in attendance, furiously swapping business cards, telling anyone who'll listen how impressive they are and preening like there's no tomorrow. A string quartet provides the musical backdrop. Kinda hard to boogie to, but these Negroes would probably die before allowing a drop of sweat to hit their custom-tailored threads.

A buzz goes through the room when Danielson is spotted.

Several men and a handful of stunning women make a beeline for him. Danielson smiles contently, back in his element.

Camille turns to me and beckons with her index finger. Damn, doesn't she know any better than to do that?

"Don't turn around now," she whispered, "but see that woman wearing her little sister's skirt? She was full of questions when I told her about my journalist brother."

A waiter decked out in white tails and a white bow tie waltzes past, carrying a tray filled with champagne glasses. I expertly snag one without upsetting the tray or slowing the waiter's momentum.

Lifting the fluted glass to my lips and taking a sip of champagne that stings my bruised lip, I slowly turn to see who Camille is talking about.

The skirt in question is painted on the mind-boggling frame of a fortysomething woman who looks like she got lost on her way to a modeling shoot. She has what's known in some quarters as big hair, majestic auburn tresses Tina Turner would kill for.

Miss Auburn is clearly a reddish-brown fish out of water. Despite her breathtaking looks, she stands all by her lonesome. Her clothing and jewelry are clearly expensive stuff, her breath undoubtedly smells spring-time fresh and she damn sure is a sight for sore eyes. The problem is her dress. It's the shortest miniskirt I've ever seen. Not that I'm in any way, shape or form offended or outraged by this.

The audacious black skirt is drawing titters and withering glances aplenty, but not from the brothers. Practically every man in the room is secretly salivating at the thought of conversing with Miss Auburn, but they fear the daggers flung by the other women in the room. The brother brave enough to approach Miss Auburn will be gossip fodder into the next century—peer pressure has erected an invisible force field around her.

"I see why she's standing," I observe slyly. "Girlfriend wouldn't have any secrets if she sat down and that skirt started riding." Camille and I laugh. "What's her claim to fame?"

"Why, you interested?" Camille responds with a grin.

"Girlfriend is a bit bimboesque."

"What do you care," Camille says bluntly. "Are you after brains or beauty? Anyway, your dance card hasn't exactly been brimming over lately."

As usual, she's taken a stiletto heel and stomped on one of my sensitive areas.

"Baltimore's most eligible bachelors aren't exactly busting *your* door down, are they?" I reply hotly.

"Oh, calm down," Camille replies guilelessly. "Take a chill pill. It was only a joke."

"Nothing's ever said totally in jest, is it?"

Camille shoots me a quick look, her face registering genuine surprise.

"Girl, you've outdone yourself this time," a woman wearing a neon-yellow ensemble coos phonily, tugging at Camille's arm. "And I just loooove that dress. Where on earth did you find it?"

Meow.

Girlfriend, you don't want to go there, I laugh under my breath.

I expertly reel in a second glass of champagne from a waiter zinging by, then stroll away before Camille and Madame Yellow Dress unsheathe their claws. For all I care, these self-important, golf-playing, BMW-driving Negroes can talk about me from now until doomsday: I have some rap for Miss Auburn.

Relieved that her quarantine is finally over, Miss Auburn gives me a grateful, coquettish smile as I approach. She's a shipwrecked maiden adrift in a sea of hostile sharks, excitedly watching her knight in shining armor approach in a lifeboat.

"My name is Darryl Billups," I tell her with mock formality, extending my hand. "My sister is hosting this affair." Two harpies holding drinks and whispering furiously stare at me and Miss Auburn, mouths downturned. One what-the-hell-are-you-looking-at glower sends the troglodytes scurrying off to get into someone else's business. Get a life.

"You know who I am. What's your name?"

Miss Auburn seems flummoxed by that question. She screws up her face à la Kato Kaelin before answering. "Monica Marshall. My friends call me Monica. Is nicknameless a word? I have one of those names you can't make into a nickname. Come to think of it, Darryl is like that, too. What's your sign?"

Oh, God. Why did I come over? A quick glance at Monica's skirt and shapely brown legs remind me.

"You know who one talented actor is?" Monica says, prattling on and looking at me intensely. "That guy who plays Steve Erkle on *Family Matters*. What's his name?"

It's time to make a graceful exit. If push comes to shove, I can always claim to be searching for a fresh champagne glass and just disappear.

Fortunately, Camille, perceptive soul, comes to my rescue.

"Darryl, there's someone I'd like you to meet," she says, tugging at my J. C. Penney sport jacket.

A crestfallen look sweeps Monica's cute face.

"Nice meeting you, Monica," I say, easing away. "Take care."

"Maybe we'll run into each other somewhere?"

"Well, you know Darryl works at the *Herald*," Camille says impishly. "If you give him a call, maybe the two of you can hook up."

Monica's face brightens. "I'd love that," she says, looking at me hopefully.

"Uh, yeah, uhhhmmm, you never know," I mumble, quickly backpedaling and narrowly missing a waiter carrying a silver tray of hors d'oeuvres.

Camille is laughing out loud by this point, but I don't even notice. I'm too busy looking in horror at the entrance door to the reception room.

Cornelius Lawrence! What the hell is he doing here?

The Clarence Thomas of journalism strides grandly into the room, glad-handing as though running for office. I don't know which is more of a shock—running into him here when I'm supposed to be under the weather, or seeing him in the company of black people instead of snorkeling up some white editor's ass.

"Who invited him?" I snap, turning my back to Cornelius, who has on a charcoal-gray suit, black wing tips and pants ever so slightly high-water.

"Who?" Camille asks, looking around.

"Him! The tall, pudgy guy in the gray suit."

"I don't know him. I invited the woman with him, Stephanie Lawrence. She works in the mayor's office. Why—what's wrong with you?"

I scoot behind Camille to avoid Cornelius. If the *Herald*'s editors hear I was out socializing, they'd assume I could have come to work instead of taking off sick.

"Can't explain now," I say quickly. "Gotta go. See ya."

Evaporating into the crowd, I move toward the door, while Cornelius and his wife flow in the direction of Camille.

"Darryl! Darryl Billups!" someone calls out loudly. It's Fredi Norment, the emergency room doctor who'd released me from the hospital earlier today.

Cornelius is now looking my way with a knowing smirk.

"I'm really surprised to see you here," Dr. Norment says. "I thought you'd be home in bed, taking it easy."

"That *definitely* would have been the smart thing to do," I respond, giving Cornelius the evil eye. "I do feel a little under the weather, so I'm going to head on home. Thanks for everything you did for me in the hospital."

Before Dr. Norment can respond, I'm moving out the door and headed for the elevator.

I just know Cornelius can't wait to tell on uppity Darryl Billups, a troublemaking shirker if there ever was one. Merriwether would be overjoyed to receive that little bit of intelligence. In fact, it might be just the final nail in the elaborate coffin I'm positive he's building for me.

By the time I reach my car in the parking lot, foreboding has displaced the lighthearted mood I enjoyed at Camille's. Something evil is afoot, and it's out to get the NAACP and Sheldon Blumberg. And maybe Darryl Billups, too.

Driving home, I'm in absolutely no hurry to get to my

loft, so naturally every traffic light I encounter blazes brilliant green.

This time there will be no checking of mail slots or message machines. When I get upstairs I'm going to wash my face, brush my teeth and belly-flop on the bed.

As I turn my key in the door leading to the foyer, I notice the hanging light in the foyer and the light on the second-floor landing are off, plunging the inside of the building into inky blackness. I don't ever recall having seen both lights out simultaneously.

The hefty inner door swings easily on its well-oiled hinges, as always. I walk slowly toward the far wall, the darkness accentuating every small sound. The change jingling in my pocket sounds like a multicar auto accident in progress.

Running my hand against the wall, I feel for a light switch and flick it on, instantly flooding the foyer in brilliant light.

I navigate the stairs quickly, feeling around in my pocket for my apartment key. I don't recall if I sensed what happened next or saw it. But just as I reach the top of the landing, I'm startled to encounter a figure crouched near my front door. Shouting involuntarily, I raise my hands over my face defensively as the assailant moves toward me.

"Darryl, it's me!" a female voice cries out.

I lurch backward on trembling legs to the second-floor light switch and snap it on.

Yolanda! She brings her hands up to shield her eyes.

"You scared the living shit out of me," I snap angrily. "What are you doing here?"

Only then do I notice the boy. About two or three years old, he clings to Yolanda's leg fiercely, indenting her thigh with his powerful grip. Blood trickles from his nose and lip, his face is filled with bruises and the left side of his head is terribly swollen.

"My God! What in the world is going on?" I reflexively move toward the toddler, but before I can get within ten feet, the boy flinches and runs behind Yolanda, whimpering.

"What's going on here?" I ask incredulously.

Yolanda just stares and remains silent. The humiliation in her eyes is so profound it pains me to see it.

TEN

THE BORED-LOOKING, MIDDLE-AGED BRUNETTE AT THE FLOCK OF Good Shepherd nursing home nodded casually to Mark Dillard, who nodded in return, then quickly scribbled his name on the sign-in sheet.

He was so preoccupied he missed the flirtatious glint in the receptionist's eye as she gazed approvingly at the trim redhead just placed on the menu. A man of few words, this one.

"Third time this week, huh, hon?"

Dillard just smiled and plopped down the sign-in clipboard, making the ballpoint pen attached to it swing a lazy arc. He wasn't trying to be rude, he was just eager to see Betty Jo Dillard, a.k.a. Nana.

It was Dillard's grandmother who'd informed his views on politicians (crooks), the military (honorable), big-band music (delightful) and African-Americans (worthless).

Nana had practically reared Dillard from the time he was ten, freeing his overburdened, single-parent mom to care for two younger children. By the time he was eleven, Dillard cursed with precocious fluency, thanks to Nana. Hurling racial epithets came as naturally as breathing and young Markie would put a hurting on Nana's Ballantine beers if she left them unattended for a minute.

Not that he had to sneak them, because Nana got pissy

drunk with regularity and tended to give him beer for amusement anyway.

Dillard shook his head, remembering how the old girl used to come home every afternoon from her janitor job at Bethlehem Steel sober as a judge, and would be talking gibberish by eight-thirty. Fortunately, she wasn't a mean drunk. No, she was one of those euphoric, giddy ones who want to hug and kiss everybody and everything.

Dillard always admired how the world never beat Nana down, except during those times she was hiding inside a Ballantine bottle.

She'd constantly impressed upon Dillard his innate superiority to African-Americans, Indians, Asians and anyone darker than he was. Never mind that Nana and three generations of Dillards before her wore the bluest of collars and were dismissed as ignorant, poor white trash by blacks and whites alike.

It was Nana's house that Dillard had moved into when she became too addled to keep it herself. Nana would be with him forever, in his heart and in the red-and-blue tattoo on his right bicep. He was going to make her remaining days as comfortable .as possible.

So visits to the Flock of Good Shepherd were a labor of love—in addition to being torture. The home's constant state of semisqualor never failed to agitate Dillard. But it was all he could afford, in conjunction with Nana's government benefits. Walking down a corridor on his way to Nana's room, Dillard frowned at the dust balls always in season under patients' beds. The scent of liniment, dried urine and greasy food loomed oppressively in the air. And as usual, there were scores of elderly people wobbling around without any apparent supervision. It was all rather dreary, depressing, secondrate. Nana deserved better than this.

"Got a light, son?"

A stooped black gentleman who didn't look a day over one hundred and fifty materialized by Dillard's side, smiling feebly.

"Sorry, Pops. Don't smoke."

The old man stopped in his tracks as though he'd slammed into an invisible wall. He'd taken the last comment as a rude directive, rather than a declaration of being nicotine-free. "Uppity goddamned cracker," he muttered as Dillard moved out of earshot. "I'll hang my foot in your smart peckerwood ass."

Dillard continued down the hallway, the encounter already forgotten.

He was a good three doors from Nana's room when he first heard her wheezing. Not surprising, considering how she'd sucked down a pack and a half of unfiltered cigarettes a day for several decades.

But what worried Dillard was that now Nana's mind seemed to be failing. Some days she'd sit and talk about old times as though they'd occurred minutes ago. But on the bad days, which came more and more frequently, she would stare blankly at Dillard as though he were a stranger.

Wondering which Nana would appear today, Dillard strolled through the door slowly, lest he startle his grandmother.

"Aft'noon, Nana," he said quietly.

She stared at him for several seconds, her eyes magnified into large, milky marbles by her spectacles. Her long hair was the yellowish shade of old newspaper. Her wrinkled feet, which were full of bunions and calluses, barely touched the floor as she sat on the side of her bed.

"Markie, dat you? Come 'ere, boy."

Grinning, Dillard walked over to his grandmother and embraced her in a gentle bear hug, feeling her sharp spine and ribs poking through parchment-paper skin. Her old one-piece, blue-and-white house dress held a classic old folks aroma, a mixture of liniment and mildew.

"Howya feelin', Nana?"

"Not bad for a broad who ain't had a man in fifty years and a beer in forty-nine," Nana shot back, flashing rotten teeth. Dillard laughed, knowing what to expect next. There wasn't a damn thing wrong with Nana, not today anyway.

"Can ya git me a beer, hon?" she said, her smile gone, her expression deadly earnest.

"Weeeeeell, Nana, you know what the rules say—"

"Fuck dem rules," Nana screeched, her tiny body vibrating with outrage. "I asked couldya git me a goddamned beer?"

Dillard realized he wasn't supposed to sneak beer into the nursing home. He also realized Nana wasn't about to take no for an answer. She started to hyperventilate, her breath coming in short gasps.

Dillard calmly grabbed a small aerosol can of inhalant and handed it to his grandmother.

Pfffft, pffffft, pfffffft.

"Why do you aggravate yourself like that?" Dillard asked in a scolding tone. "You know what always happens." He'd seen coughing attacks so bad that she'd turned blue and lost control of her bladder.

Nana merely held up a gnarled hand, ordering silence until she regained her breath and composure.

"Tell you what, I'll see what I can do, okay?"

"That's my boy," she gasped, grabbing Dillard with a cool, waxlike hand. "I knowed that if anyone would come and see me here, it would be my Markie."

Her glasses magnified the puddles of tears welling in her eyes. Feeling his own eyes getting moist, Dillard looked away.

"Don't be gettin' all sentimental on me now," he said in a mock growl. But Nana's tears were flowing freely now and Dillard knew his weren't far behind. Plus, unpredictable Rick Allen was still outside in the Camaro, sweltering in the South Baltimore heat.

"Look, Nana, I gotta go," Dillard said, emotion making his voice catch.

"Bring me a cold one next time, boy."

Her comment snapped the spell. They looked at each other and laughed, radiating mutual admiration and affection. Still looking at Nana, Dillard made a snap decision. He walked over to the door, shut it and returned to Nana's bedside.

"Nana, if I tell you a big secret, you can't tell a soul."

The milky owl eyes peered up at him. Dillard bent down theatrically until his mouth was inches away from his grandmother's ear.

"Nana, me and some other people are going to bomb the NAACP's national headquarters."

The milky eyes widened to the size of basketballs. Dillard was stunned by what his grandmother did next. She reared her head back and cut loose a laugh that sounded like a creaky wheel.

Holding her sides, she started crying, only this time it was tears of mirth that streamed through the gullies of her weathered face. Gasping by now and motioning for the inhaler, the old woman squirted two quick bursts down her windpipe, her sides still quaking.

Turning his head quizzically, Dillard waited for the laughter to stop. What on earth was so funny? He expected Nana to be impressed, possibly even awestruck. But overcome with laughter?

"Just gonna blow those niggers up, huh?" she finally managed to wheeze. "Markie, you somethin' else. Bring beer next time, hear me, boy?"

With that a whole new giggling spasm overtook Nana. Still clutching her inhaler, she keeled over on the bed, kicking her shriveled legs.

Feeling crushed, Dillard bent down and kissed his grandmother, who looked up at him and started laughing even harder. She snagged his hand as he stood up and gave it a weak squeeze.

Her wheezing laughter followed Dillard all the way down the hall. Each chuckle was a reproachful slap to his psyche and his ego. He had made his second major misstep of the morning, because there was nothing to gain from telling Nana about his plans. He'd wanted her to be proud of him and she'd responded by splitting her sides.

Well, even if she spilled the beans, who'd believe a nursing-home resident showing early signs of Alzheimer's? Dillard had no way of knowing Nana thought his statement had merely been an outlandish joke.

Dillard was in a foul mood walking out of the nursing home. When the receptionist called out a cheerful goodbye, he merely grunted and kept moving.

Allen was out of the damn car again!

This time he was yakking away on a nearby pay phone. Looking at the Camaro, Dillard could see something flashing and glittering near the steering wheel. His car keys!

Allen obviously saw Dillard, but showed no signs of being in a hurry to end his conversation.

Reaching through the passenger window and pulling out the ignition key, Dillard strode briskly toward Allen, who slammed the phone down and walked indifferently toward the Camaro. A collision between the men—if not today, then in the very near future—was clearly inevitable.

"Who you talking to?"

"My girl. Why?"

"Get in the car."

They cruised the blistering blacktop silently, not really paying attention to a soft rock station on the radio. Every now and then a street corner would be overflowing with children frolicking in cold geysers of water streaming from opened fire hydrants. In some instances poor black and white children played together, not yet infected by the debilitating sickness that long ago had consumed Dillard.

He had a uncomfortable sense that Allen was trying to precipitate something. He was being subjected to goading, manipulative behavior. The kind that gets under your skin the deepest. This was a new, alarming wrinkle in their relationship and as he drove, Dillard tried to pinpoint its genesis.

"Who's in the nursing home?"

None of your goddamn business, was on the tip of Dillard's tongue, but he wisely swallowed it. Big picture. Think big picture.

"A relative."

"Who?"

"You wouldn't know if I told you, Rick. Just a relative, okay?"

"Got you a piece of trim working there, don't you?" Allen said, his acne-scarred face twisted into a juvenile leer.

Dillard took a deep breath and looked in the rearview mirror. A blue-and-white city police car rode about two car lengths behind his Camaro. The speedometer was showing thirty-three miles per hour, two below the speed limit.

"Got a cop behind us," Dillard said in a low voice, as if acknowledging it too loudly might draw the officer's attention. At the next major intersection he pulled into the left turn lane, leading to Dundalk. The police car put on its turn signal and continued shadowing Dillard. He prayed for the light to remain green so he could make a left and keep moving. Naturally it turned red.

"Stop being so goddamned obvious in that side mirror," he snapped at Allen, who was really looking at a miniskirted woman on the sidewalk.

Damn! Allen hadn't asked to participate in this peculiar rendezvous and now his head was being bitten off at every turn.

The green left-turn arrow flashed on and Dillard eased onto Thurgood Marshall Boulevard, taking pains not to give his car too much gas and make the tires chirp. For three blocks he crept along in the right lane, giving the police car an opportunity to pass. But it stuck to the Camaro like glue, retracing Dillard's tire tracks.

He could see that the officers—one black, one white—appeared to be looking for something.

"You carry a switchblade, right?" Dillard mumbled to Allen, who nodded.

"Lemme have it."

Sweating profusely, Allen turned slowly to look at Dillard, who had an oily sheen on his forehead. Otherwise he appeared unaffected by the heat.

Looking alarmed, Allen hesitantly reached into one of his pants pockets and slowly pulled out his switchblade. He placed it lightly in Dillard's outstretched palm.

"Don't do nothin' crazy, okay?"

Coming from the daredevil of the group! Dillard gazed at Allen and was shocked by his concerned appearance. Maybe he wasn't so tough after all.

Flicking on his right-turn signal, Dillard braked gradually and eased his car toward the curb, stopping in front of several row houses and a funeral parlor. The cop car followed suit, its blue lights flashing. It seemed both officers were out of their car and standing on either side of the Camaro before the police vehicle had come to a full stop.

The white cop came up on the driver's side, stopping about a foot behind the door. A small piece of lettuce from his lunchtime taco was wedged in his mustache.

"Turn your engine off, please."

"What's the problem, officer?"

"Your left brake light is out. See your license and registration?" The officer was sleepwalking, going through the motions, Dillard observed to his relief. Must be "Fuck with Dillard Day" among law enforcement agencies.

As they waited for Dillard to produce the appropriate paperwork, both cops stooped to peer inside the car. They seemed particularly interested in Allen, who was doing a great imitation of a long-haired, sweating statue.

"Wait here, please."

Both cops returned to their motorized lair and sat in the air-conditioning for a minute before doing anything. Dillard noticed that the white cop started writing without getting on the radio. The white cop returned alone with a repair order, the black lawman not even bothering to accompany him.

Without taking his eyes from the rearview mirror, Dillard felt for the switchblade he'd placed in the center console. He ran his hand over the knife, picked it up and tapped Allen on the leg with it.

Allen coolly took the weapon and placed it under his left leg.

When the cop reappeared beside the Camaro, Dillard's eyes were flashing and he was smiling a smug, shit-eatin' grin.

"Get this thing repaired in fifteen days and you can avoid

a hundred-dollar fine,'' the police officer said, pushing the citation book and a pen through the driver's window. "Take your repair receipt to court with you, okay?"

"Sure thing, Officer. I shoulda fixed it a long time ago."

Still smiling, Dillard handed the citation book back to the cop, who tore off Dillard's copy and left.

The police car peeled away first and made a quick right, taking the officers down a narrow, one-way street.

"You drive," Dillard said quietly as the cops disappeared from view. "I ain't having too much luck behind the wheel today. You handle a stick, right?"

"Yep."

When he got out of the car to change places, there was a noticeable tremble in Dillard's hands. Allen, on the other hand, was cool and implacable. Maybe he would be valuable to the NAACP mission after all.

In one window of the funeral parlor they'd stopped in front of, a white curtain slowly inched back into place. Maybe it was the owner, disappointed that the traffic stop hadn't produced more business.

When the Camaro finally got moving with Allen behind the wheel, it leapt and jerked away from the curb like an enraged rodeo bronco. If Allen ever really had driven a stick, this had to be the second time. Dillard sank into his seat without comment.

It's just one of those days. Just one of those days.

They did the bucking-bronco routine for about a mile, when Allen unexpectedly stopped. He turned off the engine and hunched forward in his seat, looking everywhere but at Dillard. Allen's fingers were intertwined with the steering wheel and his sweat-soaked hair gave him a greasy look.

"I don't think I should go home," he said in a voice that signaled his decision was final. Allen was straining to remain impassive, but Dillard could see something was troubling him.

"What's the problem? Don't you need anything at your apartment?"

"If what you say is true, my place is probably full of pigs

right now," Allen said in a clipped tone. "I've got five guns in my place . . ." His voice trailed off. ". . . and about three ounces of dope."

Sucking in his breath, Dillard slowly processed that last bit of info. Either Allen was the biggest pothead in Baltimore, something he'd never seen evidence of, or he was dealing big-time. It wasn't even noon yet—would the surprises ever stop?

"If you don't go home, what are you gonna do, Rick? Where ya gonna stay?"

His caring tone caught Allen off guard.

"I've got a lady friend I can crash with. I'll be all right."

Dillard knew that was a damned lie. "Want me to give you a ride to her house? That's the least I can do."

"Naw, she's at work right now. Anyway, I don't have a key."

Watching Allen all but squirm, Dillard felt ablaze with shame. Because of his carelessness, his companion was unable to go home. Or return to work.

"Well, come on back to my house while you plot your next move. I can float you a few bucks."

Looking uncomfortable and hesitant, Allen agreed to go with Dillard.

The fat neighbor was still sunning herself on the stoop as the Camaro parked in the same spot it had vacated. Dillard's house felt cool because the top windows had been left open, letting in a refreshing breeze that blew dust everywhere. It was so thick both men sneezed a couple of times after they entered the house.

As before, Dillard offered Allen a cold beer that was refused. So Dillard kept it and they sat down at the kitchen table.

"I'm sorry, man, I let you down. I should have been more careful," Dillard mumbled in a barely audible voice.

Reaching across the table, Allen grasped Dillard's hand warmly and shook it. "Nothin' you coulda done, man. The jungle bunnies are outta control in Baltimore with that crack and carjacking and shit."

"Ain't it the truth. I just can't figure out why he had a white guy with him . . ." Allen was still buying that story about how his pickup disappeared. Good. "I have a clean pair of jeans and a T-shirt if you want to take a shower and get out of those clothes."

"Sure, man. Appreciate it."

" 'Cause I don't think your lady friend would appreciate being around your smelly ass right now," Dillard said with a wink. "Let's head upstairs."

A washcloth and a towel were retrieved from a small linen closet at the top of the stairs. Pointing Allen toward the bathroom, Dillard walked in the direction of his bedroom to get clean clothes.

A pine chest of drawers held faded blue jeans Dillard wore to work on his car. A blue-and-yellow National Rifle Association T-shirt completed the ensemble.

Dillard carried the clothes to the bathroom. "Oh, yeah."

Doubling back to the bedroom, he got a clean pair of underwear and some athletic socks from his chest of drawers, then returned to the bathroom and knocked on the door. The shower was running so forcefully that Allen didn't hear the knock, so Dillard opened the door, allowing steam to gush into the hallway.

Allen's clothes lay in an odoriferous pile beside the bathtub. He showered in silence behind a thick blue plastic shower curtain, oblivious to Dillard's presence.

Laying the clean clothes on the water reservoir for the toilet, Dillard picked up Allen's soiled ones, which were wet with perspiration.

"I brought you some clean clothes."

Dillard's voice shocked Allen, who thought he'd locked the door.

"Okay, man, thanks. I'll be out in a minute."

Without saying anything, Dillard took the dirty clothes with him. It would be a nice gesture to throw the clothes in the washer and dryer, given all the trouble he'd caused.

He walked double time to the door leading to the basement because he didn't want to hold Allen's threads a second longer than necessary. Near the top of the rickety wooden stairs he flicked on the light switch, illuminating an unshaded ceiling bulb. It cast its harsh light on a basement whose dusty rock walls were painted olive green.

Dillard went down the shaky steps slowly. He wanted them to be dangerous and unstable because no one had any business being in his domain, where his workbench, assault rifle and shotgun were located. In a distant corner were some free weights and a stationary bike generally put to use twice a week.

Dillard reflexively searched through Allen's pants pockets so the washing machine wouldn't ruin their contents. Fifty-nine cents in change was in one pocket, along with a silver switchblade. Another pocket yielded a black, vibrating pager and four keys on a key ring, including one with a Lexus logo! Dillard frowned. What were those things doing there?

He'd originally intended to merely take Allen's wallet out and lay it on the washing machine, but now his curiosity was piqued.

A high-pitched shriek resonated through the water pipes, warning that Allen was turning off the shower.

Moving quickly, Dillard fished a nondescript brown leather wallet from the back pocket of Allen's pants. Two crisp twenty-dollar bills were neatly tucked inside the wallet, along with three crinkled George Washingtons. There was no driver's license or credit cards, but there was a cash-machine receipt for a forty-dollar withdrawal. The money had been taken out that morning at 7:31 A.M., leaving a balance of $2,187.93.

What Dillard saw next made him blink several times. Printed on the top of the ATM withdrawal slip was BALTIMORE CITY POLICE & FIRE DEPARTMENT CREDIT UNION. What on earth was that about?

Searching through the wallet again, Dillard found what appeared to be a single business card tucked between the two twenty-dollar bills. On closer examination it turned out to be two cards stuck together. They were identical and read: "Detective Sherman Brown." Printed just beneath the name was BALTIMORE CITY POLICE DEPARTMENT. Criminal Investigation Bureau. Huh?

Why would Allen have two cards for this detective character, unless . . . Allen and Sherman Brown were one and the same?!

Dillard's mouth formed a perfectly round circle, but no sound came out. Things were coming into focus now. Rick Allen, Detective Brown—whatever his name was—hadn't wanted Dillard to drive him to Dundalk because his story about a bachelor pad in Dundalk was just that—a goddamn story. And the reason Allen always egged on Dillard and the others to commit senseless acts of violence was starting to make sense, too.

Come to think of it, hadn't Allen been the last one to join the group?

The growing realization that Allen was probably an infiltrator slowly crystallized inside Dillard's brain, taking on a horrible life of its own. It was bad enough that there might be a mole in the group, but the fact that it was Allen hit like a sucker punch. He was the one Dillard viewed as being most like himself, despite the nettlesome qualities.

So the betrayal hurt as though from a brother or a son.

Dillard stared at the wallet balefully, wishing it hadn't conveyed such depressing news.

Replacing the ATM machine slip and two business cards gingerly, he scooped up the wallet and the rest of Allen's belongings and carried them upstairs. He made it to the top floor just as Allen was leaving the bathroom, dressed in the clothes his host had provided. Allen was in mid-yawn and vigorously rubbing a towel through his stringy hair when he saw Dillard.

"I took your clothes downstairs and put them in the washing machine," Dillard said, smiling benignly as he handed the switchblade, loose change, keys and wallet to Allen, who smelled of deodorant soap and resembled a Homo sapiens again. He immediately stopped drying his hair and gave Dillard a gaze penetrating enough to see the other man's soul.

Looking at the NRA T-shirt on Allen, Dillard imagined

wires, a microphone and a portable transmitter just beneath the shirt's flowing folds.

"I'm gonna call the fellas on over," he said easily, monitoring Allen out of the corner of his eye. If Allen was an undercover cop or an informant, he was a damn good one. The young man paused half a beat before responding to Dillard, his angular face never changing its stony, impassive expression.

"Oh, yeah? Why, what's up?"

"I think we've got ourselves a little crisis with your pickup, don't you?" Dillard said evenly. His thoughts were on the nine-millimeter on the top shelf of the kitchen cabinet, and how quickly he could get to it if necessary. Where Allen was concerned, Dillard had already opted for the worst-case scenario: namely, that Allen was the enemy and had to be dealt with.

But one who wouldn't be allowed to impede the NAACP bombing under any circumstance.

"You don't think it can wait until everyone gets off from work?" Allen asked, looking at Dillard closely.

"No, I don't think it can wait that long. Plus, it's time to see who in the group is for real and who's blowing smoke up everybody's ass."

"Fucking A, man," Allen cried out without hesitation. "Let's do it. Let's get the fucking show on the road."

You don't have to worry about that, my friend, Dillard thought, looking through veiled eyes at someone who had gone from being a brother to an other.

ELEVEN

THE INSISTENT CHIRPING OF A TEAKETTLE AND THE MUFFLED staccato of popcorn kernels exploding inside a microwave oven mercifully obliterate the uneasy silence in my apartment.

Unsure of what to do or say, I just stand in the living room and watch Yolanda and the little boy she cradles protectively in her arms as she sits cross-legged on the floor. She speaks tenderly to the child, or, more accurately, rhythmically coos and clucks her tongue to a secret cadence only they share.

It takes just a few seconds to intuitively understand they are mother and son. That would have been disappointing under ordinary circumstances. But at the moment, Yolanda's availability, marital status, etc., aren't exactly pressing concerns.

A magnificent burgundy bruise roughly the size and shape of a nectarine has blossomed under the boy's left eye, which is nearly swollen shut. The cuts and scrapes on his face look to be a few hours old, if that. Without saying a word, I get a fresh washcloth out of the closet, run a burst of cool tap water over it and wrap it around an ice cube.

I hand the makeshift cold compress to Yolanda, who takes it without thanks and absently dabs at her son's eye.

He immediately starts bucking and wriggling like a speared catfish, butting his head into his mother's chest to break her embrace. He also begins whimpering, the first sound he's uttered since entering my apartment.

I walk over to the agitated pair and squat directly in front of Yolanda.

"Would you like to explain what's going on?" I'm starting to feel like an interloper in my own home. Plus, why should I even have to ask for an explanation? It should be the first thing out of Yolanda's mouth, without prompting.

Her bottom lip starts quivering while the top one remains still, as though hardwired to a different nervous system. Towering pride makes Yolanda reluctant to weep in front of me, nor does she wish to appear weak in front of her son.

But the emotions of a terrifically trying day are on the verge of cascading to the surface. Taking a deep breath, she moves her son from her lap.

"Can we please talk about it later?" she asks weakly, staring at the floor.

"No. Absolutely not. Tell me where you got my address from and why you came here at ten-thirty with a little boy who looks like he's been in a prize fight. Now!"

I'm yelling without even realizing it, making Yolanda recoil as if my words carry physical force.

"Can I use your bathroom, please?"

Without waiting for an answer Yolanda gets up and walks briskly toward the bathroom as though she owns the joint. Even in her bleakest hour she can still manage to be imperious.

The ventilation fan in the bathroom whirs as soon as the door closes, and I hear the toilet flush twice in rapid succession.

Like an arthritic old man, the little boy slowly rises and follows his mother on gimpy legs. He stands by the bathroom door and stares at me with round eyes full of trepidation. He reminds me of a terror-stricken organ grinder's monkey.

"What's your name, little man?"

I extend my hand and start walking toward him.

"Mama," he whispers so quietly that for a moment I'm not sure he said anything. "Mama, Mama, Mama," the child begins to yell loudly as I move closer. Not content to disturb my neighbors with his yelling, the boy starts banging on the door and wildly twisting the brass knob, leaving smudgy paw prints.

By now I don't care what Yolanda has to say: It's best if she and her semicrazed munchkin leave.

"Jamal, wait a minute, baby," a weary, tremulous voice on the other side of the door commands. "Just give Mommy a second, okay?"

Yolanda emerges with her eyes red, puffy and watery and she refuses to look at me. Even so, she's still attractive. I notice her right knee is scraped and oozing a trickle of blood through a hole in her jeans.

"What were you doing in the bathroom?" I ask accusatorially. "Is this all related to drugs or something?"

Actually, Yolanda retreated to the bathroom so I wouldn't see her sobbing. The world has been kicking her ass all day; now come insinuations she's a drug fiend.

"Come on, baby," she says, scooping Jamal under her arm and heading for the door. "We ain't gotta put up with this shit." She's out the door and headed down the stairwell before I realize what she's doing.

Damn, I don't need this.

I live on a block with plenty of yuppies on it, but by this time of night the street and the surrounding neighborhood are teeming with toy gangstas from a nearby housing project. Yolanda and her son are lambs headed to slaughter if they don't have a car.

Swearing, I jog to the stove to turn off the flame under the teakettle, then run to the door to catch Yolanda. Being raised by decent, God-fearing parents can be a curse sometimes.

"HEY! Hold up a minute," I shout at Yolanda, who's already reached the bottom step. Downstairs, Mrs. Wentworth takes this as a signal to start tip-tapping on the ceiling with a broom handle, as though riotous noise is an everyday occurrence in my apartment.

"I never said you had to leave," I shout at Yolanda's back

as she breezes through the foyer. "I only asked what you were doing."

Had she been by herself, Yolanda would have jetted without a backward glance. She didn't take crap from men, which partially explained her present predicament. But this time she had to take her son's welfare into account.

Nearly gagging on humble pie, Yolanda turns around and slowly starts back toward the steps.

I watch this from the top of the stairs, where I'm secretly praying they'll ignore me and keep going. That way, at least I could have gotten some rest with a clear conscience. Damn!

And to think that before tonight I would have given *anything* to get her into my apartment.

Slumping like she has a date with the executioner, Yolanda slinks upstairs, clutching Jamal's tiny hand. They'll have to depend on the kindness of a stranger tonight, one named Darryl.

Staring at them, I wonder if Yolanda is about to make some kind of emotional appeal, because she and her son sure look pitiful climbing the stairs. They make a one-story flight seem like Mount Everest.

With matching hangdog expressions, she and Jamal stroll past me wordlessly and reenter my apartment.

I remain in the hallway for a brief moment, mulling over what to do. This is alien territory, this stuff of allowing strange women and their bloody children to saunter into my abode in the middle of the night.

My sixth sense, the one that I always regret ignoring, is desperately trying to get my attention. "Don't let 'em in," it whispers. "You're tired, you have to go to work tomorrow morning and you don't know this woman from Adam. Call the police and let them handle her mess. Don't get involved!" The admonition makes perfect sense to me. I can't think of a reason not to follow it.

So naturally I decide to gamble and extend a helping hand to Yolanda. But if I see any twitching, scratching or other signs of drug abuse, her ass is history.

I close the door to my apartment, then slowly turn to face

Yolanda, who stands near the kitchen counter. Half scowling, I fold my arms expectantly.

"I remembered you from the hospital," Yolanda says, fidgeting uncomfortably. "I got your telephone number and address from Directory Assistance." She frowns, appreciating how lame that sounds, even if it is the truth. All the while Jamal is clutching her leg and jamming his head against her crotch as though trying to disappear back into the womb.

"Why? Why me? You mean there's not another soul in Baltimore you can turn to?"

Yolanda just sighs. While it's true she owes me an explanation, she's not keen on being interrogated.

"Do you mind," she asks finally in a soft, lyrical voice, "if I put my son down somewhere? Then I'll tell you what happened and why we're here. I'll tell you everything."

Truth be told, this whole deal doesn't feel right. The little warning voice in my head has grown from a whisper to a full-fledged shriek.

"The road to hell is paved with good intentions," I grumble.

"Huh?"

"Nuthin'. Let me find a sheet to spread over the couch. I'll be right back."

I pull a faded white sheet for a twin bed out of the linen closet. I haven't used it in eons—it's been at least twenty years since I last slept on a twin. Then, after lifting out a worn blue washcloth for good measure, I carry both items into the living room, where Yolanda has stretched Jamal out on the floor and is taking off his shoes. He's already sound asleep, having experienced a day that would lay low most adults, much less a three-year-old. As I gaze at Jamal, who seems terribly world-weary, my heart goes out to him.

Yolanda is bone tired and running out of steam as she spreads the sheet across the sofa. Too fatigued to even smooth out the wrinkles, she leaves it exactly as it unfurled. Seeing the bags under her eyes, I try to imagine how she might look in her forties and beyond. Cute as hell, is how.

On the verge of carrying Jamal to the sofa, Yolanda suddenly stops. "You smoke?" she asks in a voice that makes it clear she hopes I don't.

"No."

"Neither do I," she says, sounding relieved. "Jamal be havin' asthma sometimes and cigarette smoke is bad for him."

Be havin' asthma? My eyebrows arch. Mauled English has about the same effect on me as chalk screeching across a blackboard, but I say nothing.

Finished tucking in her son, Yolanda kisses his forehead and walks over to me.

"Let's sit over here," I suggest, waving at the kitchen table. "Want some tea or popcorn?"

"Thank you."

Yolanda watches silently as I dump three teaspoons of sugar into my tea. Little bubbles rise to the surface each time, popping without a trace. Watching the bubbles, Yolanda yearns to make her troubles do the same thing.

Fiercely private and proud, she's prepared to pour out her soul simply because I have something she and her son desperately need—a roof over their heads.

"When I got home from work today, Jamal was crying and bleeding," she says, looking right through me. "The guy I live with has a booze problem. He never hit Jamal before today, because Jamal ain't his."

I see tears pooling in Yolanda's eyes. For a reason I can't explain, I feel vaguely uncomfortable making her justify the terrible imposition she's putting me through.

"What happened to your knee?"

"I felt like going upside his head when I saw Jamal. I got in his face and he pushed me down on the floor. Boone had gotten drunk like that one other time and put his hands on me. I told him if he ever did it again, I was gone. So I left— I didn't even get my clothes."

Despite a strong popcorn odor in the apartment, I pick up a scent from Yolanda that smells like tangerines. Her eyelids are starting to droop noticeably.

"Why did you come here?"

"My mother and my stepfather moved to Houston last year. I have a sister who still lives in Baltimore, but she's always telling me I'm stupid for dealing with Boone in the first place because he's a violent loser. I couldn't turn to her. I don't have nowhere else to go and you seemed like a nice guy when I met you in the hospital . . . plus I figured you'd know what to do, being a reporter and all."

"How about a hotel? Don't you have a credit card?"

A credit card! Yolanda locks her eyes onto mine, to see if I'm poking fun at her. "No," a tiny voice replies, "I don't. If we could spend the night on your couch, I'd really appreciate it. We'll leave in the morning. I promise."

Making a snap call, I decide Yolanda is a decent woman down on her luck and won't slit my throat at midnight for a fistful of crack dollars.

I briefly consider offering my unexpected houseguests the loft but change my mind, picturing Jamal tumbling down the black spiral staircase, à la Eddie Murphy's Aunt Bunnie. It would be a shame to play Good Samaritan and get a lawsuit for my trouble.

"You guys can crash on the sleeper couch. This is only a one-bedroom apartment," I tell her apologetically.

Yolanda swallows twice. "Thank you very much," she murmurs in a vanquished monotone. "We really appreciate it."

The microwave popcorn has popped a little too long and is scorched, not the way I like it. Yolanda, on the other hand, immediately starts shoving handfuls of the stuff past her high cheekbones.

"Would you like a sandwich?"

Yolanda catches herself and starts nibbling demurely at the popcorn she was inhaling madly a second earlier. "That's okay. I'm about to get some sleep."

"That makes two of us. I'll leave a towel, a washcloth and some more sheets on the kitchen counter. See you in the morning."

"Good night."

Walking toward the bathroom to wash up, I feel good

about myself and my decision. But piety and goodwill turn to hostility around 2 A.M. Saturday morning. Jamal starts screaming gibberish in his sleep and flaying at an imaginary attacker. I'm actually trembling with fear and anger as I head back to my bedroom, because I had forgotten anyone was in the apartment.

The same thing happens again at 5:30.

When my alarm goes off at 8:15, I feel like sandpaper has been surgically implanted under my eyelids. I've been gracious, civil and hospitable to a fault—now it's time to show my guests the door.

I'll get these two out of here, call in sick, then spend the day sleeping, I think groggily. My head pounds from sleep deprivation.

When I get into the living room, Yolanda and her long limbs are sprawled over the couch, but Jamal is nowhere to be found. A rustling noise comes from the direction of the kitchen.

I find Jamal near the pantry, clutching a bag of sour-cream-and-onion potato chips and wearing soaking-wet, miniature Fruit of the Looms.

Standing in the middle of a rapidly expanding puddle of brown maple syrup, his hand frozen in mid-reach over the potato chip bag, Jamal stares at me with deer-caught-in-the-headlights eyes.

"Why, you little— One, two, three, four . . ."

Yolanda plods around the corner, wiping sleep from her eyes just as I reach eight.

TWELVE

ORACLES DON'T USUALLY HANG OUT IN BARBERSHOPS, BUT JE-
rome Miller ain't your typical oracle.

Sixty years old if he's a day, Mr. Jerome was shearing
naps off my round head before I could walk. And I know he
weighs at least three hundred pounds—so how does he glide
around Miller's Barbershop like a sixteen-year-old weighing
a buck-oh-nine?

When I see his massive body bouncing around, I always
think of the nimble circus bear riding a unicycle and holding
a parasol. None of that "woe-is-me, getting-old-is-a-bitch"
stuff from Mr. Jerome.

With a shop at the corner of North and Greenmount ave-
nues, an inner-city area where angels, whites and booshie
folk dare not tread, Mr. Jerome is a longtime community
fixture. He's a throwback to the days when rap was something
brothers gave up to foxy mamas.

Mr. Jerome missed his calling. Big time. The man can out-
Oprah Miss Winfrey. He has a way of making you open up
in front of total strangers, while he probes and tinkers with
your psyche. But it's always done with the aim of strengthen-
ing you, making you better.

As long as Mr. Jerome is around, I know one brother
who'll never pay a dime to a shrink or a spiritual adviser.

It's a little after 10 A.M. and my eyelids refuse to stay

open as I wait for a dignified-looking gentleman with a gray handlebar mustache to finish getting his hair cut. I waited around my apartment for Yolanda to clean up the mess in the kitchen; then she and Jamal left to see a pediatrician.

Rather than lay my weary head down, I decided to seek out Mr. Jerome. There's one customer in front of me, an impatient young brother wearing a cheap-looking brown suit. He's scowling and looking at his watch like he has a Fortune 500 company to run. On a Saturday, no less.

"Listen to that wheezing—even yo' windpipe is *overweight*. Wonder you can even breathe."

A hefty brown paw turns the customer's head to the side roughly, making the seated man's noggin look like a peach in a catcher's mitt. A pair of electric hair clippers glides toward an unruly, snow-white sideburn.

"Whadja say, Henry? I still got enough pep ta yank you outta that chair and dust off your bony ass. Anyway, you just jealous. It's been forty-five years since I stole Bonita from you and you still mad. Let it go, Henry, let it go. Not my fault I drives the ladies wild."

"Hhhhmmmppph. Miller, only thing you drive wild is eh'-body working at Benny's Barbecue Shack. They're tireda seeing your big ass five times a day."

"He always did have a little man's complex, little black Napoleon here," Mr. Jerome says, turning to me. I smile and remain silent, not feeling I've earned the right to trade barbs with two old heads who helped pave the way for my generation.

"Nigga, please. You always have been fulla shit!"

Mr. Jerome and Henry both laugh heartily, momentarily oblivious to everyone else in the barbershop as they play out their long-running shtick.

You have to operate on a fast-moving frequency to appreciate the full breadth of Mr. Jerome's nonstop yammering and joshing. On the surface he seems a jovial old cutup making easy banter to make the day go by. Don't be fooled. Mr. Jerome is one of the deepest brothers I know, and I've met some impressive folks.

Not only does he read me better than I read myself most of the time, he's an old head who's been around the block and is eager to pass on what he's learned during the journey. Incredibly, all he asks in return is a willingness to listen, a talent I seldom see in his clientele. Unfortunately a lot of brothers, especially younger ones, have a pride/ego thing going on that's a formidable barrier to learning.

So a good many of Mr. Jerome's pearls are lost on arrogant, violence-prone swine who wear ignorance as a badge of honor. What's that old, fat fart got to say that I wanna hear? Nothin'!

To be fair, some people are scared off by Mr. Jerome's ability to talk a hole in the side of your head. That and his constant belching. Within five minutes of sitting in his chair you don't have to guess what his last meal was.

I don't particularly care for that, but I endure it because of what I draw from my association with Mr. Jerome. However, if he should ever start flitting around the barbershop, passing gas from that big behind of his, that would be another story.

Mr. Jerome puts a few finishing touches on the nape of his friend's neck, a snick of the clippers here and there, then presents a hand-held mirror with a grand sweep of his arm.

"Jerome, you never could cut hair worth a damn," Henry says, grinning. "How much is the damage?"

"You been comin' in here every two weeks for the last forty years. You still don't know how much I charge?" Mr. Jerome looks at me again and shakes his head. "Damn shame, ain't it, young brother? Come on, Henry, I ain't got time to be playin' with you."

Their transaction complete, Mr. Jerome unloosens the protective bib from around Henry's neck and snatches it away with a flourish, like a magician displaying his grandest trick. A small whisk broom flicks a few strands of gray hair from Henry's shoulders and he springs out of the barber chair, exhibiting a spryness every bit a match for Mr. Jerome's.

"You take care now, Henry. Tell Martha I says hello."

"Yessir, yessir. I'll do that. Be seeing you in church."

"You can count on it," Mr. Jerome says softly, gently laying a hand on his friend's back.

The Fortune 500 CEO is up and plopping himself down in Mr. Jerome's chair before Henry makes it to the door.

"Just cut the loose ends and give me a straight line in the back," the CEO orders brusquely.

"All right, young fella. Want me to shape it around the sides?"

"That's okay. I'm late for work."

"Gotcha." *Buuuurrumph.*

The CEO's eyes widen in disbelief. Mount Vesuvius has just erupted right behind his head, which I'm sure has further endeared him to Mr. Jerome. Mr. Jerome does what he usually does: continue working as though nothing's happened. He affixes a paper strip around the CEO's neck, raises the protective bib in the air, then flicks it so forcefully it pops, scattering the remnants of Henry's haircut. Then Mr. Jerome affixes it around the CEO's neck.

No "Excuse me, I beg your pardon," nothing. I'm willing to bet his wife won't let him so much as hiccup at home without apologizing profusely. So he goes on a rampage at Miller's.

Now the clippers are buzzing around the CEO's head like a huge, angry black hornet. This continues for about two minutes, until Mr. Jerome suddenly pulls the clippers away, parking them in midair about six inches from the CEO's head.

"Whadja think of the Million Man March, young brother?" Mr. Jerome asks with a smile that lights up the shop.

The CEO's eyes roll ever so slightly and he mumbles something incomprehensible. The clippers leave their midair parking space and return to work. Like I said, Mr. Jerome ain't everyone's cup of tea.

When the CEO leaves, he all but flings two five-dollar bills in the chair and dashes out the door. I'm not that old, but I can remember when black folks were by and large courteous to one another, especially where elders were involved. When did it become fashionable to be so damn rude?

"Ten dollars closer to retirement," Mr. Jerome says, calmly picking up the bills and carrying them to his cash register. "What can I do fo' you, young Mr. Billups?"

This catches me off guard momentarily, because I came here more for advice than for a haircut. "I guess you could take a little off the sides."

"I think I can manage that."

The clippers come on with a *crack!* and are soon buzzing around my right temple.

"You was just in here four days ago. Got a hot date tonight?" Mr. Jerome asks with a laugh.

"Uh, no, sir. I wish that were the case."

"Uh-huh. I see. Well, somethin' must be percolatin' in that brain of yours, then." He puts his hand on my head to turn it. His touch is reassuring, making me feel for a fleeting moment that I'm nine years old again and without a care in the world.

I feel even better once I begin to pour out my story about Yolanda and her unexpected visit. I'll get to the anonymous phone calls later.

"Lemme ask you a question," Mr. Jerome finally says after letting me prattle on. "If it was jess this girl by herself, would you let her stay for a little while? For a couple of days or so?"

"I don't know. For a little while, maybe. Why?"

"Why would you let her stay?" Mr. Jerome asks, ignoring my question.

I hadn't really thought about that. "I dunno—you know . . ." Fat fingers push my chin toward my chest.

"Naw, I don't know."

"Because she seems like a decent person . . . I know for a fact she has a job. And she's fine as wine, too. Girlfriend's got it going on."

"So why should it be any different jess 'cause she has a son? Is that the real problem here? You willing to help out a pretty lady, but not if she has a little boy who's down on his luck, too?"

Before I came in here, offering to let Yolanda stay in my place for a few days seemed like a stretch, damned illogical.

Plus, I like having my space. There's nothing wrong with that.

But sitting here listening to Mr. Jerome, I think it's reasonable to at least contemplate helping her out a little more.

"Of course, I ain't saying do somethin' stupid. You need to check this woman out," Mr. Jerome says, reading my mind. "But if she does check out, at the end of the day you will have done somethin' valuable and worthwhile. Black people are so afraid of each other these days, and so slow to give each other a helping hand. What does that say about us?"

The real question he was posing was, what does it say about Darryl Billups if I just turn Yolanda and her son out?

"Betcha worried about what yo' mama and daddy will say and think, right? And yo' boys? What's most important? That's what you need to decide."

He's right. But for once, he hasn't made my decision any easier. When I tell Mr. Jerome about the threats to the NAACP and to Blumberg, he cuts off his clippers and lays them beside a glass cylinder filled with blue disinfectant, scissors and combs. Then he walks around my chair and stands directly in front of me.

"Son, who have you told about these threats? Have you contacted the police?"

"Yessir, I made a call to somebody in Homicide yesterday."

"You're a smart boy, Darryl. Jess like you figured out what to do there, you'll figure out what to do with your lady friend," Mr. Jerome says simply. End of conversation.

When he's finished cutting my hair and I reach for my wallet, Mr. Jerome assumes the pose of a cop stopping traffic. "You can pay me by doing the right thing. And from what I know of you, Darryl, that's like money in the bank."

Mr. Jerome gives me one of his beatific smiles and I'm out the door, less sure now of what to do than when I entered Miller's Barbershop.

THIRTEEN

MARK DILLARD HADN'T EVEN OPENED HIS MOUTH AND FLOP sweat was already on his forehead and cheeks. He swallowed, unnerved by three pairs of somber, inquisitive eyes drinking in his every move. Could they see the tic in his left eye?

What Rick Allen, Harold Boyles and Robert Simmes saw was a man coolly in control and comfortable with that. With the exception of Allen, the other two men eagerly awaited Dillard's explanation for the emergency afternoon meeting in his home.

Relax, Mark, relax. You only need to convince Boyles and Simmes. That's only two people. Allen doesn't matter. Visualizing himself sitting in his kitchen and just shooting the breeze with two buddies, Dillard felt some of his anxiety and tension drain away. Better not get too relaxed, though, because if ever a talk demanded evangelical zeal, this was it.

Persuading someone to kill a fellow human being generally isn't an easy thing to do. It takes the military months and years to transform its personnel into efficient killing machines. Dillard didn't have the luxury of waiting that long.

He regretted not having taken a moment or two to write his thoughts down on paper. He'd been too busy keeping tabs on Allen since finding that police department stuff in his wallet a few hours ago. Allen had been slightly on edge. Before Boyles and Simmes arrived, Allen had come up with two lame excuses why he couldn't attend the meeting. Dillard had been adamant about Allen being there.

His situation needed to be dealt with.

Looking glummer than usual, Boyles sat with his hairy arms crossed over his ample belly. The oldest member of the group at forty-one, Boyles was the most analytical and the least likely to be swayed by an emotional appeal.

At the moment, he was fixated on his job with Baltimore's solid-waste department. After eight years of riding garbage trucks in rain, snow and blistering heat, Boyles had been up for a supervisory desk job and more money.

And a nigger snatched it! More accurately, it had been handed to him on a silver platter.

Boyles learned yesterday that his promotion had gone to a black co-worker with two years less seniority than he had. Never bothering to ask why his black colleague had gotten the job, Boyles had gone on a raging, invective-filled tirade about affirmative action and how it was ruining the country.

Earlier today, he had transferred to a different sanitation district. No way in hell would he work under some darkie who was handed the extra pay and benefits rightfully Boyles's.

Like Dillard, lanky Simmes was ex-military—Marine Corps, to be exact. Simmes was the joker of the group, the one with a talent for coaxing a laugh from trying situations. A handyman who'd held a succession of odd jobs since leaving the Marines seven years ago, Simmes was a wizard at working with his hands.

That didn't interest Dillard so much as Simmes's knowledge of explosives gained in the service. Sitting at Dillard's kitchen table and absentmindedly stroking his chin, Simmes looked as if he might be dreaming up a practical joke. He wouldn't accept any old cock-and-bull story about the disappearance of the pickup and the dynamite, though.

Baltimore City undercover police detective Sherman Brown, a.k.a. Rick Allen, sat stiffly in his chair, staying in character. Brown had gone to the police credit union's ATM machine that morning and had forgotten to dispose of his

ATM receipt. What Brown didn't know was that his three-year-old daughter had found two of Daddy's business cards and innocently stuffed them in his wallet.

And Brown hadn't worn a concealed mike, in his haste to meet with Dillard in the morning. Not having one might make it easier to bluff his way out of trouble. On the other hand, his police colleagues would know instantly if the shit hit the fan.

Dillard cleared his throat, fighting the urge to suck down another cold one to steady his nerves. Make-or-break time.

"I guess everybody is wondering why I called you here," he said, standing ramrod-straight, hands at his sides. "Here's the deal."

Dillard enthusiastically recounted the same hijacking tale he'd told to Allen, taking care not to alter a single detail. He wove the tale far more forcefully and expressively the second time around, starting to convince himself it had actually happened that way.

Allen listened impassively, but Simmes clucked his tongue disapprovingly and nodded from time to time. Boyles's preoccupied air fell away and when his eyes connected with Dillard's they were concerned and supportive.

Dillard could feel Boyles and Simmes being reeled in. As they got more and more in sync with him, Dillard's words flowed more and more easily.

"Are we just going to pass through life without taking a stand, or are we going to dig in like men and do something about the niggers and kikes and spics ruining this country?"

Boyles wondered if Dillard was reading his mind. "Yeah, it's time to stand up and do something," he shouted, scooting forward in his chair. "The only thing some people respect is force."

"Exactly," Dillard said, pausing to let Boyles's words sink in. "That is the *only* thing our enemies understand."

"Goddamn right," Allen sang out. "It's time to teach those motherfuckers whose country this is. It's time they learned a lesson."

Dillard ignored Allen's comments and continued to press

forward. His heart was pounding, sweat poured down his face and spittle flew as he held forth before his ragtag militia. It was exhilarating. Dillard was soaring on waves of oratory he'd always suspected were bottled up inside.

Dillard ranted on about how society's moral decline, combined with the entitlement mentalities of minorities, was hurting every man in the room. Along with every hardworking, law-abiding white man in the United States.

Ignoring the fact that every U.S. President, Apollo moon-walker and Fortune 500 CEO belonged to the same club, Boyles, Allen and Simmes chimed in with examples of how reverse discrimination was giving blacks everything on a platter.

Baltimore City was dismissed as having gone to pot after blacks took over city government.

"If anybody in this room doesn't believe Baltimore is now spook central, they put the national headquarters of the number one coon organization, the NAACP, right in our city."

"The NAACP couldn't even exist if Jew bastards like Sheldon Blumberg weren't always giving them handouts," Simmes growled. "I bet," he said, laughing, "They serve watermelon bagels in the NAACP cafeteria."

Perfect. Simmes was unwittingly playing into Dillard's hands.

His core audience, Boyles and Simmes, was clearly getting the message. And beginning to feel the sense of urgency Dillard felt.

It was crucial to move beyond kitchen-table rhetoric to action. Since Blumberg's name had been brought up, now was as good a time as any to unveil his plan.

"You're right, Bob," Dillard said, dramatically lowering his voice. "Kikes and niggers are two of the biggest enemies this country has. I know how we can hurt both with one stone."

His rapt audience sat waiting.

"Blumberg gives money to the NAACP and to those liberal politicians who just *love* affirmative action. Somebody needs to take out Blumberg."

Dillard paused, eager to see who would take up the gauntlet.

"Why don't we do it?" It was Allen, looking positively gleeful at the prospect of hastening Sheldon Blumberg's demise. "If one of us went through Desert Storm, we can take out an old, rich Jew, can't we?"

Boyles and Simmes looked at Allen, then at each other. Nary a word passed their lips.

"I think Rick is absolutely right," Dillard said slowly. "Why should we continue to watch Blumberg destroy our community—our country—and not do a damned thing about it? Plus, you know what else I think? I think we should make the sanitation department pay for how they fucked over Harry." Dillard knew that would push Boyles's hot button.

"How would you do that?" Boyles asked skeptically.

"I think we should leave them something to remember you by," Dillard said cryptically. "But first things first. I think we need to take care of Blumberg before we do anything else. What do you fellas think?"

He walked over to the refrigerator and retrieved beers. Everyone took one except Allen.

"Doesn't Blumberg carry a shitload of security wherever he goes?" Simmes asked. "But come to think of it, ol' JFK had a bodyguard or two, didn't he?" Everyone laughed.

"I've got a wife and two kids and a mortgage," Boyles said slowly. "What good would it do me to get mixed up in some shit that might send me to jail?"

"Harry, if you can't, or won't, stand on your hind legs, maybe you don't want to be part of the group," Dillard said bluntly. "If you want to keep losing promotions to every jigaboo that wanders in, that's your right. But I think me and the others are going to stand up and stop getting screwed for once."

The men were so engrossed in their meeting that it was 9 P.M. before anyone realized it. The sun was starting to set, its ruby rays backlighting, shimmering dust particles floating in the air.

"I never said anything about not standing up for my

rights," Boyles said weakly. "But hell, you're talking about killing people."

"That's exactly right, Harry. That's what we're talking about. Because we're at war, in case you hadn't noticed. If you don't believe it, look at your next paycheck and see if it has your raise in it. These are drastic times—we need drastic measures."

Boyles still didn't look convinced. Nor had Dillard expected instant unanimity. Not everyone can pull the trigger when another person is in the crosshairs. Another hook would be necessary to get Boyles on board.

"Okay, tell you what. Remember when I mentioned leaving the sanitation department a little calling card?" Dillard said, walking back toward the refrigerator to get another round of beers. This time Allen accepted one, but took only two birdlike sips.

"How about if some of the garbage cans on the route you just transferred from had surprises waiting in them on trash-pickup days? Like pipe bombs?"

Boyles winced. He felt a fraternal bond with most of the trash collectors on his old route. Even, he was reluctant to admit, some of the black ones. Plus, he could envision the horror of picking up a trash can and having it explode in his face. Anyway, his beef was with sanitation management, not the rank and file.

"That's not a good idea," Boyles said quietly. "A lot of decent people would get fucked up."

"Okay, then, how about if we blew up a few sanitation department garbage trucks? Some of their expensive new models?"

Boyles's eyes lit up, but he said nothing for a few seconds as he mulled over the proposition. "Count me in on that," he said finally. "Just let me know what I have to do."

With Boyles, the violence would have to be incremental, Dillard mused. The trick would be to get him to make the switch from hurting garbage trucks to hurting people.

It was time to take Simmes's temperature now.

"Bob, what's your take on Blumberg?"

Simmes slowly pulled the edge of his hand across his throat. "I agree with you, Mark," Simmes drawled. His Kentucky accent had a way of surfacing at unexpected times. "Blumberg ain't no friend of mine."

Dillard looked at Allen, who nodded his head once. Dillard smelled fear in the air. Crossing his arms, he moved slowly to a window and peered out. Children were running up and down the sidewalk, screaming and laughing, exultant they could act like banshees till sunset thanks to summer vacation.

Allen stole a glance at Boyles, who shrugged. No telling what Dillard was up to.

Like an impressionist who turns his back and swivels around with a new persona, Dillard was wearing a homicidal mask when he faced his colleagues again. Taking a few dramatic strides, he stopped directly in front of Allen, whose nerve endings were jangling. His policeman's sixth sense told him he would soon be sternly tested.

"The final thing we need to discuss," Dillard said, staring a hole into Allen's forehead, "is how we should deal with infiltrators. How 'bout it, Bob—what do you think?"

Scratching his head, Simmes smiled grimly. "Seeing as how he could bring all of us down and put us under the jail, I say we kill the motherfucker. How about another cold one, Mark?"

Dillard fetched another long-necked beer from the fridge and flipped off the cap with a bottle opener, not bothering to pick the cap from the floor.

"What about you, Harry?"

Less violence-prone than the others, but not wishing to appear a pantywaist, Boyles weighed his words carefully. "Depends on the situation."

"If an informant was about to put your ass in jail and snatch you from your beautiful family, then what?"

"Well . . . I could see maybe having to hurt somebody in that situation."

Allen sat stock-still, trying to memorize the exact kitchen cabinet shelf where Dillard had stashed his nine-millimeter.

He was also going over a mental picture of the lock on the front door and how it opened.

"And, Rick," Dillard said slowly, "what do you think? How should we deal with some piece of shit who's spying on us?"

Allen jumped up so quickly that his long brown hair arced toward the ceiling. Pumping his right fist in the air, he further startled everyone by shouting, "I say we off the sonofabitch!"

Momentarily taken aback, Dillard recovered quickly. He chuckled softly and shook his head, as if to say, "That crazy Allen!" Boyles and Simmes joined in. Dillard's smile vanished as quickly as it had appeared. "Okay . . . fair enough. Got a little question for you, Rick. Would you mind showing us your wallet?"

"My wallet? What's up, man, need a couple of dollars?"

Boyles laughed. Simmes, sensing something was up, didn't.

Figuring he could easily explain the police credit union's ATM slip in his wallet, Allen handed it to Dillard, who turned it upside down and dumped the contents of the brown leather wallet onto the kitchen table. Two business cards for Detective Sherman Brown, Baltimore City Police Department Criminal Investigations Bureau were the last items to flutter out. Little silver detectives' badges embossed on them glinted red in the cherry sunshine.

Boyles's and Simmes's mouths flopped open simultaneously. Their expressions mirrored Sherman Brown's, who could have passed out when he saw two of his business cards on the table.

Looking closely at Brown, hands on hips, Dillard picked up one of the cards between his thumb and forefinger and tauntingly held it in Brown's face. "Why do you have two cop cards in your wallet, Rick? Are all your cards on the table now?"

"What is this, some kind of joke, man?" a bewildered Brown asked, looking from face to face. "Are you trying to set me up?"

"Got that backward, don't you—*Detective Brown?*"

Katie! How had his three-year-old gotten his wallet? Oh, my God, no! No! This is not happening. Don't show any fear.

Brown shot up in his chair again, ready to take on all comers this time. Backing up rapidly, he positioned himself between Dillard and the kitchen cabinet where the gun was.

"You have got to be fucking kidding," he said in a loud voice. "Somebody put that shit in my wallet." He shot an accusatorial glare at Dillard.

"Really?" Now Dillard was inching toward Brown, who had backed against the kitchen sink. Mouths agape, Boyles and Simmes remained glued to their seats, stunned by the unexpected drama.

"This shit is crazy, man! What's wrong with you? You know I ain't no fucking cop!" Without turning his back, Brown reached behind him, feeling for a drawer that might contain a butcher knife. With his other hand he reached into his pants pocket, after his switchblade.

Pushing his chair back, Simmes stood up.

It seemed to Brown that Simmes had never been *that* tall before. Then Dillard lunged. As he streaked toward Brown like a wolf, his gray eyes seemed to be shimmering with fury.

Sidestepping Dillard, Brown swung with the ferocity of a man fighting for his life. The blow hit Dillard squarely in his midsection and he crumpled to the kitchen floor, holding his stomach and gasping in agony. But there was to be no respite; Simmes was grappling with Brown before Dillard had finished falling.

I must see Katie and Sylvia again! Brown told himself.

Dishes, chairs, even the kitchen table went crashing to the floor as the two men wrestled through the kitchen and into the living room. Brown was starting to get the upper hand when he noticed Dillard rise and stand on tiptoe. Oh, my God! Now Dillard was groping along the top shelf of the cabinet.

Boyles had joined the battle by now and, with the help of Simmes, tossed the flailing Brown onto a glass-and-pine coffee table. The thick glass shattered on contact, sending a three-inch-long shard plunging into Brown's back and impaling a kidney. He sprawled awkwardly on the living room floor, his legs elevated on the pine frame of the table.

The odd thing was, Brown never screamed. The pain was so excruciating that tears flowed from his eyes, but he never shouted or moaned. He instinctively knew his blood supply was ebbing and he would need to make every motion count. Thrashing around and screaming would only accelerate his decline—it was critical that he think clearly.

Reaching behind him, he fingered the daggerlike shard of glass embedded in his back. It was slippery with O-negative blood. Brown gave the shard a quick tug, but instead of dislodging it, he succeeded only in slicing his right ring finger and pinkie down to the bone.

"You've got to get me to a hospital," he said in a near whisper, pain and the onset of shock making his voice sound strained. He looked at Boyles, who seemed to have more of the milk of human kindness than Simmes or Dillard. "You can't leave me here to die."

Boyles's response was to retch the contents of his stomach all over Dillard's living room floor.

Moving quickly, Dillard slammed shut the windows in the kitchen and living room, shuttered the blinds and drew the curtains tight. The day had begun with him firing bullets at a cop and now a mortally wounded one was on his living room floor, bleeding on the throw rug. The air was thick with the odor of Boyles's beery vomit.

Simmes still hadn't gotten up after tumbling to the floor with Brown and Boyles. Pain seared through his right collarbone and when he stood up, he heard the horrible sound of bone against bone.

"Maybe we should drive him to a hospital," Simmes said through clenched teeth. "I think I need to go, too."

"WHAT IF HE'S A COP?" Dillard screamed as forcefully as he could, an ill-considered move since adjoining homes flanked his row house. "I don't know about you, but I don't feel like going to jail."

"I told you, I ain't no fuckin' cop," Brown grunted, determined to maintain his cover.

"Then how did those cards and that ATM slip get in your wallet?"

"My cousin is a cop," Brown said, fighting light-headedness. "I went to see him this morning and he gave me a couple of his cards. Got me some money while I was there, too."

Brown's tears were flowing faster, more from fear than from pain. He didn't want to die on the living room floor of some psychopath and his band of angry losers. His breathing was becoming increasingly shallow and he could feel delirium setting in.

"You gotta get me to a hospital, man," he said in a barely audible voice. "I'm dyin'."

Dillard decided right then that Allen, Brown—whoever he was—was just going to have to die. He couldn't chance this man turning out to be an undercover policeman. Snapping on the television set in the living room, he turned up the volume as far as it would go. The voice of an attractive woman complaining about cat litter odor boomed through the house.

Nodding for Simmes and Boyles to follow him, Dillard walked to the door leading to the basement. "We can't take this guy to any hospital," he said simply. "He might be a cop."

"I'm sure going to a doctor," Simmes said, grimacing.

"Whaddaya mean we can't take him to a hospital?" Boyles said, his eyes growing larger by the second. "He might be a cop. I don't want nothing to do with killing no cop."

"What do you mean you don't want nothing to do with it?" Dillard shouted. "How do you think he got there on the floor, bleeding? He's there because of you, Harry! YOU pushed him onto that table, in case you forgot."

Boyles's ruddy complexion had turned ashen. He was looking beyond Dillard, into the living room. Utilizing sheer will-power, Brown had somehow gotten his oxygen-deprived body erect and was walking haltingly across the living room toward the front door. His hand was outstretched to twist the lock when he collapsed with a thud, a red trail marking his meandering path.

A sitcom on the TV incongruously filled the house with sidesplitting laughter.

Brown was unconscious when Dillard reached him, his expression serene now instead of pained.

"You can get us into the city incinerator, right?" Dillard barked at Boyles.

"Uh, yeah. Why?"

"Figure it out, Harry."

"We'll need to burn that rug, too," a wincing Simmes interjected.

"Look, Mark, I gotta go home," Boyles whined in a quavering tone. "I told Doris I would only be at your house for a little while. We're supposed to go out to dinner."

"Well, goddammit, call Doris back and tell her you're going to be longer than you thought," Dillard snapped. With Simmes injured, Dillard was going to need help transporting Brown, and he wasn't going to do it by himself. Plus, Boyles had a beat-up van they could use.

"Lemme tell you something," Dillard continued. "You're in this shit up to your eyeballs, my friend. There's no turning back. You have helped kill a Baltimore City police officer. Am I making myself clear? Call your wife and tell her you'll be in later."

"But he's not dead yet."

"He will be."

"What do I tell Doris?"

Dillard shrugged. "What the fuck do I care? Just do it."

Boyles stammered through a conversation that had him constantly on the defensive. "No, I ain't been drinkin'. No, nothing's wrong. Yes, Mark is here—wanna talk to him?"

An Orioles game was blasting over the TV when Brown finally died around ten o'clock. Simmes, who'd been given the job of keeping an eye on Brown, saw him shudder a couple of times, then sigh. In the basement, Dillard and Boyles were busily crumpling old newspapers and stuffing them into plastic lawn and leaf bags, a task Boyles performed in stunned silence.

Carefully positioning Brown's body on the throw rug, they rolled it around him, hiding a large burgundy bloodstain. Dillard drove Boyles's van into the alley behind his house and loaded Brown into the van first, with Boyles's help. Then they carried out ten bulging lawn and leaf bags and tossed them on top of their makeshift body bag.

Simmes, his right arm dangling uselessly by his side, stood in the alley watching for cops and nosy neighbors. A pit bull in one backyard bayed noisily the entire time, as though it had spotted Satan.

Had the neighbors looked out their windows, they wouldn't have seen much. Young boys playing with a BB gun had broken the streetlamp in the alley. And thick clouds from a fast-moving storm obscured a full moon.

In any event, Dillard and Boyles weren't lollygagging: They transported Brown's body and the lawn and leaf bags from the house to the van in a little under three minutes.

Dillard hastily locked his back door, herded his compatriots into the van and departed immediately. Boyles drove, since it was his vehicle, and because he could get them past the gate at the city's incinerator and waste-energy facility on Russell Street. Dillard sat in the passenger seat while Simmes sat on the floor of the van, which had only two seats.

When the van inched toward the incinerator building's main gate, Boyles couldn't have been more nervous or suspicious-looking if he'd tried.

"Hey, Harry. What brings you out here this time of night?" a surprised guard asked casually.

Boyles answered with a chuckle that was too loud and too long. The guard looked at him oddly, then peered into the van at Dillard and Simmes, whose eyes remained downcast.

"Just cleaning out my garage and figured I'd throw this stuff away. Don't wanna give the boys too much to haul Monday."

"Why didn't you just go to the Cold Spring landfill?"

"It's closed this time of night."

"Oh, yeah. What you got in there, anyway?"

Boyles appeared stunned, then looked over at Dillard.

Answer him, dumb ass, Dillard's look said. Say something. Anything!

"Just chopped up the ol' lady, Bill. You know how it is." More inappropriate, nervous laughter.

"If you've got any more of what you've been smoking or drinking, Harry, gimme some," the guard said, waving the van past. He returned to his little guard station and settled in front of a portable TV, his face a ghostly bluish white.

"Why don't you just tack a sign on the truck that says 'Dead man inside?'." Dillard snapped.

"Don't fuck with me," Boyles roared back as he drove slowly toward the incinerator building. "This may shock you, but this shit ain't somethin' I do on a regular basis."

"Knock it off, both of ya," Simmes barked. "We're not outta here yet."

Fortunately for them, the thunder of yellow bulldozers attacking mountains of trash and green city dump trucks carrying in more refuse drowned out their edgy bickering.

Boyles parked beside a waist-high river of stinking garbage that crept by the van on a metal conveyor belt. When it reached the incinerator furnace, the conveyor belt elevated about two stories, where it dumped rotten food, disposable diapers and the rest of society's flotsam into the maw of a mechanical inferno. The garbage had been subjected to a process that removed most of the metal in it.

Another sound began to fill the air now, a droning hum so powerful that it resonated inside everyone's chest cavity. It came from the fans that pumped air into the incinerator, as well as from emissions equipment cleaning the white-hot gases streaking up the smokestack and into the cloudy Baltimore sky. But most of the noise came from powerful steam turbines that ingeniously used heat from burning garbage to generate electricity for the city.   •

A black woman searching the conveyor belt for renegade bits of metal nodded at Boyles, who nodded back. Dillard frowned disapprovingly as the van came to a stop.

"Can we unload this stuff here?"

"Yeah. We can just throw everything on the conveyor belt."

"Okay, let's start with the bags. I'll let you know when to put the throw rug on."

Boyles opened the back of the van as a bulldozer went zooming by, its shovel missing the van by less than a foot. The atmosphere inside the incinerator building was one of controlled chaos.

"Start handing out the bags." Dillard began passing lawn and leaf bags to Boyles, who gently placed them on the conveyor belt. The woman worker approached after the third bag went on.

"No metal, right?"

"You got it, Cynthia. Just trash."

She turned on the thick rubber heel of her work boot and strode away, toward some other matter requiring her attention.

"Let's take out the rug after this bag," Dillard said, shouting over the noise and keeping an eye on the woman as she walked away. The men grabbed either end of the rug and nonchalantly carried it to the conveyor belt. So much adrenaline was at work that the rug seemed weightless.

Six lawn and leaf bags were placed on and around the rug containing the body of Detective Sherman Brown, which slowly floated up the gently inclining conveyor belt into the mouth of incinerator No. 2. Boyles, Dillard and Simmes never saw the rug disappear down the chute into the roaring flames below. Once consigned to the twelve-hundred-degree temperature inside the furnace, Brown's body was quickly converted into silvery ash.

No one watching television or using the microwave in Baltimore at that moment could have guessed what macabre fuel source was helping power his or her gizmo.

It was raining like crazy when Dillard, Boyles and Simmes left the incinerator building. Small pieces of hail mixed with the precipitation sounded like pebbles bouncing off the van's roof.

The enormity of their crime was just beginning to settle into the group's collective consciousness. Simmes, stoically enduring the pain of a broken collarbone, moaned softly every time the van hit a bump or a pothole. A hospital visit was in his future.

Boyles was so oblivious to his surroundings, so distant and uncomprehending, that he almost blew right through two stoplights. The only thing that snapped him into the present was screamed warnings from Dillard. A long, sleepless night was in Boyles's future.

Dillard, who would sleep well that night, eagerly anticipated his future.

"Within a week we're going to kill Sheldon Blumberg," he said to no one in particular.

Pain and preoccupation had clouded Boyles's and Simmes's minds to the point where neither heard, or cared about, Dillard's bold declaration.

FOURTEEN

YOLANDA IS HUGGING ME JOYFULLY, WE'RE SMILING AND ALL IS right with the world.

Self-absorbed, selfish Mr. Bachelor has just done the right thing: I've told Yolanda she and Jamal can stay for two weeks. If they turn out to be the houseguests from hell and this experiment goes dramatically sour, I can always ask them to leave earlier.

Yolanda does a happy little jig from me to Jamal, whom she hugs and whirls around in the air.

"I promise you won't regret this," she says, grabbing my hand. "You just don't know how much this means to us . . ." Tears start flowing down Yolanda's beautiful cheeks. "We'll give you some money for rent and your electric bill," Yolanda says finally. "And I'll buy all of our food, so you won't have to worry about that."

"That works for me. I hope you guys don't mind the living room couch?" Goodbye privacy.

"No, no, definitely not. Thank you so much, Darryl. Thank you."

"Hey, no problem," I say, smiling at Yolanda. "Uh, I hope you aren't insulted by this, but I would really appreciate it if you could give me a little something as a security deposit. Whatever you think is fair."

This request takes some of the wind out of Yolanda's sails. Her smile dims and she flashes me a quick, pained look.

"Sure, no problem. I can go to the bank and get you two hundred dollars today, if that's okay. I'll get it back when I leave, right?"

"That's a deal."

"I would like to ask one other favor of you, though," Yolanda says slowly, looking embarrassed.

Uh-oh. I should have known this wouldn't be simple. Come on, Yolanda, don't kill the warm, fuzzy feeling right off the bat.

"Sure, if I can. What is it?"

"Me and Jamal don't have any clean clothes, we don't have toothbrushes, we don't have anything. I had to leave boyfriend's crib in a hurry. Can you go over there with me to get some of my stuff?"

"Is your boyfriend home right now?"

That prompts a grimace. "No, he should be at work. And please don't call him my boyfriend." Which is exactly what she called him five seconds ago.

So with Yolanda at the wheel of her twelve-year-old subcompact and me driving my little black Japanese coupe, we head toward East Baltimore, toward The Pit, and a small apartment complex at 1231 Frank Robinson Way.

Little black boys armed with water guns big enough to fill the Hoover Dam are chasing girls up and down the sidewalk in front of 1231 when we pull up. I hear the girls' delighted, mock-indignant screams as I turn off my engine.

Having already seen her boyfriend's propensity for violence, I'm guessing he's a macho asshole. So with any luck, this will be an in-and-out operation and we can be on our way without encountering him.

So naturally her boyfriend's blue Lexus eases into the space directly behind my car. I don't even have to ask, I just know it's him.

Wearing a pair of inky-black shades, carefree, ignorant Cool Daddy bobs his head to the radio. When he gets out of his car, I see he's wearing a green tank top so the world can see he's been working out and has arms like Magilla Gorilla. He looks to be about two inches shorter than I am.

My last fight was in the tenth grade, when I whipped a bully named David Jefferson who had been goading me for a month. I'd hoped that would be my last fight and that I could retire victorious.

As soon as Jamal spots the thirty-one-year-old punk who blackened his eye last night, he starts screaming.

The man-child swaggers past me to Yolanda, who's already out of her car. I quickly exit mine.

"Back already, bitch?"

Yolanda gazes at her cretinous former companion with sheer revulsion. Did she actually love this baboon, or was he just a reclamation project?

"I just came back to get my stuff, Boone," Yolanda says icily, not even making eye contact. "My cousin Darryl came to help."

Boone glances briefly at me in a way that indicates I'm of less consequence than the street grime under his tan boots. He's too busy scheming to worry about me. "Come on, baby," he says in a smooth-as-honey voice as he roughly encircles Yolanda's waist in his arms. "Daddy said he was sorry."

"Get OFF me, Boone," Yolanda says, snatching herself from his grip. "Did you hear me? I said I came back to get my things."

"Just let the lady get her stuff," I say in a neutral and nonconfrontational voice.

"Just let the lady get her stuff?" Boone repeats in a taunting falsetto. "Who did you say this faggot was? Your cousin!"

Now he's so close I can smell last night's liquor. "You never mentioned no Cousin Darryl to me before. Who is you, punk?"

I can feel animosity and aggression churning off Boone like heat from a raging fire. But I don't fear him as I gaze at his ugly little face. I just feel profound disgust, because I've peeped Boone's hole card. He's nothing but an overblown bully, a latter-day David Jefferson. Only this one's such a coward he can't perform his misdeeds without a bottle.

"Lemme tell you something," I say with deceptive calmness. "First of all, you better get your monkey-lookin' ass outta my face. Second, if you want to talk about punks, let's talk about men who hit women and children. Because that's what a PUNK is."

Boone continues wolfing but backs away a few steps, realizing he may have misjudged things. "Ohhhhh! Why I gotta be all that, huh? I got your punk, all right." In keeping with his thoroughly classy persona, Boone grabs his genitals. Now it's my turn to ig him.

"Let's go get your stuff, Yolanda. I don't have time for this silly bullshit." Grabbing her by the elbow, I guide her toward her car and she reaches into the backseat to grab Jamal.

"You better walk away," Boone yells at the top of his lungs. " 'Cause I'll fuck you up!"

I think I understand where all of Boone's misplaced rage is coming from. If I looked like a warthog, had bad breath and an IQ of seventy, I'd be mad, too.

"And you better not take nothin' that don't belong to you, bitch!"

Yolanda freezes in her tracks. You'd think the *b* word was tethered to a choke chain around her neck. Jamal looks at her with a puzzled expression.

"Come on, Yolanda. He's just pushing your buttons—can't you see that? He just wants to drag you down to his level. Don't give him the satisfaction."

By now girlfriend's nostrils are flaring and she's clearly ready for an ugly domestic scene I want no part of. I grab her elbow again and push her toward the apartment building.

Boone is silent, apparently having exhausted his repertoire of witty, scintillating remarks.

Me and Yolanda take seven suitcases of clothing out of the cramped, cluttered apartment she shared with Godzilla. She does pause long enough to repeatedly smash a framed picture of herself, Boone and Jamal, sending slivers of glass flying into the carpet.

"Is he Jamal's father?"

Yolanda massages the back of her neck and looks around the apartment. "Unfortunately, he is," she answers in a tired voice. That contradicts what she said earlier about Boone not being Jamal's father.

"It's none of my business, but you two don't exactly seem like the perfect couple."

"What can I tell you? He wasn't always the monster you saw today. And I was young and dumb and didn't believe in abortion. Still don't. Boone tried to keep things together for a long time and we were doing okay until liquor entered the picture."

Coming across a pair of handcuffs, I silently pick them up in front of Yolanda.

Instead of blushing, she never misses a beat. "Hey, different strokes for different folks," she says matter-of-factly.

"Hhhhmmmmm."

"Do you mind if we concentrate on getting my clothes so we can get out of here, please?"

There's no question how Jamal feels. He never moves from the front door and whimpers the entire time we're in the apartment.

When we get outside with the first load of clothes, Boone is sitting on the hood of *my* car, looking like he's ready to go to war!

"Now he's pushing *your* buttons," Yoldanda whispers as we struggle with several suitcases. Boone offers no assistance, nor does he look as if the thought ever entered his thick head. "You gonna let him take *you* there?"

"No, I'm not going to let him take me anywhere, but he is getting off my car."

But before a showdown can materialize, Boone slides off the hood, clambers coolly into his Lexus and glides away before we reach him. I guess he just wanted to see with his own eyes whether Yolanda was bluffing. Now you know, chump.

When I sneak a glance to see if Yolanda appears sad, the only thing registering on her face is relief. Lucifer is finally out of the picture.

After the U-Haul routine is out of the way and the bulk of Yolanda's and Jamal's belongings is safely inside my apartment, we all go to a little soul food restaurant on Pennsylvania Avenue, Miss Kelly's, for a noontime breakfast.

Wonder of wonders: Yolanda sits across from me with a look of pure adoration on her face. No doubt because I stood up to her ex-caveman, Boone. It feels damn good to have her look at me that way. But why couldn't she have done it because of my intellect or strength of character? Or for caring enough to take her and her child—total strangers—off the street? Why did I have to sink into Neanderthal mode for her to view me in a flattering new light?

Now that I've shown a willingness to fight in the street like a brutish animal, my stock has gone up. What kind of twisted view is that?!

At least Jamal is consistent. He still flinches every time he thinks I'm going to get within three feet of him. And he monitors me warily.

Our waitress, a sweet wisp of a lady around sixty who has a single gold tooth in her mouth, takes our order, then asks what we want to drink. "Y'all a nice-looking family," she says before moving off toward the kitchen.

A nice-looking family!!!

I can feel my cheeks burning. Yolanda looks vaguely embarrassed, too.

"I don't know what you two have planned," I tell Yolanda, "but when we leave here I'm going to bed. I'm feeling pretty beat."

"I, uh, have Jamal in Saturday day care," Yolanda says, her inflection indicating something else is on her mind. "I was thinking that after all we've been through, I might keep him with me today and let him get some rest. If that's okay with you."

"As long as he doesn't keep me awake."

Breakfast arrives, and soon the only sound in the booth is the smacking of lips.

Jamal chews his food so vigorously you'd think he was mad at it. Despite being the smallest person at the table, Jamal finishes first and immediately hounds his mother for the remaining pieces of bacon on her plate.

After we finish I split the check with Yolanda; then me and my "nice-looking family" head back to my apartment. If I've ever had a more difficult time staying awake driving six blocks, I'm hard-pressed to recall it.

"You know where the linen closet is. Good night," I mumble before I march into my bedroom and collapse on the bed.

Wouldn't you know I dream about Boone as soon as I drop off! Boone and Yolanda.

Followed by a horrific nightmare of the NAACP building tumbling to the ground in a sickening cloud of dust and smoke. It bothers me so much I can't go back to sleep, despite my fatigue.

Sighing, I get out of bed, put on some clothes and wash up quietly. Saturday is a workday, so I might as well head to the *Herald*.

FIFTEEN

SHELDON BLUMBERG WAS MURDERED SO EFFICIENTLY THAT HO-
micide detectives immediately suspected a professional hit.
Which would have elicited a self-congratulatory smirk from
Mark Dillard.

Gunshot victims smoked during crimes of passion or by
panicky gunmen usually wind up like whiffle balls, Swiss
cheese on the hoof. Blumberg merely had a single-entry
wound to his right temple; there was no exit wound. The
fragmentation bullet fired into his head worked as designed,
instantly transforming his brain into a puree of gray matter
and blood vessels. One of Baltimore's most fabled philanthropists was dead and gone before his head thudded against the
steering wheel of his gray Volvo station wagon.

There was no indication of a struggle and none of Blumberg's neighbors saw or heard anything amiss, even though
the shooting took place in Blumberg's driveway sometime
between seven-thirty and seven forty-five Saturday morning,
homicide detective Philip Gardner noted disgustedly. Not
even a man two houses down, tending to his squash garden,
had noticed anything unusual before Blumberg slumped onto
his car horn, jarring the neighborhood and Baltimore into a
state of shock.

Gardner sighed and chomped down on an already tired
wad of gum. Mayor Clifford Shaw had been notified and was

148

en route to the scene. Soon he'd be in front of the TV cameras, jaw set, face grim. Solemnly vowing Blumberg's killer or killers would be swiftly apprehended and brought to justice.

Which would place Gardner atop a cattle prod. Positioned inside a pressure cooker. Located inside the fourth circle of hell.

The media would grill the mayor, who would lean on the police commissioner, who would castigate the homicide captain, who would ride Gardner until a suspect was collared. The search for this perpetrator would be a meat-grinding, stomach-wrenching bitch, Gardner knew all too well. During investigations of this magnitude, he rarely spent more than forty minutes a day at police headquarters. Life there was akin to being nibbled to death by ducks.

Gardner was one of several police officers tromping through the grass and shrubbery around Blumberg's expansive Victorian home in Roland Park, a middle- to upper-class northern Baltimore enclave. Blumberg had prided himself in having retained "the common touch," which was why he'd driven a faded, 1984 Volvo. And why he'd refused to ensconce himself in a palatial estate or a gated community. Instead, he had remained in the house he and his wife called home for thirty-five years.

That preference, and his habit of letting his security detail off on weekends, had cost him his life.

"Come on, Sheldon, give it up, baby. Tell me who capped your rich ass and save me a world of grief," Gardner said, brushing away Blumberg's comb-over with a gloved hand to examine the entry wound. "Was it business? Your old lady pissed at you? Whazup, bro'?"

The car yielded the fingerprints of Blumberg, his wife and a security detail member whose alibi was airtight. The rear seat contained the only clues Baltimore police had to work with: a spent nine-millimeter shell casing that had been struck by the firing pin of a Beretta. And granules of dirt that could have come from one of six construction sites in northern Baltimore County.

In accordance with Jewish tradition, Blumberg was quickly eulogized and planted in the soil. During a special memorial service at the convention center, it was hard to determine who wept more vigorously—friends and relatives or representatives of the various liberal and civil rights organizations dependent on The Blumberg Foundation.

Flags across the state fluttered at half-staff for days, the state legislature created a Sheldon Blumberg Day, and a Baltimore TV station ran a cloying half-hour special on Blumberg's life.

Detectives investigated radio talk-show callers who excoriated Blumberg and his "pinko legacy." The legwork yielded nothing.

Mad Dawg Murdoch didn't just say what I thought he said. No way. I listened to a cassette in my car, instead of turning on the radio while driving to work. This is the first I've heard of it.

"Man, did you hear somebody offed Super Jew this morning?"

"What are you talking about, Dawg?"

"Somebody killed Sheldon Blumberg."

Grabbing the lanky Dawg by his collar, I pull him down to my level. "Is this some kind of fucking joke? Are *you* the one who's been calling me? Because if you have—"

"What the hell's your problem, man?" a startled Dawg growls, yanking free and shoving me in the chest.

"What did you just say to me? Repeat exactly what you just said."

"I said Blumberg got shot this morning. Why are you freaking out?"

Disbelieving and light-headed, I squat next to the elevator. *This shit is for real!* There's always been the thought in the back of my mind that I've been dealing with a crackpot.

"What's wrong with you, Darryl?"

"Nothing, Dawg," I croak feebly. "Feeling a little under the weather after my run-in in the alley, that's all."

"You okay? Want me to run you to the doctor or somethin'?"

"Naw, Dawg, I'm cool. Just give me a couple of minutes and I'll meet you upstairs, okay, partner?"

"You're buggin', man. You need to get yourself in check," Dawg says, annoyed. Can't say I blame him.

After he leaves, I go into the first-floor men's room. Latching onto a sink with a death grip, I turn on cold water and splash some on my face.

When I stand erect, a pained-looking young brother with water droplets on his brown face appears in the mirror. Why do I feel somehow responsible for Blumberg's death? I left a message on Detective Phil Gardner's machine—was there something else I could have done?

Maybe Dawg was wrong; maybe he didn't have the slightest idea what he was talking about. Maybe I'm going to go to the newsroom, turn on my computer and find some April Fool message on my computer. Then I'll cuss him out and we'll have a good laugh.

But that hope is shot down as soon as I exit the elevator on the fifth floor. The newsroom is packed with energized editors, reporters and editorial assistants, which is unheard of on a Saturday.

There's electricity in the air that crackles only when a major news story is unfolding. Everyone is moving around purposefully, solemnly, at a pace a click or two above normal.

A revelation burns through the fog. This is *my* story. I'm the police reporter, have been for the past five years. Five years of giving up my Saturdays and having Sunday-to-Monday weekends has finally paid off with a blockbuster.

I'm not being callous or unfeeling. Regardless of whether I'm linked to Blumberg's demise or not, covering it is my job.

"Darryl!"

Tom Merriwether walks toward me with that queer, crablike gait of his, trailed by a distinctly uncomfortable-looking R. Charles Covington III.

"You're in today, right?" he asks brusquely.

"Yep, I'm in for my regular Saturday cop shift. Looks like we've got a juicy one today with Blumberg."

Merriwether gives no indication of having heard my last remark.

"Good. Since you're on the clock, I need you to call Jewish organizations and community spokesmen in the area and get some Blumberg quotes. We'll wrap that into the story and give you a contributing tag."

A contributing tag is where your name appears at the end of a story, giving you credit for helping to gather information. Why do I need a contributing tag if I'm writing the story?

"Right, Tom. I'm writing the main bar, too, right?"

"No. You are not." The words hover briefly in midair before slapping me in the face. R. Charles is suddenly fascinated by the tips of his shoes. Merriwether snorts and turns to walk off.

"Excuse me! I'm the police reporter, right? R. Charles was still covering City Hall the last time I looked. Why is he doing a story off the police beat? *MY STORY?* I don't get called in on major stories out of City Hall. What are you doing this for, you—"

"I only intend to say this once, because we need to hurry and get this story in the paper. First of all, it wasn't clear, Darryl, whether you would even be showing up for work today. I'm sure," Merriwether adds, pausing theatrically, "you must be tired after cutting the rug at that function where Cornelius saw you last night. Second, R. Charles can bring to bear writing and news-gathering abilities that you simply can't. Not to put too fine a point on it, the average person writing a letter to his or her mother writes better than you do, Darryl. If you have any questions about anything I've just said, we can take that up later."

Having said his piece, Merriwether walks off.

You arrogant, supercilious pencil-neck, talentless, kiss-ass son of a bitch! I would gladly relinquish this job for the pleasure of dragging him outside and stomping him into the employee parking lot. This just isn't fair. It is NOT fair, goddammit.

I've never, ever claimed to be God's gift to journalism, but I'm pretty decent after seven years in this business. I know damn well my writing and reporting are above average. You bastard!

I stalk out of the newsroom, nearly knocking over Mad Dawg, who's on his way to cover an afternoon Orioles game.

"What up, homes? Still buggin'?"

I just grumble unintelligibly and breeze by. No question Dawg deserves an apology or an explanation, but not now. I'll take care of that later.

Fit to be tied, I stalk to an elevator and slam the button for the basement floor. When the elevator door closes, I brush one of my shoes against it, wisely pulling up at the last second instead of giving the door a hard kick. Why should I break my toe because Merriwether is a poor judge of talent? And an asshole? Would my hobbling around in a cast change that?

The elevator door opens into the cavernous pressroom in the bowels of the building. Six idle, two-story presses loom before me like hulking sentinels. An elderly pressman stands beside one with a toolbox and an oil can, doing routine maintenance work. He turns briefly to see who's invaded his domain, waves a grimy hand, then returns to work. It's quiet as a chapel down here.

The soda machine in the pressmen's break room accepts my crumpled dollar bill on the third try, and dispenses a frigid grape soda. I sit down inside the break room, which reeks of stale cigarette smoke, and press the soda can against the back of my neck. And close my eyes.

A thought floats into my head that pushes Merriwether to the background, where he belongs: If Blumberg is dead, maybe these fools really are going after the NAACP!

Still rubbing the cold soda can against my neck, I get back on the elevator and push the fifth-floor button. Blumberg may be gone, but at least I can get on the phone and warn someone about the NAACP threat.

When the elevator gets to the first floor, it stops and the door opens. In walk a grim Managing Editor Walter Watkins and the *Herald*'s wunderkind publisher, Francis Birch. Both are wearing polo shirts, shorts and golf shoes. The Blumberg shooting dragged them off the links.

"Hello, Darryl," Watkins says with the graveness of someone headed to a state funeral. "Looks like a helluva story landed in your lap."

"Well, that's the way I figure it, too, Mr. Watkins," I say slowly, picking my words with care. "But Merriwether tossed it to the City Hall reporter."

Watkins waggles an unlit, telephone-pole cigar between his teeth. "That's interesting," he says noncommittally. "I'll talk to Tom about it. Real shame about old Shel, though. Took one in the head inside his car."

I nod, not letting on that's the first detail I've heard.

A red number five glows inside the elevator and Watkins holds the door for Birch, then waves for me past. "Time to get cracking, kid." He winks. "You've got a big story to tackle."

Whatever you say, big guy. Paddle Merriwether if you have to, but just make sure I get what's rightfully mine. Namely, the lead story in tomorrow's paper. The *Herald* sells 230,000 papers on Sunday, its best circulation day.

Back at my desk, I pick up the phone and dial the police bomb squad.

"Sergeant East, police tactical section and bomb squad. How can I help you?"

"This is Darryl Billups and I'm the *Herald*'s police reporter. I'm calling to report a bomb threat against the NAACP."

"Do tell."

"Beg your pardon?"

"Look, Mr. Billups, we get about ten to twelve NAACP threats every week. Not to mention the IRS, the federal courthouse—even your wonderful institution."

"No, you don't understand. This is different. This came from someone who warned Sheldon Blumberg was going to get killed today."

Sergeant East is all ears now. "Go ahead, keep talking."

I run through the frequency and nature of the Androgynous One's calls. "So can you send someone down there to go through the building and check things out?" I ask anxiously.

"I'm afraid we don't work that way. There aren't a whole lot of city police officers who do bomb squad work, so we can't mobilize unless we have a report that a bomb is actually in place."

"Even though I got those calls predicting Blumberg's shooting?"

"Unfortunately, that's the way it goes."

Next, I try to call the NAACP and get a recorded message that office hours are Monday through Friday.

Grimacing, I hang up and start putting together a phone list of Jewish sources. Tapping into a computerized source list maintained by the metro desk gets me five phone numbers. A call to the home of the *Herald*'s religion writer nets seven more numbers. Armed with these valuable digits, I start working the phone when, out of the corner of my eye, I see Merriwether enter Watkins's office.

Through the office window I see Watkins jab at the air with his stogie, a chastened-looking Merriwether saying one or two words, then leaving the office. I focus on my computer screen.

"Do you have a moment?" I hear someone snarl.

I turn to look up at Merriwether, whose entire face is red and whose eyes look like they might burst from his head. His fists are clenched. I smile sweetly and speak in a voice that would put the front-desk receptionist to shame.

"Yes, Tom, may I help you?"

"I'm sick and tired of your insubordinate attitude, you son of a bitch!"

Oh, shit! Why did he have to go in there? Why did this simple redneck just curse me?

I get up from my chair, rising an inch taller than Merriwether, who shuffles backward a couple of steps.

"Tom," I say, conveying just the right mixture of calm and menace, "my performance evaluations around here aren't based on attitude, so there's no reason to discuss it. You can't measure it or quantify it—it doesn't have a damn thing to do with anything. Secondly, if you *ever* call me out my name again, we can take it outside and I'll kick your narrow ass. If you think I'm bluffing, try it.''

His mean-looking eyes widen, then quickly narrow. ''That a threat, Darryl?''

''No brag, Tom. Just fact.''

''You have three hours to finish the Blumberg story. Instead of sending it to the metro desk, send it directly to my computer so I can personally edit it.''

I nod. Sure thing, Tom. So you can rewrite it in your deadly, pedestrian prose.

Since I'm such an insubordinate son of a bitch, maybe I should send Watkins an unedited copy of the Blumberg story, too.

My desk phone starts ringing, which Merriwether mercifully takes as a cue to get out of my face.

''Hello.''

Silence. I know instantly who it is. My heart drops.

''Do you believe me now?'' There's no hint of gloating, no I-told-you-so intonation. Sad and subdued is more like it.

''Yes. Yes, I definitely do. Were you involved with the murder?''

Quietly taking my phone tap from my desk drawer, I attach it to the telephone. My tape recorder doesn't have a microcassette in it, nor can I find one. Damn.

''No, Darryl. What do you take me for? I'm no murderer.''

''I don't know what you are, frankly. I do know one thing—it's possible that you may be charged with being an accomplice to Blumberg's shooting.''

Light laughter, then a pause as that reality hits home. The voice is a little less certain and assured.

''No . . . I don't think that's possible. I don't think it is.''

''Who killed Blumberg?''

Nothing comes across the line, not even static.

''Hello? Are you still there?''

''Yes.''

''Who killed Sheldon Blumberg?''

"More than one person. Two, possibly three." Just enough hesitation to sound genuine.

"You don't know?"

"I wasn't there. I know one of the people—I'm not sure."

"Look, let's knock off this secret-agent stuff. Let's meet somewhere."

"Uhhhmm, I don't know. He might kill me if he knows I've been talking to you." The response is skittish, nervous. Am I dealing with a woman?

"Hey, I won't bite you. You must have thought I was a decent guy, else you wouldn't have started calling me in the first place."

"Save the charm, Darryl." The Androgynous One is sounding confident and in charge again. "But you're right, you are a good person."

"Do I know you?"

A slight cough crackles across the line. "Yeah, you know me."

"Refresh my memory, then."

"I'm not ready for that . . . I'd better go."

"Come on, let's meet somewhere."

"Lemme think on it."

"Is the NAACP bombing still on?"

"Sure is. Bye." Click.

Jotting down Blumberg's address, I grab my notepad, tape recorder and walkie-talkie. I e-mail Merriwether that I'm headed to the crime scene, get a press car from the motor pool, then set out for Roland Park.

In front of the *Herald*, walking along the sidewalk toward the employee parking lot, is R. Charles, who motions to me. I put on my emergency flashers and pull over to the curb.

"I just want you to know the last thing I want to do on a Saturday is come to work and cover a police story," he says, oblivious to the backhanded insult. "The Blumberg thing wasn't my idea, okay? Cornelius Lawrence was originally supposed to sub for you, but Merriwether called me after Blumberg got shot."

"Hey, it's cool. I know you weren't trying to stab me in the back."

R. Charles reaches through the open passenger window and shakes my hand. In the five years I've been working at the *Herald*, this is the longest exchange we've ever had.

When I reach Roland Park, I can barely drive down Blumberg's street. About three hundred people are milling about, most of them looking lost, helpless and angry. It didn't take long for word to get out that one of Baltimore's most revered figures has been senselessly slain.

Detective Philip Gardner is about to pull off just as I get to Blumberg's house. I slowly veer in front of his unmarked car, prompting him to stare at me belligerently until he realizes who I am.

Police technicians are taking pictures of a gray Volvo station wagon in the driveway from every conceivable angle. Two television reporters are doing stand-up reports in front of the house.

"Outta my way, Darryl. Gotta run down to headquarters," Gardner says gruffly.

"I have to talk to you right now," I reply, hopping out of my car. "It's about Blumberg—I may have something that can help."

"Yeah? What's that?"

I yank open the door to Gardner's police car and plop onto the passenger seat, sitting on an empty fast-food wrapper. The ashtray is full of cigarette butts, including two with plum lipstick stains.

"I left a message for you at work yesterday that somebody was making threats on Blumberg. Did you get my message?"

Gardner snaps open his little notepad. "No. I wasn't at work yesterday and I was supposed to be off today, too. But I got called in." He gestures at the bedlam surrounding us. "Who made the threats?"

"I don't know. The calls have been anonymous."

"How long has this been going on, Darryl?"

"The last couple of days." My eyes inadvertently shift to the floor.

"You must get crank calls all the time, huh?"

I could kiss Gardner for that, instead of chastising me or playing the blame game.

"You got that right," I say, shooting him a grateful look. "I thought this might be just another one, but obviously I was wrong."

"You wouldn't believe the number of homicide threats we receive each week. And how many of them can we act on? Not one, unless the President's name comes up. When was the last Blumberg call?"

"About fifteen minutes ago." I ask Gardner what he can tell me on the record, and he zips through a dry recitation of what little he knows.

"Anything you can tell me off the record?"

"Just that if I don't have a suspect in the next fifteen minutes, I'll probably be at the *Herald* tomorrow filling out applications." He laughs. Grace under pressure. One of the things I like about Gardner.

I interview a few of Blumberg's neighbors and some well-known Jewish community leaders present, then head back downtown.

When I reenter the newsroom, everyone looks up as I stride in. Like when the conductor strolls before his orchestra, baton at the ready. Time to make some 1A music. But first I ask an editorial assistant to go to the library and fetch the clip file on Blumberg, then bring it to my desk.

"What did you find out in Roland Park?" It's Merriwether, who's looking antsy and apprehensive. He may work in a pressure-packed profession, but he has never handled pressure terribly well.

"They don't really know much at this point. No potential suspects or motive, although they did find a nine-millimeter shell casing in his car."

"We already knew that," Merriwether says distantly, his mind whirling. "Okay, here's the deal. Irving Beatty is going to write a retrospective on Blumberg that recaps his life and times. Instead of folding the Jewish angle into your story, Jim Smilow is going to write a sidebar covering that.

"You're going to concern yourself with what happened today. I want to know if he ever feuded with a neighbor, if there were ever death threats and why his security detail wasn't on duty. To the extent you can, given our time constraints, find out if there may be a disgruntled ex-employee fired from one of Blumberg's businesses.

"Reactions from the mayor, from charities funded by The Blumberg Foundation and from politicians he funded need to be in your story. Our statehouse reporter in Annapolis is sending you some stuff and I'll have another reporter feed you man-on-the-street quotes."

I scribble all this down in my notepad, struggling to keep up.

"We on the same page?" he asks.

"You're aware that we knew of a death threat on Blumberg yesterday, right?"

Merriwether slowly brings his hand to his mouth, terror-stricken. "What are you talking about?"

"I told Barbara Rubenstein about it yesterday. Plus, the person called again today."

Merriwether literally runs to Rubenstein's desk as I follow.

"Barbara," he says in a voice high-pitched with fear, "did Darryl tell you yesterday that a caller warned Blumberg might be killed?"

Incredibly, she denies I told her.

"Remember you said you were busy and that you would call me back?" I ask incredulously.

"I said that, but you *definitely* didn't say anything about a Blumberg shooting, Darryl!" Rubenstein says loudly, hands on hips.

"I've heard enough," Merriwether shouts. "Let's deal with the task at hand."

Anger and adrenaline are at play as I set out to write something 230,000 people will eagerly review when they get their newspapers tomorrow. Time never fails to fly on deadline. After three hours that seem like fifteen minutes, I've produced a story with comprehensive reporting and good writing.

After two quick reads for typos and inaccuracies, I make a copy of the story for safekeeping, then send the original to Merriwether. Regardless of what he says, I know I've smacked the ball out of the park.

"How's that piece coming along, young man?" It's Watkins. The telephone-pole stogie has been reduced to a mere nub he nibbles at contentedly.

"I just sent it over to Merriwether," I reply innocently. "He says he wants to edit it personally."

"Good, good. I think I'll sit in on that, because Shel was a very good friend. Did you ever have the pleasure of meeting him?"

"No, I can't say that I did, but he appeared to have done a lot of good things."

"Indeed he did." Watkins's face takes on a dreamy cast. "He did a lot of good for Baltimore. I can't believe he's gone."

I glance up at Watkins, who's lost in his thoughts. A tear forms in the corner of his left eye and he quickly turns away and coughs. Reaching into one of my desk drawers, I pull out a tissue and discreetly hand it to Watkins, who blows his nose. The effect is that of a foghorn going off in my right ear.

"Mr. Watkins, I think you'll find that my story gives Blumberg a proper send-off," I say quietly.

Watkins casually tosses the tissue into the wastebasket beside my desk and lightly rubs his hands. "I have no doubt of that, Darryl," he says, moving off toward my nemesis's desk.

Hah! Sic 'em, Watkins. Go get 'em, boy!

Watkins pulls up a chair beside Merriwether's desk and the two of them spend about half an hour editing my story. Every now and then Watkins's stubby fingers will point at the computer screen and I'll see Merriwether's type something.

I use the time to call police and fire departments in the Baltimore area to make sure nothing else is going on. Blumberg may be dead, but life goes on. Once it's clear the city's quiet, I call my apartment to see what Yolanda and Jamal have been up to. I've been feeling a little uneasy about them being in my place.

At least Yolanda has enough sense not to answer my phone. The answering machine picks up on the fourth ring.

"Hey, it's Darryl," I say in a booming voice. "Go ahead and pick up the phone."

"Hello." It feels strange to call my apartment and have a female answer.

"Just got a little break here, so I figured I'd see what you guys are up to." I hope that doesn't sound accusatorial.

"Not much. I went to the bank this morning to get you some money." A nervous little laugh. "I'll have a surprise for you when you get here."

That catches me totally off guard. "Really! What kind of surprise?"

"It wouldn't be a surprise if I told, now would it?" Yolanda giggles.

I'm not sure which is more startling, the fact that she's gone out of her way to do something just for me, or hearing her giggle.

"Fair enough. I should be home around nine or so."

"We'll be here when you come home."

"Bye."

"That was a first-rate piece of writing, Darryl. We barely had to change a comma."

I look up to find Watkins and Merriwether standing by my desk.

"Thank you, Mr. Watkins."

"That was a nice job, very nice job," Merriwether chimes in with a sick-looking grin. Insincere, two-faced invertebrate.

"There are a couple of things we'd like you to slip into the story, though," Watkins says, frowning slightly.

"Fire away."

"It would be a good idea to call some prominent area businessmen and find out if most of them have security people. And it would be nice to know if Shel's murder will impact the way these businessmen conduct themselves. Can you think of anything else, Tom?"

"No, not at all. I think your suggestions put the icing on the cake."

My personal credo is to never get too high or too low based on what happens at work. Because it's dangerous for any black man in America to let a white-dominated company unduly affect his sense of happiness or self-worth.

Despite that, I'm floating as I place telephone calls to several high-profile Baltimore businesspeople. It's always a good feeling to be recognized for doing quality work.

The early edition of the Sunday paper is out by five-thirty. WELL-KNOWN PHILANTHROPIST SLAIN is the banner headline across the front page. The story occupies the front page's two right-hand columns and the byline reads: By Darryl L. Billups.

I sit and admire the paper for several minutes, then run around the newsroom looking for additional copies to take home. Heading back to my desk, I read my story as though I'm John Q. Citizen who's just bought the paper. The litmus test is: What would I want to know about the shooting and about Blumberg that's not in the paper?

After a quick read, I'm curious if Blumberg and his wife were having marital difficulties, or if Blumberg may have had a mistress. If those are the only holes I can manage to come up with, that's not bad.

Weekend editor Daniel Chapin gives me the all-clear at 9 P.M. As I walk out of the newsroom I catch Merriwether scrunched down in his chair, staring balefully as I go by.

Fine. I didn't come here to be his bosom buddy anyway. All I want is for him to respect me as a journalist. Besides, Merriwether can't spoil my mood tonight. 'Cause I'm Da Man.

Plus, I have a strong hunch—no, that's too weak—I *know* that I won't be around this place too much longer. *The New York Times* or *The Washington Post,* maybe, but not here. I've still got a lot of growing and learning to do in my profession and I'm not sure if the *Herald* is capable of teaching me much more.

In the meantime, I'm on Page One with the Sunday paper's biggest story. During the drive home, I feel like sticking my head out the window and shouting that bit of information to everyone I encounter.

Wonder what Yolanda's surprise could be?

Walking up the stairs to my apartment door, it dawns on me that something's out of the ordinary. Digging in my pockets for my key, sniffing the air like a bloodhound, I figure it out. The odor of food cooking is on the second-floor landing, and it's coming from under my door.

When the door swings open, I can't believe my eyes. Or nose or ears.

A Will Downing CD plays softly on a boom box Yolanda retrieved from her apartment this morning. And the succulent smell of meat and bread envelope me, just wash over me and do wonderful things to my nostrils.

Smiling shyly and looking like he just joined the Fruit of Islam, Jamal sits at the dinner table wearing a dark blue suit, a white shirt and a blue bow tie. There are three place settings at the table, with glasses containing red wine at two of them. Freshly cut red and white carnations provide a decorative touch in the middle of the table.

But Yolanda is the real visual centerpiece. Wearing a tan, one-piece cotton dress that clings to every curve and hollow of her lithe body, she has on eyeliner and red lipstick instead of her trademark gold. The cold waves in her reddish-brown hair seem just-pressed, and her black-and-bronze earrings swing gracefully.

Yolanda looks like a goddess from the pages of *Essence.* How do you cook and look that beautiful?

My mouth flies open as I stand outside the door, trying to adjust to the exotic stimuli bombarding my senses. I want to stroll in all nonchalant, like I encounter this sort of thing every day, but can't pull it off.

Extending her arm, Yolanda hands me a white business envelope that appears to be stuffed with money. At least it feels like dollars bills are inside. That's my best guess, not being used to receiving envelopes filled with cash.

She takes care of business first. I like that.

"I hope you don't mind that I cooked dinner for you,"

Yolanda says anxiously, biting her lower lip. "But I figured it was the least I could do after all you've done for Jamal and me."

I slowly walk through the front door of my apartment. At least I thought it was mine, but I'm not so sure now. It dawns on me that I've never seen Yolanda or Jamal wearing decent clothes before tonight.

Coming home to this in my bachelor pad is oddly pleasant and uncomfortable at the same time. I'm used to having my space, to enjoying my privacy once I get home. A lot of times I don't even bother to answer the phone.

On the other hand, being greeted by the aroma of a home-cooked meal is hardly a bad state of affairs. And seeing Yolanda looking like this is . . . Lawd, have mercy! Help me, Jesus.

Yolanda is eyeing me strangely, probably because I have yet to comment one way or the other.

"This is, uh, different. It's definitely a surprise. Thanks for cooking dinner." I lift the envelope and hold it against the ceiling light. "What's this?"

"That's a little something to cover Jamal and me for our two weeks. We pay our way." She's starting to look more relaxed, now that it appears her experiment is going over well and she's gotten money into my hands.

Ripping open the envelope, I see an army of twenty-dollar bills. Eighteen of them, to be exact.

"Hey, you really don't—"

"It's not a problem," Yolanda interrupts. "Jamal and me, we appreciate what you're doing, but we don't want no charity." A bemused grin creases her face. "Are you going to come in or what?"

True enough, I'm only six inches inside the door and haven't closed it yet.

Blue flames flare under three pots on my stove as I drop eight copies of the Sunday paper onto the floor with a thud. Jamal nearly jumps out of his skin, scurries down from the table and grabs his mama's leg. Yolanda caresses his head lovingly and pats him twice on the back.

"Why do you have so many copies of the paper?"

I pick up one and proudly point to the banner headline and my byline.

"You wrote this?" Incredulity, as though I can't be telling the truth.

"Just finished it a few hours ago."

Admiration and awe sweep across her face. "Congratulations."

"Thanks. So what have you concocted in my kitchen?"

"Why don't you go wash your hands, and it will be ready when you come out." A chagrined expression. "It's kind of late in the game, but—are you even hungry?"

I just laugh and walk to the bathroom. Dealing with women has taught me it would be a good idea to eat Yolanda's meal whether I'm famished or not. When I emerge from the bathroom, most of the lights in my apartment have been dimmed, except for a lamp and a light on the stove. Yolanda has made a grilled, sliced roast sirloin of beef in peppercorn mustard and red onion marmalade, along with cabbage and string beans. The smell alone is out of this world.

Having expected meat loaf or something along those lines, I stare at her in astonishment.

"Bet you didn't think a ghetto girl knew how to make stuff like that, huh?" she says, laughing heartily. Very perceptive of her. I start to protest weakly, but she cuts me off. "Let's eat."

Girlfriend has also made rolls from scratch, which she pulls out of the oven, dumps into a small wicker basket and covers with a cloth napkin.

I'm all set to tear into dinner, but Yolanda very methodically adjusts everyone's silverware, makes sure Jamal's bib is on just so, then insists that I bless our meal. I'm tempted to say, "Good bread, good meat, good Lord, let's eat," but I don't think that would go over.

As I suspected, girlfriend can burn! I gorge on sirloin of beef until I nearly bust a gut, and put a hurtin' on the home-made rolls. The wine ain't bad either—three glasses have

given me a very nice glow and made me horny as hell.
Yolanda appears to be pretty relaxed herself after two glasses.

Over the span of about an hour we have progressed beyond
tentative, feel-each-other-out chitchat to an honest discussion
of our dreams, fears and secrets.

Like a lot of people—black and white—I sometimes fall
into a trap of assessing a brother's or sister's intelligence
based on speech. I figured Yolanda, with her infinitive-
splitting self, didn't have it going on in the brainpower department. How wrong I was.

She's got a quick mind, a warped, twisted sense of
humor—like me—and enviable reserves of common sense.
And I like the way she cuts to the heart of an issue quickly
and makes snap, no-holds-barred assessments. And she's a
fox, too! Puuhhhleeze!

I can't believe some of the things I'm telling her, or that
she's telling me. Like my ambition to run a newspaper and
have a wife and three kids someday. I nearly tell her about
the wet dream in the hospital before getting my tongue in
check at the last second. No more wine for me!

She tells me that life is passing her by, that she would
have made a pretty good journalist had things fallen into
place the way she'd hoped and planned. And that the last
two years of living with Boone have been an absolute hell,
but she endured them because of Jamal. And that Boone was
a selfish, unimaginative lover in bed.

It's all starting to click. Dinner, lights down low, Will
Downing on the box, wine, frank talk about knocking boots.
Is she trying to seduce me? Or is that a typically male way
of thinking—reducing everything to sexual terms? That old
saying about men being on a lifelong quest to reenter the
womb is basically true.

Maybe this is all simply a kind gesture. Whatever, I'm
going to remain a gentleman. I will ignore the fat nipples
poking through Yolanda's dress, will act like I don't even
see them.

When the three of us finish eating, Yolanda clears the table and brings out a luscious-looking lemon meringue pie sitting on a plate.

I laugh. "Oh, come on. Don't tell me you make perfect lemon meringue, too!"

She feigns being offended. "And why couldn't I—is that such a stretch?"

"After tonight's dinner and our conversation, I see that nothing is a stretch where you're concerned." I hadn't meant to say that. But judging from Yolanda's reaction, it was the perfect thing to say.

She casts her eyes downward and looks slightly ill at ease. "Thanks a lot, Darryl. It really means a lot to hear you say that, because the last couple of days haven't exactly been great for my self-esteem," she says in a near whisper.

"Hey, I'm not just throwing you a line," I tell her. "That's the truth."

What I'm really thinking is how I'd love to lick those white flecks of meringue off her top lip. Then I'd lock Jamal in my bedroom and drive his mom wild with pleasure until the sun comes up. I stare into her enchanting eyes just a little too long, and a little too longingly, then stand and rub my stomach.

"Yolanda, this was the best surprise I've had since I've been in this apartment. Thank you very much."

Rising also, she comes toward me and plants an innocent peck on my cheek. Jamal springs up instantly and wraps his arms protectively around his mother's left thigh.

"Look, I, uh, know you didn't have to do none of this. You took a real chance on us and I can't tell you how much we appreciate it."

Yolanda lifts Jamal and gives him a giant bear hug. He smiles contentedly. Where's *my* bear hug?

"Hey, you cooked all this great food, so I'll go ahead and wash the dishes."

"No way. I told you this was my treat."

Know any men who argue with women over doing the dishes? Me either.

There's a different vibe in the air with Yolanda and Jamal

here. One that brings out a calmer side of me. However, the vibe may be long gone after a week or so of this. Hell, it might depart as soon as this red wine wears off. But for the time being, it makes me feel serene and centered. And I must reluctantly admit that I like it.

As was the case in the hospital, I have a climactic fantasy about Yolanda after I go to bed. Only this time I'm very much awake and responsible for bringing things to a boil.

I wonder if she's having a similar experience out there on the couch?

SIXTEEN

Mark Dillard had gotten to be quite popular with granite-faced police detectives unable to find a parking spot anywhere else in Baltimore except in front of his house.

They glared at him like he'd plopped from a pooper-scooper. Their eyes warned they'd make Rodney King's beating look like a harmless fraternity hazing.

Two days after Sherman Brown's disappearance, a cadre of muscular officers toting assault rifles and wearing bulletproof jackets conducted a midnight search of Dillard's home. Swinging him around like a sack of potatoes, they flung Dillard into a police van and drove him to headquarters.

He was accused of driving a van full of stolen dynamite and of taking a shot at U.S. Park Policeman John Burke. Incredibly, a public defender not only got Dillard's charges dismissed, but made it possible for Dillard to leave. The search warrant had been improperly executed! Also, nothing of evidentiary value had been found.

The encounter only strengthened Dillard's resolve. He'd die before anyone took him into custody again.

Correctly guessing that his phones at home and at work had been turned into law enforcement party lines, Dillard had taken to meeting Harry Boyles and Bob Simmes on the fly, usually inside Boyles's van as it trundled along city highways

170

and byways. Dillard called his cohorts from pay phones and never twice from the same one.

With each passing day, Boyles was shedding more of his cautious reserve and becoming more a part of the *brotherhood*. At first he had to be coerced with blunt reminders of his role in Sheldon Blumberg's death. Dillard had bullied Boyles into driving the getaway car out of Sheldon Blumberg's neighborhood. And Boyles had been forced to toss Dillard's nine-millimeter into the lake at Druid Hill Park.

However, a funny thing was happening—as Boyles's complicity grew, so did his enthusiasm. Now it was usually he who initiated the meetings between himself, Dillard and Simmes, whose broken collarbone was still on the mend.

Simmes's quick wit and ready laugh weren't on display as in the past. Dillard hoped the change was just a result of the ex-Marine's aches and pains, because he was their explosives guru and they needed him on top of his game.

Quiet as it was kept, Dillard was having major misgivings about the Blumberg shooting. Not about using a slim jim to break into Blumberg's Volvo, or waiting in the backseat twenty minutes to pump a bullet into the unsuspecting businessman's balding head. Dillard regretted having overlooked the propaganda value of the shooting. He should have called a television station—or at least the *Herald*—to establish a white supremacist, quasi-militia tie to Blumberg's death.

And it was galling to him that when he finally became Baltimore's man of the hour, no one knew. In his heart of hearts he suspected most people dismissed him as a poor-white-trash nobody.

That hadn't stopped him from persuading Simmes and Boyles they needed to plant a pipe bomb at the city sanitation facility Boyles had just transferred from, where that black boy had taken Boyles's promotion. Boyles had agreed to return to his old workplace, place the bomb on one of the garbage trucks and leave before a timer detonated the device. Simmes's task was to assemble the bomb, giving Dillard a chance to gauge his expertise.

The men sincerely believed the world would be a better

place because of their principled lawlessness. They were ushering in a society lacking entitlements, and with an emphasis on personal responsibility and unquestioned Caucasian dominion.

Each man had read and reread *The Turner Diaries*, designating the racist manifesto their unofficial Bible. In fact, they'd briefly discussed the book before meeting one Thursday night at Ruby's, a crowded, dimly lit bar in the Highlandtown section of Baltimore. Not only would the booming country music drown out their conversation, but a detective would stick out like a sore thumb.

Under the table, Simmes gripped a tan athletic bag containing his explosives handiwork.

"What did you bring that for?" Dillard asked brusquely, motioning for a waitress. A thick pall of cigarette smoke nearly obscured a thin, pale girl on the other side of the room wearing a buzz cut. Nodding, she continued taking another table's order.

"Should I have left it in Boyles's van?" Simmes responded with an enigmatic smile. "So the cops could find it and throw all our asses in jail?"

"Guess you got a point there," Dillard shouted over noise. "Got a cigarette, man?"

Simmes grunted softly. Tucked inside the rolled-up left sleeve of his T-shirt, in plain view, was a pack of cigarettes. The thought of giving Dillard a free cigarette actually seemed to pain him. Dillard and Boyles glanced at each other and started laughing so hard, tears rolled down their cheeks. Even Simmes had to chuckle at himself.

The slim waitress made her way toward their table, bobbing and feinting around chairs, tables and drunken patrons as she carried three beer bottles.

Dillard nodded in the direction of Simmes. "You don't guess Jack Benny here used cut-rate gunpowder, do you?" Boyles and Simmes both laughed, surprised by the rare display of levity.

It took only two rounds of beers to finalize the plan for the sanitation department bombing. The pipe bomb was set to go off at eight-thirty the morning of July 2nd, two days after Sheldon Blumberg's slaying. Around 5 A.M., long before most of his former co-workers arrived for work, Boyles was to enter his old place of employment and simply set the device between the cab of one of the garbage trucks and the forty-gallon diesel fuel tank.

Which is precisely what he did. To his relief, he didn't run into anyone who might recognize him. Looking for one of the new garbage trucks the city had purchased only four months ago, Boyles found three sitting side by side near the huge maintenance garage. He picked the middle vehicle, No. 507. Gingerly shoving the athletic bag into a tight space between the right fuel tank and the cab of the truck, where the driver would be less likely to see it, Boyles smiled. That would teach them to take what was his and cause his family to suffer. This time affirmative action had victimized a man who chose to stand up, rather than meekly roll over.

Unbeknownst to Boyles, No. 507 wasn't going to roll through the streets of Baltimore that morning. Instead, it was scheduled for routine maintenance and was slowly driven into the maintenance garage at 8:03.

At 8:29, sanitation department employees working in the maintenance garage were stunned by a thunderous report accompanied by an orange fireball that fanned across the ceiling of the maintenance garage. As panicked workers scattered, grease, oil and aerosol cans ignited, setting seven other trucks parked inside the maintenance garage ablaze.

The old brick-and-wood building was consumed by a stubborn six-alarm blaze that took firefighters four hours to control and sent a spectacular plume of black smoke towering over the East Baltimore skyline. City mechanic Joel Kocinski, who was under truck No. 507 when the bomb went off, was incinerated in the inferno. Kocinski was Harold Boyles's best friend.

At eight-forty, once he was sure the bomb had detonated, Dillard used a pay phone to call a local television station. He was patched through to the producer of the local morning news show. Covering the phone with a handkerchief in an attempt to disguise his voice, Dillard said a local militia group had bombed the sanitation department facility to protest the decline of American values and the rise of affirmative action. Pausing tantalizingly, he added that the group had also been responsible for the death of philanthropist Sheldon Blumberg. Then he hung up, calmly wiped his fingerprints off the phone and drove to work.

Hanging onto a garbage truck tooling through downtown Baltimore, Boyles was grappling with second and third thoughts about what he'd done. And when he saw plumes of black smoke billowing into the sky somewhere in East Baltimore, no one had to tell him what had happened. He knew intuitively it had something to do with the bomb. The bomb *he* had planted.

The longest three hours of his life were spent riding through downtown Baltimore listening to the distant whine of fire sirens and wishing that someone—anyone—would bring news about the conflagration just over the horizon. He felt like running up to passersby, grabbing them by the shoulders and imploring them to disclose what was on fire. Boyles nearly lost his breakfast when the dispatch center called over the radio to say the East Baltimore maintenance facility was burning to the ground.

"Did anybody get hurt?" he asked in a panicky voice. The other members of his truck's crew stared at him. "Hey, I worked there for twelve years. I know all those guys."

"Got me, chief." The driver of Boyle's truck shrugged. "I know some people over there, too."

As they cleared their last street of trash cans filled to the brim with garbage, word came over the radio that one person was missing in the fire.

"Ohhh, Gawd," Boyles moaned, clapping a hand against his forehead. "Who? Who is it?"

When Boyles's truck rolled back to the South Baltimore facility where it was maintained, a large American-made sedan eased in behind it and stopped. Two city homicide detectives hopped out, guns drawn.

"Whichaya guys is Harold Boyles?"

"Me. Why, w-w-what's going on?"

Boyles's other crew members stood around him, watching dumbfounded.

"City Homicide," one of the cops said, flashing a badge. "We want you to come downtown with us to answer some questions."

"About what? About what? I ain't killed nobody. What's going on?"

"We want to ask you about that fire at the East Baltimore sanitation garage today. A guy named Joel Kocinski got killed. Hey!"

Just as one of the detectives reached out to grab Boyles's arm, he crumpled to the ground, his legs splayed awkwardly. He came to in time to hear the *whoop, whoop, whoop* of the city ambulance that took him to Mercy Medical Center, trailed by the two homicide detectives. After a quick checkup, Boyles was taken to police headquarters for a tag-team grilling that arson investigators joined in on.

Initially he could barely hear the questions over the sound of his pathetic, nonstop blubbering. And there was another sound in the interrogation room, that of Joel Kocinski's voice asking over and over: "How could you do that, Harry? I'm your son's godfather!"

Boyles's trash hauler's union arranged to have one of the city's top criminal defense attorneys come to police headquarters and represent Boyles. Sometime around 1 A.M., after Boyles had steadfastly denied any involvement in the bombing and refused to give up Dillard or Simmes, Boyles's attorney angrily shouted it was time to fish or cut bait. Boyles was reluctantly allowed to go free.

Predictably, Baltimore's news media went into an orgasmic feeding frenzy when the existence of an anonymous call linking the garage bombing to a militia movement was disclosed. Making the story even juicier was a link to the still-unsolved slaying of civic pillar Sheldon Blumberg.

A bedraggled and inconsolable Boyles had been home an hour when his wife heard a *pop!* from the area of their upstairs bathroom. Kneeling in front of the commode, Boyles had begged God for forgiveness, then shot himself once in the chest with a rickety .22-caliber revolver.

In the *Herald*'s newsroom that morning, Tom Merriwether was overheard joking that Boyles could at least have killed himself in time to make the paper's final edition.

SEVENTEEN

THE PIERCING SHRIEKS OF AN ENRAGED NINE-MONTH-OLD JOLTED Cornelius Lawrence from a deep and satisfying sleep.

He rolled over groggily and opened one eye in the general direction of his digital alarm. An angry red 5:32 glared back through the darkness. It appeared he was going to be cruelly deprived of nearly an hour of precious shut-eye. There was no way Stephanie couldn't hear their daughter's rambunctious wailing.

Turning toward his better half, Cornelius could barely discern her motionless outline. He could see where this was going—a conspiracy to dupe the only male in the household. Exhaling through his teeth, he swung his feet over the side of the bed and ran his feet along the carpet until they bumped into his slippers.

"Stef!"

Getting no response, Cornelius stood erect slowly, making his right knee pop.

Women.

Although it was dark, he was able to navigate by memory past the sharp and unforgiving edge of the wooden end table and through the frame of the bedroom door. He turned left and trudged down the hallway, veering slightly to the right, where he knew a booby trap of stacked newspapers would be waiting.

He passed the bathroom and groped for the doorknob of the second door on the right. It opened with a creak. Cornelius slid his hand along the wall and felt for the light switch. He clicked it on, revealing a pair of squinting black eyes that bored directly into his from behind the bars of an oak crib.

Angelique's nappy brown hair was matted with sweat, and twin rivers of tears glistened on her fat, mahogany cheeks. Cornelius's irritation and his heart melted in the same instant.

"What's wrong, Pooky?"

The baby stopped in mid-scream as soon as she heard her father's reassuring voice. Maybe it was Cornelius's imagination, but he thought he saw a fleeting look of indignation, as though her servant hadn't hustled quickly enough to suit the queen.

The transgression forgiven, Angelique stood up in the crib, chubby outstretched arms issuing an unspoken demand to be picked up.

"What's wrong with Dadum's Pookums?" Cornelius cooed. He brushed his forehead against a mobile of brightly colored spheres and blocks suspended over his daughter's crib as he lifted his baby up. "Come on, Pookums."

Because Angelique had been sleeping through the night for at least a month and a half, Cornelius guessed a full diaper or a nightmare was behind this outburst. Instead of courageously thrusting his hand into Angelique's disposable diaper, as he'd seen Stef do, he tugged at the waistband and peeked inside. It looked dry. Bad dream.

He held his daughter tight and she responded by wrapping her wee arms around his neck and wearily resting her head on his shoulder.

This is what it's all about, Cornelius thought. He always felt totally at peace when in the company of his beautiful women. He was tempted to stand there and hold his daughter until she went to sleep, even if it meant getting to the *Baltimore Herald* late. He'd waited until age thirty-two to start a family and fully intended to drink in every second of being a father.

Cornelius enjoyed being a reporter at the *Herald,* the only work he'd ever done since graduating from college ten years ago. But now that Angelique was on the scene, he viewed work differently. He still put in long hours perfecting his craft; it was just that perfection was no longer an end in itself. The goal now was to get promoted to assistant city editor. That would bring an increase in pay, making it easier for him to take care of his growing financial responsibilities.

It seemed simple enough to him. Why couldn't Stephanie see things that way?

In the six years they had been married, she'd always allowed him to ply his trade as he saw fit. To compensate for his absences, she had poured more time and effort into her public relations job with the mayor's office. However, now she was adamant about doing a nine-to-five, and was beginning to insist that Cornelius do the same. Which annoyed him, because she knew perfectly well that newspaper journalism wasn't a nine-to-five job.

Last night, when he'd gotten home at nine-thirty after covering an auto workers strike, she'd heatedly accused him of putting his job over his family. When he sarcastically remarked that the auto workers had been damn inconsiderate to announce their strike at five o'clock, she'd dissolved into tears and stormed into their bedroom.

His response was to stay up until midnight, reading news magazines and drinking rum and Coke, something he rarely did.

"Doesn't seem terribly logical, does it, Pooky," Cornelius whispered to his daughter, who didn't react. The calming presence of Daddy had already ushered in the sandman. Cornelius gently pried her fingers from around his neck and held his baby in front of him.

If God had ever created anything more beautiful than Angelique, Cornelius would love to see what it was.

She wore a little white nightgown decorated with pink clowns and bunny rabbits. Her stubby toes peeked out from the bottom of the gown. Beautiful little brown angel.

Cornelius held her in front of him for several seconds,

committing her face and body to memory, before gently laying her back in the crib.

Tiptoeing to the door, he turned out the light. There was a brief stirring in the crib. Rather than try to close the creaky door, he left it open and tiptoed back to his bedroom, skillfully sidestepping the stack of newspapers in the hallway again. Once in his bedroom, Cornelius slowly closed the door behind him, then purposely plopped hard into bed.

"Is the baby okay?"

Her voice didn't sound sleepy at all, like she'd been awake all along.

"Yep. She's fine," Cornelius answered irritatedly. "You didn't hear her crying?"

There was a pause as he lay on his back, staring at the blackness.

"C, I'm sorry about last night." Stephanie had always preferred calling her husband "C"—even back in their dating days—rather than Cornelius.

"Forget it, Stef," he replied meanly.

There was another brief silence before she crept over to his side of the bed and started nuzzling his ear. She had taken off her pajamas—he felt her soft skin against his.

If he lived to be one hundred, he would never understand women.

"There's about to be a rape in here," she growled in his ear. "How much you want to bet it doesn't appear in the *Herald?*"

"Come on, Stef, stop," Cornelius protested weakly. He knew that rebuffing his wife in order to make it to the *Herald* by 8:30 A.M. would be suicidal. Plus, their sex life had fallen off since Angelique's birth, so he wasn't about to throw water on the flickering flames.

Moving with the swiftness of a tigress, Stephanie was on top of Cornelius and attacking him with a ferocity that caught him by surprise.

He must have dozed off afterward, because the next time he looked at the clock, it said 7:51.

Damn.

Alone on the bed, dressed in his birthday suit and surrounded by tussled sheets, Cornelius felt lethargic and satisfied.

The door to the bathroom was closed, muffling the sound of water running.

"Stef!"

The bathroom door suddenly jerked open, but no one was there. Stephanie slowly stuck her head, which was wrapped in a peach-colored towel, around the corner. White foam flowed from her mouth, which was closed around a green toothbrush. She shot Cornelius a comical look.

Except he was in no mood for levity.

"See what time it is?" he asked, gesturing angrily toward the clock. "You know I try to get to work at eight-thirty, so why didn't you wake me up?"

Her expression darkened instantly and she ducked back around the corner. When Stephanie reappeared, the toothbrush was gone. She stood framed in the doorway, buck naked and frowning. Dark-skinned, with high cheekbones and luscious lips that were beautiful with or without lipstick, Stephanie was about ten pounds heavier than her pre-baby weight, but still shapely.

Hands placed firmly on her hourglass hips, she was ready to do battle.

"You've been killing yourself for those people ever since I've known you," she said in a clipped voice. "What has it gotten you, C? What? An extra twenty dollars a week every year? Why on earth do you kill yourself to get there every morning at eight-thirty when everyone else drifts in after nine? Who's even there to notice, C? Who?"

"But you know—" Cornelius tried to interject. However, his wife was on a roll. They seldom argued and were so openly affectionate that their friends had dubbed them The Love Connection. But experience had taught Cornelius that when his wife was in this mode, meaningful discourse was impossible.

"Don't interrupt me, C," she said, voice rising as she waggled her right index finger. "I am sick of waking up in an empty bed, do you hear me? Sick. I'm tired of killing myself in the mornings to get Angelique to day care, then dragging myself to work while you sit at the *Herald* and have a leisurely cup of coffee. C, I have needs, too.''

By now Stephanie's eyes were brimming with tears, and she wore an anguished expression as though she had gone too far in confronting her husband.

Cornelius, who was sitting up in bed, silently counted to ten before articulating his thoughts. ''Stef, I don't need this,'' he said, straining to modulate his voice and not yell. ''You know the extra things I do at work are so you and Angelique will be able to live comfortably.''

''Do you really do those things for us, C?'' Stephanie asked, crying quietly. ''Do you really? Or are they really for Cornelius Lawrence?'' With that, she disappeared around the doorframe, leaving the door open.

The sound of running water filled the bedroom.

Cornelius's brain was a jumble of potential responses, most of them devastatingly witty and sarcastic and hurtful. He wisely opted to say nothing. In all honesty, he wasn't one hundred percent sure his boundless ambition at the *Herald* was just for the welfare of his family.

He hated it when his wife got the last word, especially when she was right.

At least Angelique would still love him.

Cornelius stood up, walked over to the closet and snatched his blue terry-cloth robe off a hanger. He marched into his baby's room and stood by her crib for a moment, watching her sleep. Instead of the saintly expression she usually wore, the baby was frowning, wordlessly casting a vote with her mother.

''So you think Daddy is out for number one, too?'' Cornelius whispered, bending over to kiss his daughter. No sooner had his lips brushed her face than Angelique smiled, laughed and turned over.

''Thank you, Pooky.''

Cornelius turned to see his wife standing in the doorway, wearing panties and a bra.

"Honey, can we talk for a moment?" she said in a quiet, almost timid voice.

"When I tried to say something, you cut me off," Cornelius answered brusquely. "Plus, I would think that you got everything you needed to say out of your system, wouldn't you?"

"C, please!"

Cornelius walked toward the door to leave his daughter's bedroom. "Excuse me," he said roughly to his wife, who quickly stepped aside to let him pass.

He went back to their bedroom and got a clean towel out of the closet. Then he went into the bathroom and slammed the door behind him, immediately feeling childish. Cornelius adjusted the shower so that it was hot and streaming out with such velocity that it pricked his skin.

He was feeling contrite. And exasperated. And more than a little selfish. It was true that he hadn't made a single attempt to help transport Angelique to or from day care since Stephanie had returned to work five months ago. He would make an effort to help out.

Once he'd made that mental concession, righteous indignation began to reassert itself. So what if his push to get promoted at the *Herald* benefited him? It would be a plus for his family, too. He'd invested too much of his sweat and tears to turn back now.

After Stephanie's hormones stop raging, she'll come to understand that, Cornelius told himself as he turned off the shower and began toweling himself dry. Wrapping his towel around his waist, Cornelius stepped from the bathroom. The air in the bedroom gripped him in a wonderfully cool embrace after the saunalike bathroom.

His wife had left the closet door open, revealing her clothes neatly hung on the left side of the narrow closet, Cornelius's on the right.

A weight gain over the past two years made Cornelius's suits appear too small. As a result, his arms and legs looked like swollen pieces of bratwurst sprouting from his pudgy body, Darryl Billups had observed.

Never have liked Darryl, Cornelius mused as he rummaged through his suit collection, picking a soulless gray number that would have done his accountant proud.

Darryl had called Cornelius "a denatured Negro" because Cornelius preferred listening to soothing string concertos, rather than the head-blasting racket of some sociopathic rapper. And because he subscribed to *Golf Digest* to keep tabs on a sport his uncle had taught him to love at the age of ten.

Cornelius wasn't oblivious to *Herald* murmurings—mainly out of Darryl's ignorant mouth—that he was an Uncle Tom. Being shunned and ridiculed by his own cut to the core. But his goal was to eventually run the *Herald*, not make black friends at work. So the slights and cracks only served to make him more determined. If anyone didn't like it, tough shit.

To advance in a white organization, Cornelius knew whites had to feel comfortable around him. On those days when work was over and he hung out with metro editor Tom Merriwether at a nearby watering hole, it wasn't because he adored Merriwether. Or the fair-haired white boys who glided in Merriwether's orbit.

That after-hours schmoozing was all about raising comfort levels. Period.

He wasn't ashamed of his African-American heritage. But ultimately, his sensibilities were shaped and molded by America more so than by Africa. And the dominant group in America happened to be white, so he planned to study them till he knew them like the back of his hand.

He would display a commitment to excellence that Ray Charles could see.

He would continue to socialize with white editors and reporters. And when all the black reporters congregated at the same lunch table in the *Herald* cafeteria, he would continue to avoid it like the plague. To voluntarily segregate himself and clannishly stick with blacks would deprive him of experiences and contacts that might prove valuable to his career progression.

Still, the ostracism he encountered from other black *Herald* journalists stung on several levels. First, no one ever invited him to sit down and share his point of view. Second, it seemed that the so-called brothers and sisters harbored more stereotypes about how a *real* black man should talk, walk and act than whites.

I'll show all the doubters and second-guessers, Cornelius told himself as he put on a white Oxford shirt, then picked a blue-and-red paisley tie to go with it.

That goes for Stef, too. And especially you, Darryl, you hypocritical, self-righteous jackass.

I'll show all of you, because there's no stopping a capable man with a plan.

Cornelius couldn't wait to enter the *Herald* so he could put the final touches on his.

EIGHTEEN

THE YEARS OF BOOTLICKING AND OBSEQUIOUS BEHAVIOR HAVE finally yielded pay dirt: Cornelius Lawrence is getting promoted to assistant metro editor.

The announcement hasn't even been posted on the bulletin board yet, but I can tell from the smug, shit-eating look on Cornelius's face that it's true. He's on the phone right now, excitedly jabbering away to someone.

"Maybe it's not all bad," Mad Dawg Murdoch says hopefully as he stands over my desk. "Maybe he was doing the Uncle Tom thing just to get the job, and once he's in there he'll be down for the cause."

I roll my eyes evilly. "That's the same thing a lot of people hoped about Clarence Thomas. Seen any change in his behavior?"

"Hey, brother, I'm just trying to find a silver lining here. It can't be all bad."

"Dawg, I guess it ain't bad for you," I answer with a sigh. "You work in sports."

"Sho' you right," Dawg says, chuckling with malicious glee. "And I'm glad, too, 'cause I'd have to smack that imitation white boy upside his handkerchief-wearing head. But you da man. If anybody can turn homeboy around and make him see the error of his apologist, gray-boy-appeasing ways, it's you. I have faith in you, my brother," Dawg says, thumping his chest.

I laugh. "Get the fuck outta here, okay? Go back to the sports plantation, where never is heard a discouraging word."

"Yassuh, boss," Dawg says. "But you jess wait till da oberseer git his hands on you. Oooooweeee."

Da oberseer indeed. I know one of the first things Cornelius is going to do is come down hard on a brother or sister to prove his impartiality. And given the boundless respect and admiration Cornelius and I share, dare I wonder who his first victim might be?

Watching Cornelius, a part of me acknowledges a little jealousy, too. Because if I'm ever going to realize my dream of running a paper, I'll need to make that first step into management like Cornelius just has.

The white smoke officially wafts out of the chimney when Merriwether tacks a memo on the newsroom bulletin board. Cornelius is filling a slot vacated by Barbara Rubenstein, who's riding her daddy's coattails to *The New York Times*. Within minutes I receive five e-mail messages from black reporters nervous about Cornelius's potential negative impact on their careers.

A steady stream of well-wishers, all white, march over to Cornelius's desk to offer congratulations. If I were a bigger person I would go over and offer my hand, too. But—God forgive me—one of my faults is that I can nurture the hell out of a grudge. And when you've made it abundantly clear that you ain't in my corner, I don't have much use for you.

Besides, best wishes coming from another black journalist would mean nothing to someone like Cornelius. So I just sit at my desk and make believe I can't see or hear anything taking place three desks away.

Ch, ch, ch, chaaaang! Ch, ch, ch, chaaang! I snag the receiver of my desk phone after the second annoying ring.

"Hello, Darryl." The Androgynous One, sounding unusually cool and dispassionate today. I involuntarily suck in a lungful of air. Nothing good ever follows these calls, only death and misfortune.

"So we meet again. What glad tidings do you bring?"

Fumbling quietly, I hook my microcassette recorder to the phone line so I can tape the rest of the conversation.

"So where are you now?" I ask.

"Oh, Darryl!" A light laugh tinkles out. "You never give up, do you? I'm at a pay phone."

"I don't mean to insult you, but are you a man or a woman?"

"What do you think?"

"You don't get it, do you? This isn't some silly-ass game. Real people are dying while you twiddle your goddamn thumbs. If you just want to play stupid little games and won't help me catch these bastards, stop calling me, goddammit. Got that?"

My reply is met with silence interspersed with faint pops of static.

"Because as far as I'm concerned, you're no different from those dirtbags," I shout. "You might as well have pulled the trigger yourself, for all the blood that's on your hands. Did you ever stop and think about that?"

"I'm a woman."

"Glad to hear that, lady. Do you want to keep more innocent people from getting killed, or do you want to keep playing out this Agatha Christie shit?"

"It's hard to talk to you when you're like this."

"Let's stop talking, then. Let's *do* something and bring this thing to a close. Who killed Sheldon Blumberg and Joel Kocinski?"

Click!

Sensing someone, I turn around and look directly into Cornelius Lawrence's face. His brow is a mass of horizontal lines.

"Who was *that?*"

"First of all, why are you eavesdropping? You have no right to do that. Did someone tell you that your promotion gives you the right to invade people's privacy?" My voice has risen an octave from when I was speaking to the Androgynous One.

"Let's go into Merriwether's office, Darryl. I need to talk to you," Cornelius says in a cajoling, conspiratorial voice. As if we're bosom buddies now, after years of antagonism.

I start to tell him where to go, but remember he's now my superior, at least as far as titles are concerned. "I need to make some calls to do a follow-up on the sanitation bombing. What do you want to talk about?"

"We shouldn't discuss it out here," Cornelius says easily, smiling. "That's why I suggested we go where we can have some privacy."

Wondering what he has up his sleeve, I reluctantly rise from my chair and follow him to Merriwether's office. Cornelius closes the door behind us and motions for me to sit down. Incredibly, he pulls Merriwether's chair out from under the desk and grandly plops his pudgy ass in it.

"Can I get you something to drink, a soda or something?" Cornelius asks unctuously. This Negro hasn't officially been promoted an hour yet, and already he's buggin'.

"Come on, man, let's cut to the chase," I say, my voice now low and gravelly. "If you're looking for me to congratulate you on your promotion, that ain't gonna happen. What exactly do you want? Because I've got to knock that story out."

"Okay, okay, fair enough." Acres of white teeth. "Wait here a sec. I'll be right back." Striding quickly across the office, Cornelius gently closes the door behind him and breaks into a gallop the minute his feet hit the newsroom floor.

The framed picture of Ronald Reagan is staring reproachfully when Cornelius returns about five minutes later with Merriwether in tow. Oh! So that's where he's going with this. Straight to massuh. Should have known.

Watching the hyena and the vulture approach, I feel the muscles in my midsection tense.

"Darryl," Merriwether says in a neutral tone, "I've just received a most disturbing bit of information." He pauses and gazes at me benignly. I guess this is where I'm supposed to break down and confess my sins, like on *Perry Mason*.

Instead, I just stare at Merriwether blankly. Out of the corner of my eye I notice Cornelius has taken on some of his mentor's mannerisms, like the dainty way Merriwether crosses his legs.

"Corny thought he overheard you talking to someone who might be connected with the Blumberg shooting and the sanitation bombing. Is that correct, Darryl?"

"I don't understand what this is all about, Tom. Cornelius was eavesdropping on a conversation of mine, which he has no business doing—"

"First, let me say that Corny is one of the most honest, upstanding young men I know, so his listening to your conversation was in no way intentional," Merriwether says, shaping the air with his hands. "But that's not the issue here. The issue is: Did you have a secret source that could have enhanced our coverage of Blumberg's slaying and the sanitation bombing? Or that could have prevented them from happening in the first place?"

I sigh and look at Cornelius disgustedly. Is there any hope for you, brother?

"Tom, we went over this Saturday with Barbara Rubenstein."

Merriwether clicks his ballpoint pen and begins taking notes. That's an ominous sign.

"What did this person or persons say to you?"

I pause, knowing full well Cornelius has probably conveyed hearing something about "blood on your hands." Merriwether puts down his notepad and steeples his fingers under his chin. Anyone familiar with body language knows steepled fingers are a sign the speaker feels superior to his or her audience.

"The person told me that a group of white supremacists was out to kill Sheldon Blumberg," I say slowly.

Swiveling his head on that narrow little neck, Merriwether looks at Cornelius incredulously.

"Let me see if I have this down correctly," Merriwether says. "You knew that someone was going to shoot Blumberg, but you didn't tell the newspaper that you work for. Why?"

I sigh loudly. "Tom, I already told you I called Barbara Rubenstein on Friday, when the caller gave me a date for Blumberg's killing. And I called Homicide Detective Phil Gardner right before I called Barbara."

"How long have you been talking to this person?"

"A few days. The first call was last week, er, Wednesday. The day I went into the hospital."

"And you failed to notify us immediately. Why?"

"Tom, I don't have to tell you pranksters and crackpots call this paper all the time with outrageous claims and statements. Until I got a concrete date, I figured this was just another crazy. While we're on the subject, the same caller is threatening to blow up the NAACP."

Merriwether ignores that. "How many times has this individual called you?"

"Probably about four or five times," I respond, fidgeting in my seat.

"Did it ever occur to you to inform anybody about the phone calls?" Cornelius asks. I didn't see massuh give Toby permission to speak.

"I did inform someone," I reply indignantly. "I said that already."

Rising from his chair, Merriwether theatrically drops his pen and notepad.

"I've said this before," he says, head tilted upward, arms behind his back. "But we run a *news*paper here. We collect news. That's what we, or specifically you, do for a living. You have received critical details about the biggest Baltimore murder in twenty years and you share that information with the police instead of us! Who's paying your salary, us or them? Why are we bothering to pay you?"

When I look up at Merriwether's face, instead of anger there's euphoria. Beaming, he sits behind his desk and dials the phone.

"Hello. Yeah, hi, Gloria. Sure, I can hold, no problem." Cradling the receiver between head and shoulder, Merriwether furiously scribbles something on his notepad.

"Hi, I was just wondering if you could come to my office

for a second or two. Yes, I understand, but I think this will be worth your while. Yessir. Fine.''

About a minute passes before managing editor Walter Watkins rumbles into Merriwether's little shoebox office. Watkins has on a hot-pink shirt with the sleeves rolled up, his blue-and-red tie is loosened and the huge cigar in his mouth is lit and trailing smoke, in clear violation of the *Herald*'s anti-smoking policy.

"That budget meeting is in five minutes," he barks at Merriwether. "What's so important?" Walking behind Merriwether's desk, Watkins fishes through the trash can, finds an empty soda can and extinguishes his huge cigar. "I'm listening!"

"There's an additional twist to Shel's murder you haven't heard," Merriwether says in a dramatic whisper.

Watkins walks over to Merriwether's couch and sits down. As though snapping out of a trance, Watkins finally recognizes that Cornelius is also in the room. "Welcome to the club, young man," he booms, extending a beefy hand to Cornelius, who grasps it eagerly. "What's the twist, Tom?"

Watkins still hasn't seen me. Maybe I've actually become invisible—God knows I'm trying hard enough.

The *Herald*'s managing editor is ashen and slack-jawed before Merriwether is done with his incriminating tale.

When Merriwether finishes, Watkins ambles over from the couch and stands in front of my chair. "All this true, young man?" He doesn't wait for an answer. "I'm not saying you could have saved my friend's life," he says, holding his cigar like a pointer. He's so close I notice he has a slight tremor in his hand. "I don't know if that's the case. But if you could have saved him and did nothing, God help your soul."

With that Watkins jams his greenish-brown cigar between his teeth and walks out of Merriwether's office.

I've just lost a powerful ally in Watkins, putting me at the mercy of Merriwether and his new henchman. Cornelius hasn't been on the job twenty-four hours and has already torched me spectacularly.

The most damaging blow dealt to me in my five years at

the *Herald* has come at the hands of another black journalist.
Stunned, I walk back to my desk and replay the sorry episode
in my head.

Me and Cornelius could have talked the whole thing out.
But his knee-jerk reaction was to shuffle over to Merriwether
and immediately blow the whistle.

Personality conflicts are one thing, but Cornelius is messing with my livelihood, my ability to pay rent and feed and
clothe myself. With the exception of Merriwether, I can't
think of a single white editor who would have done what
Cornelius just did.

I impulsively compose a letter on my computer:

July 3

Phil Watkins
Managing Editor
Baltimore Herald

Dear Phil:
*It is with regret that I inform you of my intention to
resign from the* Herald's *editorial staff, effective July
19.*

Sincerely,
Darryl Billups

Hell, I can't quit. My father always preached that you
never quit a job before finding a new one. Plus there's no way
I'm leaving around the same time some kook is threatening to
blow up the NAACP. So I start erasing the letter to Watkins.
And who should materialize beside my desk when I finish
but Cornelius!

"What do you want *now?*"

He clears his throat nervously. "We never have been particularly good friends," he says in something of an under-
statement. "But I want you to know that I wasn't trying to
ambush you in Merriwether's office."

"It's a little late for that, Cornelius," I shoot back acidly.

"You're right that I don't like you, and I know you sure as hell don't like me. That's why you ran straight to Merriwether when you could have handled the entire thing yourself. But you're filled with self-hate . . ."

"Darryl, I handled that poorly, okay?" Cornelius says. "This management thing is new to me. I'm hoping that we can put aside our differences and that you'll help me to grow in this new job and to learn from my mistakes."

Now he wants me to help him look good in his new job??!! I nearly blurt, "Nigger, have you lost your mind?" in the middle of the *Baltimore Herald*'s newsroom. Good colored boys like Cornelius are one reason black men suffer disproportionately from hypertension—and have stunted life expectancies.

I just stare at him and he moves off in the direction of his desk, head slightly bowed. Starting to get worked up, I fire off e-mail messages to the other black reporters, detailing how Cornelius hung me out to dry.

Outraged, contemptuous e-mail responses come flashing back in a matter of minutes. Mad Dawg actually comes by my desk, demanding to confront Cornelius. I plead with him to chill, to lie low, but it's good to know my boy has my back.

Having vented, I'm ready to get down to the business of being a newspaper reporter.

My sanitation-bombing story is flawless, and I wind up on Page One again. Under ordinary circumstances I would be ecstatic, but today my pleasure is curtailed. Sure hope I have a job tomorrow.

Russell Tillman's pistachio-stained fingers barely touch his keyboard as he edits my story. He has no idea how glad I am to see him tonight. Merriwether, Cornelius and the dayside crew are gone.

"That wasn't a bad job," Tillman says after he edits my piece.

"Russell, can I speak with you confidentially?"

"Sure, no problem. Do you want to stay right here or go into the break room?"

It's 10 P.M. and the newsroom is empty, save for Russell, me and a janitor. We look around and laugh simultaneously.

"I may be speaking out of school here, but when you're around other editors, do you ever hear my name come up?"

Russell's expression darkens instantly. I'm onto something.

"Without getting into details, let's just say this—you need to watch yourself around here, okay?"

"Do I need to be worried about my job?"

"You need to be concerned about safeguarding it, yeah. And you definitely did not hear this from me, and I'll deny it if you repeat it, but you need to start keeping a diary of what happens around here. Good and bad. Sending out some résumés wouldn't be a bad idea, either."

A shiver snakes its way up my back. "Sounds pretty serious to me."

Russell merely nods. "Go home and get a good night's rest, kid. Darryl, for what it's worth, I think you're one of the best reporters here."

I'm so busy thinking about his warning that I nearly run a red light on my way home.

The smell of home cooking assails my nose when I open the door to my apartment, which is dark except for a stove light. Yolanda and Jamal are sacked out on the couch and a note is propped against a vase of flowers on the kitchen table:

> *Darryl:*
> *I wasn't sure if you had ate at work, so I left a couple*
> *of burgers for you in the frig. There's some fresh corn*
> *on the cob, too.*
>
> *Yolanda*

That was a nice gesture, but I don't see how I could microwave anything and not wake up Yolanda and her son. Anyway, I don't have much of an appetite tonight. I scribble, "Thanks, I really appreciate it. That was thoughtful," on her note.

Opening the fridge, I grab a cold beer, then head to my

room and shed my work clothes. I'm in dreamland before the beer is half finished. Actually, nightmareland is more like it, another horrible dream in which the threats to detonate a bomb at the NAACP are carried out. Scores of innocent black people are lying around bleeding or being carried out of the building in body bags. A good friend of mine who works at the NAACP is in the parking lot, slumped against his car. His head has been blown off by the force of the blast.

The vision is so vivid and so upsetting, I can't go back to sleep.

NINETEEN

MARK DILLARD AND ROBERT SIMMES COULDN'T UNDERSTAND why a lone black man with salt-and-pepper hair and shades was among the mourners at Harold Boyles's grave site.

"Who's the darkie?" Dillard asked Simmes, who was decked out in his only suit, an ill-fitting, light blue number webbed with wrinkles.

Simmes shrugged. "Got me."

Neither would have suspected Phil Gardner was a city homicide detective, nor would they have guessed that two other detectives were discreetly taking pictures of mourners from a nearby van. To say that the cops were aching to collar Dillard and Simmes, and that the urge grew exponentially each day, would be putting it lightly.

"Is it my imagination, or is that nigger staring at us?" Dillard muttered. "Must be one of those spooks Harry picked up garbage with."

"Maybe we need to send the sanitation department another present," Simmes whispered, grinning.

In fact, Gardner wasn't watching the remaining members of the *brotherhood* from behind his Foster Grants. He was monitoring with interest how Boyles's widow and her two children glared ominously whenever they looked at Dillard and Simmes. Doris Boyles's intuition told her that her husband's death was somehow linked to those men. She had never liked Dillard, not from the first. Plus, she was angry that neither Dillard nor Simmes had enough common sense or manners to offer condolences.

A tangle of unvoiced questions swirls around the death of any suicide victim, but there were more than the usual surrounding Harry Boyles's. Dillard, for one, suspected Boyles's death was really Jewish-sponsored murder meant to avenge Blumberg's slaying.

He didn't believe for a second that Boyles was weak-minded enough to kill himself, especially when there was so much critically important work yet to do. Harry had been in perfectly good spirits up to the point of planting the bomb that razed the sanitation building. In fact, if Harry were still around, he would take pride in what he'd accomplished, Dillard mused.

He would never forgive Doris Boyles for the insensitive way she'd broken the news of her husband's death. "Whatever crazy shit you had Harry involved in, he killed himself over it last night," she had screamed into the phone. "I hope you're happy now, you no-good motherfucker."

The odds of him having a comforting word for Doris Boyles matched the odds of him standing beside Harry's pewter-colored casket and delivering a stirring eulogy in Latin.

Members of what Dillard called the "Jew-dominated jackal press" were just outside the cemetery gates, hoping to get an interview or a picture. Dillard had noticed one of their black lackeys in an ivory compact with THE BALTIMORE HERALD—THE TRUTH IS THE LIGHT emblazoned on both sides.

Because of their distance from the proceedings, the media horde missed the grave-site showdown between Dillard and Mrs. Harry Boyles. While talking to Simmes, Dillard noticed an alarmed expression flash across the other man's face. Dillard turned to find Doris Boyles shaking a plump finger in his face as other family members, including her teenage son, struggled to restrain her.

"You piece of shit," she sobbed, eyes rolling back in her head. "This is all your fault, you evil bastard. Get the hell out of here NOW, before I kill you, *too*." With that she fell to her knees, imploring God to take her so she could join her "beautiful Harry."

Phil Gardner looked on impassively.

"I think you need to leave," a young, well-built man said firmly, laying a massive hand on Dillard's shoulder. The gargantuan school ring on the man's finger contained a stone that looked like a polished blue boulder.

Unafraid of the muscular stud, but not wishing to cause a scene or in any way dishonor his friend's memory, Dillard quietly did as he was told. "Come on, Bob, let's get outta here," he murmured disgustedly.

"What was that all about?" Simmes asked as he and his partner strolled past plaques and tombstones dedicated to the dearly departed. Strewn haphazardly on the neatly manicured grass were bouquets of sun-baked flowers.

"Harry is definitely in a better place," Dillard snorted as they trudged toward his Camaro. "He's finally escaped the clutches of evil Shamu. I never did like that fat bitch, especially the way she used to nag him all the time."

Simmes, his arm still in a sling to protect his broken collarbone, nodded. Most people would have been stunned to be ejected from a friend's funeral by the grieving widow. But the uncommon was becoming commonplace for Dillard and for Simmes. A modern-day Butch Cassidy and the Sundance Kid was how they viewed themselves. Fighting for a noble cause. A cause Dillard was increasingly willing to die for.

Boyles's death dabbed a little more cement on the bond between the remaining partners.

When they got into Dillard's Camaro, he started the engine and cranked up the volume on his favorite soft rock station. The idea was to defeat police listening devices Dillard was convinced were in his Chevrolet.

"Know that little surprise we delivered?" he asked, using their code for the sanitation pipe bomb.

"Of course."

"Think you could make one that would go off if somebody moved it?"

Simmes grinned. He had received two long-awaited mail-order books the previous day. The first, *Science of Revolutionary Warfare,* was written by German anarchist Johann Most. Along with such enlightening matters as how to make dynamite in your home, the book covered the use of fulminate of mercury and the manufacture of nitroglycerine, gun cotton and nitrogelatine.

The other new addition to Simmes's preferred reading list, the *Special Forces Demolition Training Handbook,* contained an introduction to demolitions, advanced techniques, insurgency demolitions and an introduction to arson and incendiarism.

Combined with the explosives experience he'd gained in the military, Simmes was confident of his ability to fill whatever explosive order Dillard had in mind.

"Shouldn't be a problem. What you got up your sleeve?"

"Well, I've been thinking about Harry a lot," Dillard shouted over the radio, defeating the purpose of having it on. "It wasn't right what those people on his job did to him. I think we need to finish teaching them a lesson."

"You don't think firebombing Harry's building and barbecuing one of his co-workers taught his old bosses a lesson? Whatcha want to do next, nuke them?" Simmes laughed. Dillard didn't appreciate the flippant, irreverent query. But Simmes was the only remaining member of the team, not to mention the ordnance expert.

"I have something in mind that should keep those affirmative-action butt wipes on their toes."

Could Simmes put a pipe bomb in a garbage can and rig it so that it exploded when picked up? Dillard wanted to know.

"Are you kiddin' me? Piece of cake. My only question is, why?"

"Every time someone from the eastern sanitation district picks up a trash can, I want them to think about Harry Boyles. That's why. How fast could you throw together something like that?"

Simmes began wriggling out of his suit jacket, remembering Dillard's aversion to air-conditioning. Whipping his tie from around his neck, he casually tossed it onto the backseat. As he gazed at the fast-disappearing white obelisks and tombstones of the cemetery where his friend was about to be interred, Simmes felt a surge of cold anger.

"I could do it tonight, two days tops. And I could make it more powerful than the one that blew up the sanitation building."

"Roger that. I say we get this show on the road. Whaddaya say?"

Simmes stroked his chin contemplatively and shifted in his seat, trying to better position himself in the flow of hot, humid air cascading through the window. Although not self-delusional like Dillard, Simmes knew he wasn't put on earth just to be a handyman. He'd had his share of bad breaks in life, but preferential treatment of minorities was also to blame.

"Let's do it," Simmes said, surprised at how forcefully the words shot from his throat.

The first booby-trapped garbage can was rigged in an alley behind a Broadway Street row house, not far from Johns Hopkins Hospital. A week had passed since the bombing of the sanitation department maintenance garage, on July 2nd. Working at 3 A.M. in the morning while Dillard stood watch, Simmes took about fifteen minutes to carefully position the bomb, cover it with newspaper, then replace the can lid.

Later that morning, sanitation worker Carl Jenkins came face-to-face with Simmes's handiwork. Lying in a hospital bed and coming out from under general anesthesia, Jenkins vaguely remembered picking up a garbage can, but nothing after that. The bomb had taken Jenkins's hearing, his left eye and arm, and a significant chunk of his right thigh.

To the twisted delight of Dillard and Simmes, Jenkins happened to be black.

An anonymous male caller told the *Herald* the bombing was linked to the Blumberg slaying and the sanitation building bombing. The sanitation department was being singled out, the caller said, because it "kept giving undeserving African savages promotions on a silver platter'' while turning its back on deserving white men and women.

A second garbage-can bomb went off, on Tuesday, July 10th, a day later behind a row house on Orleans Street. Sanitation worker Ray Connor wasn't as fortunate as Jenkins. Connor was killed by a piece of shrapnel that pierced his larynx, puncturing his jugular in the process. Two of Connor's co-workers were hospitalized for shrapnel injuries, burns and shock.

Possibly because of the banner headline the first call generated, an anonymous male caller again called the *Herald* with a message similar to the first one. The second call was left in the voice mail of reporter Darryl Billups, who wrote the first garbage-can bombing story.

The FBI, the Bureau of Alcohol, Tobacco and Firearms, and the city police launched a unified search to catch the bombers, a coordinated push the likes of which had never been witnessed in Baltimore.

Mayor Clifford Shaw seemed to be on every TV channel at once, looking stern and uncompromising. He pledged a $150,000 reward for information leading to the arrest and conviction of the bombers. That amount was increased to $250,000 the following day.

The offer didn't stave off a wildcat strike by city garbage haulers, burying Baltimore in stinking mountains of uncollected garbage that putrefied in the summer heat. Emergency arrangements were made with private trash haulers to service strategic locations such as hospitals, Orioles Park at Camden Yards, the National Aquarium and HarborPlace.

But for average people, those like Dillard and Simmes, trash pickup was nonexistent. Nor would the trash collectors' union budge, its members justifiably afraid for their lives. City residents with friends and relatives in surrounding counties had taken to driving their trash to the 'burbs. Hospital emergency rooms were routinely filled with patients who had burned their garbage and were hurt by detonating aerosol cans.

Adding to the misery, a hot, humid weather system stalled

over Baltimore. The horrific smell of rotting refuse and a ubiquitous brown haze of garbage smoke kept all but the hardiest souls indoors.

Police patrols regularly cruised the harbor throughout the night to cut down on the flotilla of trash bags found bobbing in the water every morning. Roach and insect infestations soared to record levels citywide, and the streets were overrun by monster rats that only a suicidal cat on PCP would confront.

Dillard and Simmes would have been shot on sight, dragged through streets, then burned in City Hall Plaza had anyone known they were behind the sanitation bombings. Their actions and their cause were vehemently denounced on editorial pages, TV programs and around water coolers across the state.

Like an attention-starved child who'll settle for negative strokes if positive ones aren't forthcoming, Dillard reveled in the notoriety he'd generated. Simmes, on the other hand, appeared unconcerned whether reaction to the bombings was positive or negative. Dillard admired the way Simmes sailed along with equanimity, totally unfazed by the consequences of his actions.

But it was painfully obvious to Dillard that the trash-can bombings had backfired. The entire city abhorred him and everything he stood for. Besides, garbage cans weren't his ultimate objective.

Given that Dillard had finally managed to steal several cases of dynamite from two construction sites, it wouldn't be long before the NAACP building was reduced to a shattered ruin.

TWENTY

THE MELODIC, SOOTHING SOUND OF AFRICAN DRUMS PULSATES rhythmically in my head, connecting with a zone some African-Americans are reluctant to acknowledge and even more embarrassed to admit exists. Specifically, that region in the brain's left hemisphere still in sync with the Motherland after all these centuries, the zone that sets shoulders swaying, feet tapping and broad lips smiling.

Gathered around an outdoor stage, a joyous crowd of about five hundred brothers and sisters watch as an African dance troop goes through its paces, performing numbers exotic and curiously familiar. Jamal is laughing and shaking his little hips in unison with Yolanda, who's happier at this moment than I've ever seen her.

And to think that I hadn't wanted to come to AFRAM, an annual African-American celebration of arts, crafts and food held in downtown Baltimore every year. To be more accurate, I wanted to come, but not with Yolanda and her son. There's always a bevy of unattached beauties—dragging Yolanda and Jamal along would only cramp my style. At least that was my initial thinking.

"Come on, Darryl, it'll be fun," Yolanda had urged sweetly. In fact, she suggested it twice before I hesitantly agreed to go along with the program. And that was only after she'd cornered me in a moment of weakness, after I'd worked a fourteen-hour day writing about how Major Clifford Shaw settled the garbage strike by having the National Guard and the police from Baltimore and four neighboring counties inspect each of the tens of thousands of trash cans on the city's streets and in its alleyways.

I was so tired when I got home last night that I don't remember what I said, although Yolanda claims I committed to AFRAM.

So here we are. I would rather have been bitten by a snaggletoothed mule than to have loaded Jamal and Yolanda in my car earlier this Sunday morning and driven them to AFRAM. But it's funny how affairs and events that you absolutely dread often turn out to be the most fun. You can add attending AFRAM with Yolanda and Jamal to that list.

When the two of them finish shimmying and clapping after one number, Yolanda picks up her boy and playfully swings him around twice. Jamal giggles contentedly as several women—and men—in the crowd smile approvingly. This mother-and-son combo has something that's magical.

"Want to try that out?" Yolanda suddenly asks, pointing to a stand about one hundred yards away where vendors are busily selling jerk chicken.

"No problem with me."

As we walk in the direction of the stand, which has a line of about fifteen customers, Jamal squirts between me and Yolanda and clutches his mama's hand. Before I can feel any annoyance over his preemptive move, he shyly grabs the pinkie of my right hand, marking the first time he's permitted any physical contact.

When I glance over at Yolanda, she looks as shocked as I do and shrugs.

I wasn't ready to play out a cute little family scene again, which is one reason I was reluctant to be here. I *like* being a bachelor and the freedom that comes with it.

So this Kodak moment, nuclear family stuff, is a little unsettling. And yeah, there's the usual peer-pressure component. My boys, my crew—what if they roll up on me right now?

Three foxes have glided into view in the minute or so since Jamal gripped my finger, one in cream-colored jeans that had to be painted on.

Groaning under my breath, I mutter, "Lawd, have mercy!"

My head begins swiveling reflexively before my brain sends an emergency override signal. Even though Yolanda ain't my significant other, she probably wouldn't appreciate my keen appreciation of feminine beauty. So I gulp, take a deep breath, sigh and keep my eyes straight ahead.

I knew this wasn't a good idea.

Unhooking my shades from the collar of my T-shirt, I slap them against the bridge of my nose. Gonna have to check out the honies in stealth mode.

Yolanda insists on paying for the jerk chicken and our soft drinks despite my protests.

"Hey, we invited you to come along." She laughs. "It won't make or break me. Please!"

Pride may goeth before a fall, but I admire that trait in her. Because I have a lot of self-pride, too, and would have done the same thing if the roles were reversed. Plus, it's refreshing to go out with a sister who isn't trying to get elbow-deep into my wallet.

We head toward an area where several wooden picnic tables and benches have been set out. A young couple get up from a table, Yolanda pulls Jamal's hand and they run like frisky colts before anyone else parks his buns.

When I arrive, Yolanda's not even breathing hard and cutting jerk chicken with a plastic fork and knife for Jamal. "Glad you could make it, old man," she says, those beautiful, intense eyes flashing under her unruly eyebrows. I could lean across the table and plant a kiss on her succulent gold lips. I'll bet they'd taste like—

"Hello!" Yolanda says, grinning as she waves her hand in my face. "Anybody home behind those sunglasses? Sure a bright and sunny day, isn't it?" Actually, it's overcast with a slight chance of rain.

"Just trying to guard against ultraviolet rays."

"Oh, please," Yolanda says, waving her hand dismissively. "You must be used to dealing with ditzy, simple sisters who don't know what time it is. You just looking at all these women out here. No biggie," she says, pausing and looking me dead in the eye, " 'cause if I see a fine brother, I'm gonna peep him, too."

Damn! Her bluntness has me at a loss for words. So I say nothing and just sit at the table with my mouth open.

"Eat your chicken." She grins. "And close your mouth before a fly buzzes in."

Double damn! All I can do is laugh and do as I'm told.

"Not much for beating around the bush, are you?" I observe after washing down a mouthful of jerk chicken with soda pop.

"Why bother? I mean, what's the point of playing games, pretending? It's just a waste of time, and if there's one thing I never have much of, it's time."

"I hear what you're saying," I interject, biting into a roll. "But it's also possible to be in such a big hurry that life passes you by."

"Gettin' philosophical on me, huh, brother? Or is that metaphysical?"

Expecting me to be surprised, she waits for my mouth to fly open again. But being the quick study that I am, I remain poker-faced. A brief, puzzled frown flashes across Yolanda's face.

At the next table, two rude brothers in their early twenties are ogling Yolanda obnoxiously, making little comments and giggling like punk-ass schoolgirls. Why do some brothers dis one another like that? Ignorance, lack of home training, what? At any rate, Yolanda ignores them and I follow suit, but they're definitely plucking my nerves.

"For all your bluster, you're really just a softie, a closet romantic," I tell Yolanda boldly. "And with someone as fine as you around, why would I want to look at other women?"

Yolanda's jaw goes slack this time. Didn't know who you were messin' with, didya?

"Close your mouth—"

"Before a fly buzzes in," Yolanda says, finishing my sentence and capping it with a smoldering, sensual look that could melt steel. It sure is melting me, putting a funny, warm sensation in my chest.

In the middle of all this, Jamal merrily chomps away, not the least interested in anything that doesn't resemble jerk chicken. His mother rubs his head, never taking her eyes off me the entire time.

"As soon as little man gets finished eating, let's find a stall selling books," I say with a calm that belies a heart flip-flopping all over my chest.

After Jamal gets his mouth wiped by Yolanda, off we go in search of black literature, with Jamal again walking between us and holding our hands. When we turn the corner of one row of stalls, who do we run right into but Boone! Shooting the breeze with two of his boys, he looks flabbergasted when he sees us, our hands joined.

Jamal starts bawling immediately and runs behind Yolanda. Boone looks at Yolanda first, a plaintive, hurt expression on his baboonlike face. Then he glares malevolently at me, before looking at Yolanda again.

"He hurt me, he hurt me," Jamal screams at the top of his voice in between yelps. We all stand there for a moment, suspended in time, with no one quite sure what to do. Finally I grab Yolanda by the arm and pull her in the opposite direction.

"Come on, let's go this way."

Boone says something to his boys and starts shadowing us, which makes Jamal scream even louder. Yolanda looks like she might start crying, too.

Heart thumping, throat dry, I peel off to find out what Boone wants.

"What's the problem?" I ask, trying hard to keep my tone civil.

"What's the problem? You out with my woman and my son, you punk bitch, and you askin' what's up? You don't look like no cousin to me."

I move quickly toward Boone and, startled, he throws up his guard. Stopping about three inches from his face, close enough that he can feel my breath, I put Boone straight about something.

"I got your punk bitch, motherfucker. You're bad when it comes to roughing up women and children, but I'll kick your goddamn ass right here in the middle of AFRAM. WHAT do you want?"

Two unarmed security guards materialize out of nowhere, not eager to see me and Boone put a damper on everyone's fun.

"What's up, fellas?"

"Me, this lady and her son are just minding our business, trying to have a good time, and he keeps following us," I say, shaking slightly and hoping Boone doesn't see it.

"Go away, Boone," Yolanda shouts. By now passersby are slowing down and stopping, curious to see what's going down. "We don't want to be with you, can't you see that?"

"I changed my life around, baby," he says in a pleading voice. "That old stuff I used to do, the drinking, all that stuff, it's in the past now. I just want to talk to you for five minutes. Can you give me five minutes? Please?"

"Will you leave us alone if I do?" Yolanda sobs, tears streaking down her beautiful cheekbones. "I don't mean to hurt your feelings, Boone, but you just bad news. If I talk to you, will you *please* leave us alone?"

I don't trust Boone. My sixth sense is screaming for Yolanda not to talk to him. I wouldn't put it past him to pull out a gun and play out some sick murder/suicide shit.

"Do you think this is a good idea, Yolanda?"

"If it helps him put closure on things, yes. Yes, I do. Can you watch Jamal for one minute, please? It won't take long."

She and Boone move about fifteen paces away and are immediately engaged in animated conversation. Yolanda keeps swiping at the air with frustrated gestures. Boone's arms are outstretched in the manner of someone begging.

As I watch all this, Jamal is crying and clinging to my leg. "Calm down, little man," I say soothingly, picking him up. "It's all right. Stop crying." He doesn't stop, but at least the tears are flowing a little slower than before.

''What's this all about?'' asks one of the security guards, a beefy, light-skinned brother with acne.

''The man's an asshole,'' I reply, momentarily forgetting about Jamal. ''His woman left him and he just can't deal with it.''

''Oh. From looking at her, I can see why he's upset. You steal her, my brother?''

''Naw, it's nothing like that.'' I start to explain, but stop. For one thing, it's none of his business. Plus, I have enough to worry about as I lug around a weeping Jamal and try to keep tabs on Yolanda and Boone.

''I hope you guys work it out.''

''Yeah, me, too. Thanks.''

Boone's defeated stance tells me he didn't hear what he'd hoped to as Yolanda walks away, looking battle-weary.

''Come here, baby,'' she says, grabbing for Jamal and holding him tight against her chest. ''I apologize for all this,'' she mumbles in my general direction, too embarrassed to look at me. ''Do you mind if we leave now? Boone can be unpredictable sometime.''

''So you're going to concede defeat and let him ruin your afternoon,'' I say, putting my hands on my hips and striking a defiant pose. ''Just like that?''

''Let me tell you somethin','' Yolanda says quietly. ''This ain't about male ego or drawing lines in the sand. This is *all about* what's best for my son. And what's best for me. If you want to stay, be my guest. I'm leaving.''

She knows this fool better than I do. Maybe it is a dumb macho thing, but I would prefer to stay instead of being run out of the joint. Boone smolders and glowers at the three of us as we walk past, headed for an exit.

It's deadly quiet during the ride home. No one says a word and I feel myself getting more annoyed with each passing moment of silence. Despite my warning, that clown has put a damper on the afternoon.

Jamal is fast asleep, with drool dribbling down the right side of his face, when we pull up to my apartment building. I try to help Yolanda lift him out of the backseat so she can avoid straining her back. But, ever the proud one, she insists on picking him up herself, as well as carrying a bag filled with toddler supplies.

I hold open the door to the foyer and Yolanda trudges past, looking sad and remorseful. I know the last thing in the world she would ever want is my sympathy, but I feel sorry for her anyway.

"So what do you have planned for the rest of the day?" I ask, jiggling my key in the lock to my door.

"Oh, I don't know," she says with forced chipperness. "I might take Jamal to Druid Hill Park, then put down a deposit on an apartment on Liberty Heights Avenue, then drive past my sister's house later on. Right now I'm just going to lay him on the couch so he can take a nap."

"Feel like talking about what happened at AFRAM?"

"Nooooo, not really." Yolanda cuts loose a snorting, bitter little laugh. "I'd like to wake up and find the whole thing was a nightmare."

"Wait here," I tell her after getting the lock open. She looks at me oddly, but says nothing.

Opening the door slowly, I turn off the burglar alarm and glance around my apartment to make sure nothing is amiss. Only then do I enter, checking all the windows to see if any have been opened. And I check every closet in the house—even look under my bed. I've done this ever since the Androgynous One called my house.

Walking to my answering machine, I hesitantly push the button to retrieve messages. But no one called while we were out. It's a relief these days to come home and not find a message on the machine.

Satisfied that everything's cool, I motion for Yolanda to come in with Jamal. She's standing in the doorway, staring at me like I've lost my ever-loving mind.

"What was that all about?" she asks warily, holding Jamal against her chest in a protective embrace. He continues to snore.

"Oh, nothing," I say, trying to sound unconcerned and lighthearted.

"Hey, I ain't stupid," Yolanda says, clearly annoyed. "I saw what you just did and I want to know why. If there's something going on that could hurt my son—or me—I want to know what it is."

"I've been getting some threats, okay?"

"What kind of threats? From women?" Yolanda's eyes narrow suspiciously.

I laugh. "No. I wish it were that simple. Look, it's related to work and I really don't want to get into it. But you and your son are safe here. If you weren't, I wouldn't have asked you in."

Looking unconvinced, Yolanda stares at me for about ten seconds before walking over to the couch to gently put Jamal down. She takes off his shoes, pulls a sheet over her son and kisses him.

There's an awkward silence when she stands up and turns to face me.

"Darryl?"

"Yeah?"

"Sorry again about what happened today. I didn't mean to drag you into a big pile of shit." Long sigh.

"First of all, if you apologize one more time, I'll scream," I say, laughing. "Second, you really don't have it that bad. You're an intelligent, attractive woman and you and your son have each other." I point toward the ceiling. "And you have a roof over your head."

"I know. I know all that. And I'm thankful for all of the things you mentioned. It's just that, well . . . oh, never mind."

Smiling, I look Yolanda in the eye. "Don't you just hate it when people do that?"

For the first time since the Boone encounter, she smiles. Nice to see those deep dimples again. "Yep, sure do. So sue me, 'cause I ain't perfect." Seeing me wince, she smiles and affects a veddy proper British accent. "What I mean, Mr. Daniel Webster, is that I'm not perfect. Like you."

"It's about time you recognized that. Well, I'm gonna get out of here and run some errands." My hand is outstretched and about to turn the doorknob when I hear that sexy voice again.

"Darryl."

"Yesssss, Miss Yolanda. What up?"

"Would you mind staying just a little while? I know this sounds silly, but I almost feel like Boone is in here, a monster hiding in a corner or under the bed or somethin'. Or maybe I should say manster? Whatever, it's making my skin crawl."

I start to say something smart, but if anyone can empathize with the way Yolanda feels, I can.

"Well, it's not like I had anything to do that was urgent," I reply with a shrug. "Want something to drink?"

Me and Yolanda sit at the kitchen table, sipping peach-flavored iced tea and speaking softly so we don't disturb Jamal. We talk about the sanitation bombings, Mayor Shaw's administration, life in general. As we talk, I contemplate whether or not to let her in on the phone calls and the Blumberg murder.

To my surprise, Yolanda loves the Baltimore Orioles and NBA basketball, like me. We make a tentative commitment to see some baseball one day, but I can't tell if she's serious or just making small talk.

"Thanks, Darryl, I'm feeling much better," she says abruptly. We've been chewing the fat for over an hour, but it seems like only a few minutes. "I hope I didn't hold you from anything important. We'll be out of your way soon."

"You're not in the way. And I enjoyed talking to you. I'm here to listen anytime you need to talk." That first comment was a bald-faced lie, because she and her son have definitely been in my way. But I really do enjoy talking to her. In fact, I wouldn't mind continuing. To be more accurate, I *need* to talk to someone about what I broach next.

"You asked me why I was looking around the apartment when I came in," I say quickly. "Well, I'm going to tell you."

When she learns the full extent of what's been weighing on my mind, Yolanda claps her hand to her mouth, her expression aghast.

"Oh, my God," she says quietly. "Aren't you afraid?"

"Well, yeah, as a matter of fact, I am. You saw what I did when I opened the door to my place."

"Have you told anyone about this, Darryl?"

"Yes, I called a police homicide detective I know, and I talked to the bomb squad."

"And what did they say?"

"They said there are threats against organizations like the NAACP all the time and there was nothing they could do unless they had something concrete. Besides, the target date was July eleventh and today is the fifteenth—maybe it was a bluff all along.

"Did you call the NAACP?"

"And tell them what? To watch every car, van or person who goes near their building?"

"No, Darryl, that ain't the point," Yolanda replies angrily. "They need to at least know a threat is out there. They need to know the people behind Blumberg have threatened them, too. If they capped Blumberg, do you think they would kill a whole bunch of black folks?"

"I'm sure the homicide detective I talked to alerted the NAACP," I protest feebly. "And I did try to call them, but I got an answering machine."

Jamal starts rustling on the couch. Yolanda immediately springs up and tends to her son, squeezing his feet into a pair of tiny tennis shoes and giving him iced tea from her glass. Soon she's headed out the door, having replenished her carrying bag with more baby juice and those wet wipe things full of baby soap.

"What time do you think you'll be back, so I can be here to let you in?" I still haven't given Yolanda a key to my apartment, nor do I intend to.

"Lessee," she says casually, stifling a yawn and glancing at her watch. "It's about two o'clock now. I'm guessing we'll be back around six-thirty or so. If you don't have any dinner plans, I can whip together something."

"Sounds like a winner to me," I say as I open the apartment door. "And don't hesitate to call if you run into a problem in the streets, if you know what I mean. Okay?"

"Thanks, Darryl," Yolanda says, sticking out her hand and shaking mine firmly. The move catches me totally by surprise. It's just, well, odd. Stiff and formal.

Now she is laughing, undoubtedly because I'm standing beside the door looking clueless. "I just really appreciate all you've done, that's all," she says, leaning over and giving me a peck on the cheek. "Come on, Jamal."

She heads out the door and gently pulls it shut.

Really baffled now, I look through the peephole and see her standing there, gazing at my door wistfully, before she and Jamal walk downstairs.

I gave up trying to understand female behavior a long time ago.

A wonderful sensation immediately floods over me. I'm back in *my* apartment again—alone. I strip off my T-shirt and shorts and uncharacteristically toss them in the middle of the floor. Liberation! I feel like running around buck naked, clicking my heels and urinating in strategic locations to mark my territory.

But frivolity quickly disappears, instantly forced out of my head by the letters NAACP.

I impulsively grab the telephone and dial the number for Directory Assistance.

"Could I have the number for the NAACP, please?"

The phone rings twice before it's answered. "You have reached the national headquarters of the NAACP," a recorded voice intones. "Our business hours are Monday through Friday, from nine A.M.—" Frowning, I hang up. It was silly to think a real live person would be there to answer the phone on a Sunday.

Shelving my decision to run errands, I revert back to Plan A, meaning I flick on the stereo, plop down in a reclining chair and pick up a magazine. Within five minutes the magazine flutters out of my hand onto the hardwood floor. I'm out like a light, and dreaming about you-know-who.

We're strolling along a beach where the sand is pink and

very fine. Yolanda has on an aquamarine dress she pulls up to her knees to keep it from getting wet as the surf foams over our bare feet and ankles.

In the water, a few yards off the beach, Boone is up to his neck in dark green seawater. Every time the surf comes in, the water momentarily submerges him, leaving him angrily gasping for air when the surf rolls out. Boone's yelling something at us, but can't seem to move—it's as though he's anchored to the ocean bed. Which doesn't bother me or Yolanda.

She suggests we walk to a secluded section of the beach to skinny-dip. But our reverie is interrupted by a booming explosion.

I awaken with a start, breathing fast and looking around my apartment. Boom, boom, boom. Someone is banging on my door.

"Hold on a minute."

I quickly gather up my clothing, dress and go to the door, rubbing my eyes.

It's Yolanda, her athletic body framed in the doorsill. Jamal is nowhere to be found.

"Where's Jamal?" I ask in the croaky voice of someone freshly awakened.

"He's at my sister's house. She's off from work next week and decided she wanted to keep her nephew for two or three days."

I calculate quickly. That means Jamal will be gone today—Sunday—as well as Monday and possibly Tuesday.

"Oh!" Yolanda is still standing in the doorway, gazing at me with her head tilted provocatively to the side. "I'm sorry, come in, come in. Instead of eating here tonight, would you like to go to HarborPlace for dinner?" I blurt impulsively.

"Definitely. It's been so long since I was out on the town, I can't even remember the last time."

"You just have to promise me that you'll leave your wallet behind. This evening is totally on me."

"Okay, you've twisted my arm hard enough. You da man."

Is that a fact? I take a quick shower while Yolanda watches TV. At least I thought that's what she was doing, but when I leave the bathroom, she's sitting on the edge of the couch, wearing a black leather miniskirt, a pale yellow blouse and yellow stockings on those long, shapely legs.

"Where did you dress? I ask, astonished by her rapid transformation and by the way her clothes complement her beauty.

"I went upstairs in the loft, in case you came out too soon," she says in a soft, demure way. The thought of going out with her excites me so much that I hurriedly throw on a blue banded-collar shirt, tan slacks and brown leather shoes in no time flat.

She's standing near the door, cradling her purse, when I exit my bedroom. "What took you so long?" she asks coquettishly. We both crack up and head out the door.

A full moon shines brightly against a crystalline black sky as we begin the most memorable night I've had in a long time. The last time I got this excited over a date was in junior high.

"I'm really glad we have an opportunity to go out before you and Jamal leave."

Yolanda looks at me and smiles radiantly.

"Does that mean you feel the same way?" I ask, teasing.

"I'm going out with you, right?" Yolanda says, looking at me like I just left an alien spaceship. "I think you're one of those people that has to put everything into words. Am I wrong?"

"That's kind of what I do for a living," I reply with a smile.

"All right, then. Describe what chocolate ice cream tastes like. Put that into words, Mr. Smarty-pants."

"You trying to say I talk too much?"

"No. Not at all. I love listening to you talk and I admire your way with words. I envy it, actually. I just think you put too much stock in the power of words. When it comes to some things, like describing emotions and sensations, words ain't all that."

We glide up to a stoplight as I ponder that. While we wait

there, two brothers who look like they've been fiending all day come lurching toward my car. They're sweating profusely, armed with bottles of window cleaner and jostling furiously to see who can attack my windshield first.

When they're about two paces from the car, I activate my windshield washers. "See, fellas," I say loudly out the window, "I've already got one." The crackheads glare as the light turns green and I slowly pull away.

"That wasn't very cool," Yolanda says quietly.

"What did you say?"

"I said, what you just did to those two brothers wasn't cool. If you want to be totally honest, it was kind of assholish."

Stunned, I shift my manual transmission from second to third, grinding the gears slightly and making a *graaaunch!* noise, something I never do. She's absolutely right, of course. I'm just surprised to be called on it. And surprised I did it, because that's not like me. Maybe I was just showing off.

"Well, they're not really providing goods or services," I reply testily. "Why should I pay them when my car has a windshield washer and a reservoir full of fluid?"

"That's not the point, Darryl," Yolanda says in the same quiet, nonjudgmental tone. "The point is that you stripped them of their dignity. I don't pay those guys, either, but you don't have to make somebody feel like shit when you turn them away. I know what kind of person you really are," she continues, "by what you've done for me and Jamal. That wasn't the real Darryl back there at the light."

"Guilty as charged . . . Mother Teresa."

"Not hardly." Yolanda laughs. "You'll find out what kind of girl I am," she adds mysteriously.

"That a threat?" I ask, smiling broadly. "Or a promise?"

"Just a statement of fact," she replies matter-of-factly.

Darryl, you got yourself a real live wire here. If nothing else, Yolanda is definitely keeping me on my toes.

As soon as we arrive at HarborPlace, I dig three dollars out of my wallet and buy a long-stemmed rose from a flower vendor. Yolanda nearly levitates off the ground out of sheer joy when I give a little bow, then hand her the rose. Never have three dollars given so much pleasure, or been spent so wisely.

An incongruous aroma wafts across the calm black water of the harbor. It's the smell of wood burning. It's coming from a brick-oven restaurant, Dolore's, that's practically on the water's edge. Dolore's is our destination.

As we stroll through the door we're greeted by a young white guy whose red hair is neatly tied into a ponytail. "Dinner for two?" he asks pleasantly, briefly admiring Yolanda. I nod and he runs the red eraser of his pencil over a seating chart.

Tonight must be my lucky night—without a reservation, I get a seat outside on the terrace, where Yolanda and I can watch people as they casually stroll along the promenade abutting the harbor. Blacks, whites, young, old, lovers, dog walkers and people walking alone amble by, all enjoying a beautiful summer night.

I can sense Yolanda looking at me.

"That's one of my favorite pastimes, too," she says, in sync with me as usual.

"People watching, you mean?"

"Yeah. Like that guy right there with chest hair like a gorilla and the garden-hose gold chain. Now, you know he probably has daughters older than that woman he's with!"

"What makes you so sure that's not his daughter?"

Yolanda gapes at me in disbelief. "Come on, Mr. Trained Observer. Women that age don't hold hands with their fathers. And fathers and daughters don't look into each other's eyes like that . . . unless something pretty freaky is up."

"Just testing you, checking out your powers of observation. You get an A. So why is he with that tender young thing?"

"Midlife crisis, trophy-mistress situation. He kicked his wrinkled, cellulite-queen ex-wife to the curb because she made him realize he's not nineteen anymore."

"I guess that's one way of looking at it," I say as a waitress heads toward our table. "Actually, he never got divorced. His wife is home watching Oprah on the VCR, waiting for him to get back from a business meeting. That's his hot little secretary, who works at his business. You can tell he's a self-made man, because executives don't generally dress that tackily. They tend to be conservative, bland.''

''Aren't you two a pretty couple!'' It's our waitress, a short, cute little sister with dreadlocks. A quick thought flashes through my head: Do I want someone wearing dreads handling my food? Whether it's dread particles or blond strands, I hate it when someone serves me food with hair in it.

''Thank you. I think we're a stunning pair, too,'' I answer slyly, looking over at Yolanda. She rolls her eyes and flashes those beautiful dimples.

''Would you like something from the bar before dinner?'' Even though Dolore's is bustling, absolutely packed, our waitress has a charming, relaxed manner, as though we're guests in her home instead of in one of the city's busiest restaurants.

I order white wine; Yolanda, a Long Island iced tea! My eyebrows flicker skyward, but I keep my mouth shut. Girlfriend ought to know what she can and can't handle by now. Wonder if Jamal's nickname is ''iced tea''?

''So if that's his secretary,'' Yolanda says as our waitress saunters off, ''why is he holding hands with her in public?''

''Because he lives and works in Annapolis.''

''Oh. Why did they come to Baltimore?''

''Because this is where his little love-nest apartment is. Plus, whipped cream is cheaper here, and he uses a lot of it when he's sucking it off her toes. Foot fetish, you know.''

''Darryl!''

Gotcha!

Light jazz/pop music floats from an outdoor speaker as Yolanda orders more iced tea, without alcohol this time, and cavatelli with pan-seared chicken sausage. I guess I'm in white-wine mode tonight, ordering another glass along with broccoli and chicken in white wine sauce.

Usually when a couple is on a first date, they avoid conversational lapses at all costs. Yolanda and I are already comfortable enough to be at ease with the ebb and flow of our conversation. When moments of silence arise, neither of us feel pressed to fill it with meaningless chitchat.

Unlike most sisters I know, Yolanda talks only when she has something interesting to say.

Maybe it's the wine, maybe it's Yolanda, maybe it's a combination. But I am light-headed and euphoric throughout dinner. The meal has a dreamlike quality to it, from the red neon lights reflecting off the harbor to the big fat silver moon that looks like a child's toy suspended from the ceiling.

Even the food at Dolore's tastes better than usual. I'm no great fan of Italian—Dolore's got the nod tonight more for its ambiance than for anything else. It would be a perfect evening . . . if not for the threat looming over the NAACP. I can see it from our table, sitting on the harbor's edge.

"What are you thinking about?" Yolanda asks brightly.

"Oh, nothing. Why?"

"Your face got so sad all of a sudden. And worried-looking."

"I was thinking what a shame it will be for this beautiful evening to come to an end." I don't like being evasive, but I really don't want to talk about the NAACP right now. Short of going over there and standing sentry, what can I do?

Looking at Yolanda, I'm tempted to grab her hand. It seems like such a natural thing to do, but I don't want the gesture to be misinterpreted. She might think I'm too forward. Or read too much into it. I'll bet her hand feels like velvet. Erring on the side of caution, I keep my mitts to myself.

"What are you thinking?" she asks again after catching me gazing pensively at the harbor.

"Just how nice all of this is," I answer, truthfully this time. "And how comfortable I feel with you. I feel like we've known each other for a long while."

"You gettin' mushy on me, slim?" Yolanda asks. The remark lets a little air out of my mellow, romantic mood.

"No, I'm not getting *mushy,* as you call it," I answer a tad defensively. "Scratch that last observation, okay?"

"Oh, shnap!" Yolanda says, laughing lightly. "Not a little

thin-skinned, are we? Don't be upset,'' she adds, suddenly serious. ''Because I feel comfortable with you, too. That surprises me—I wasn't expecting that.''

Nobody says anything for a while after that. We just work at finishing our meals and digest what's just been said. I could blow a kiss to Yolanda's sister, whoever she is. Yolanda must be reading my mind, because she excuses herself from the table to call her sister and check on Jamal.

She's smiling broadly when she returns. ''Jamal has already had a fight with her three-year-old daughter, scared the cat half to death and now he's sleep.''

''You miss him, don't you?''

''More than life itself,'' she answers dreamily. ''But sometimes,'' she says, snapping back to her present surroundings, ''Mama needs a little time to herself.''

We both turn down dessert and walk along the HarborPlace promenade after leaving Dolore's. Going nowhere in particular, we head in the general direction of the Maryland Science Center, a spotlight-lit building looming about two blocks away.

When we stop to gawk at an extravagant yacht moored in the harbor, I screw up my courage. As Yolanda admires the luxurious furniture in the yacht and speculates about the owner, I move toward her for a kiss.

To my horror she pulls away, leaving me puckered up and kissing air. ''Heeeey! What are you doing?''

''Sorry. I wasn't trying to scare you or anything,'' I reply, rattled. ''What did you think I was doing?''

''Well, if I didn't know better,'' Yolanda says with a mischievous grin, ''I would have sworn you were trying to do this.'' With that she slowly brings her lips to mine and aggressively pushes her sweet tongue into my mouth. I feel a charge race through my body as I return her kiss and pull her against me. I've encountered some aggressive and unpredictable women, but Yolanda takes the cake.

Taking in the shocked look on my face, Yolanda starts giggling. ''What's the matter? What did you think I was trying to do?''

"I thought you were trying to take advantage of me," I answer with mock indignation, then give her a hard kiss in the middle of the promenade, not caring who's watching. A group of black teenagers clap and cheer, causing both of us to blush.

"Let's go watch a video back at my place," I suggest disingenuously.

"That sounds like a good idea to me," Yolanda replies eagerly.

We hold hands all the way back to my apartment and exchange a kiss in the foyer that should have set off the smoke detector, but somehow didn't. After going to the bathroom to "freshen up," Yolanda glides into the kitchen, where I'm pouring two glasses of wine. Sneaking up on me, she starts peppering my neck and ears with kisses, flicking her tongue ever so briefly against my skin as she does so. It would be easier to stop Niagara Falls than to hold our passion in check any longer.

We leave a trail of shoes, undergarments, even earrings on the floor in our haste to my bedroom. And that's where the rushing stops. I want to slow things down, to savor what me and Yolanda are about to share.

Moving deliberately, I massage her scalp, moving my hands gently in a circular motion. Closing her eyes, Yolanda smiles contentedly. My touch assures her she's in the hands of someone who knows what he's doing and does it well.

After lingering briefly over her temples, I land the lightest of kisses on each of Yolanda's earlobes, sending a slight shiver through her both times. When I knead the back of her neck, every vestige of tension flows from Yolanda's body.

I had intended to give her a full-body massage, but the mutual attraction is becoming too strong to ignore much longer. My tongue slides down the side of her neck, steadily moving south toward her firm breasts. Just before my tongue reaches an erect brown nipple, I stop briefly, then flick my tongue over it slowly.

"Darryl," Yolanda whispers. "Oh, m'God."

Yolanda's inner thighs are salty with sweat when I kiss

them, stopping at the edge of a lush forest whose border I bombard with kisses. Yolanda brings her hands behind her head and starts gently thrusting her hips. And flaring those nostrils.

Smoothly scooping a rubber from my nightstand, I start to put it on when Yolanda opens her eyes and snatches it out of my hands.

Pushing me down, she takes the rubber in her mouth and inhales, making the rubber inflate slightly into her mouth. Then she hovers over me and slowly encases me in rubber with her lips and tongue. After about a minute of that, I gently, but firmly, push her head away.

"We're not going to need that rubber in a second," I say, trying hard not to groan.

No one has ever brought me the ecstasy I shared with Yolanda, nor pleasured me with such imagination or vigor. So many times. In so many different sections of my apartment.

Sometime after five o'clock in the morning, we finally collapsed into a sweaty pile on my bed, damned near drained of body fluids.

When I wake up, it's noon and I have my arms around Yolanda, who's snoozing peacefully. If this is a dream, God, please don't let me wake up! I just stare at her beautiful face and body until her eyes open. Gazing around my unfamiliar bedroom, Yolanda tenses, then sees my face and smiles. And gives me a languid, sensuous kiss.

"You trying to start more trouble?"

"Yeah. As a matter of fact, I am. But it would be nice to get something to eat first. I'm starving."

"What was that all about last night? I mean—"

Yolanda gently places a finger against my lips. "Know what your problem is? You overanalyze everything. Ever try just going with the flow, instead of dissecting everything to death?"

We go with the flow the rest of Monday, after Yolanda calls in sick.

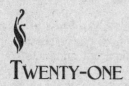

TWENTY-ONE

"SAW YOU DOWN AT HARBORPLACE WITH THAT HONEY," MAD Dawg says, doing a ludicrous, pelvis-thrusting dance in front of my desk at the *Herald*. "Whazup, Mac Daddy?" That's followed by a quizzical head tilt, like he's some six-foot-four, dread-wearing owl.

I just chuckle. He's gonna have to work for the 411. Mad Dawg's timing couldn't have been better, because I've been sitting here stewing over the Androgynous One and the NAACP.

"Guess-you-just-got-it-like-that, huh?" Dawg says, punctuating every word with one of his little thrusts. Other reporters, nosy creatures that they are, begin to turn their heads in our direction.

"Come on, Dawg," I protest. "You know when they see two or more of us together, they call security. Stop acting the fool—it's still your world, squirrel. I'm just trying to get a little nut."

"Uh-uh," Dawg replies, shaking his head fiercely. "I'm only the deputy, adjutant, assistant man when you be sportin' babes like that. Whazup? Come clean!"

Dawg's eyes damn near pop out of his head when I explain how I met Yolanda, detail our living arrangement and tell him about the wild Sunday and Monday we just shared. I'm not the kiss-and-tell type, but I had to tell somebody about my incredible fortune.

Dawg starts bowing in front of me like I'm a deity.

"Please tell me, mighty one, how I may become more Darryl-like," Dawg says, unleashing that loud, Eddie Murphy laugh of his.

"Come on, man, chill. You know I don't like these folks bein' in my business."

"Yes, my lord. As you wish. But could you please tell your humble servant one thing before I take my leave?"

"What, Dawg? WHAT?" I avoid looking at Dawg, because if I make eye contact with this fool, I'll be on the floor laughing my ass off. I can't afford that, since I know Tom Merriwether and Cornelius Lawrence probably write it down every time I so much as yawn.

"Does girlfriend have any sisters? 'Cause she's sho' nuff *fiiiiiine*. Hell, is her mama looking for anybody?"

I swivel around in my chair, turning my back to Dawg. "I gotta go to work, man. Leave me alone. You know they're laying for me."

In fact, someone must have sounded the two-black-males-in-the-newsroom alarm. Cornelius is suddenly beside my desk holding a stack of papers and frowning, no doubt fearing an overt display of Negroid behavior from me and Dawg.

"How are you doing, John?" Cornelius says crisply to Mad Dawg. He has consistently refused to recognize Dawg by the nickname every other black journalist knows him by.

"Not bad at all, Cornelius," Dawg responds, his diction exaggeratedly precise, his tone comically nasal. "And how might you be doing this fine afternoon, my good man? I trust everything is going along swimmingly? And that you are constantly on the lookout for stories that will inspire African-Americans and portray us positively?" Dawg is sneering by now.

"John, don't you have something to do over in sports?" Cornelius says curtly.

Dawg just shakes his head in a pitying way and walks off in that direction. I feel like screaming. "Take me with you!"

I really appreciate being left with a scowling, clearly agitated Cornelius, who happens to be my boss.

I turn and stare at my computer screen instead of at Cornelius, who has been trying to make nice ever since he waylaid me in Merriwether's office. I silently chide myself for always talking about sending out more résumés but never getting around to it.

"Darryl, I have something that you may find somewhat more challenging than the day-to-day shoot-'em-ups you've been covering." He plops a bunch of paperwork onto my desktop. "I want to detach you from the police beat for a week or two and give you an in-depth project you can really sink your teeth into."

When I look up, his expression is sincere, earnest.

"Really? What do you have in mind?" I respond unenthusiastically. Anything gift-wrapped by Cornelius can't be worth much. Anyway, I'm in the middle of the Blumberg murder, the sanitation-bombing investigation and a threat to bomb the NAACP, the biggest stories to hit the police beat in some time.

"We've been able to whip together some preliminary data from our library and from the police department showing an interesting correlation between police-brutality claims and the backgrounds of the alleged victims." He pauses to see if I'm following.

"Why can't Special Projects handle it?"

"They're already working on something else. Anyway, Darryl," Cornelius adds almost apologetically, "Merriwether wants you to do this."

In that instant I realize Cornelius is someone to be pitied, not despised.

"How soon were you planning to detach me from the cop beat to work on this?"

"In the interest of knocking this thing out quickly, we thought it would be a good idea to start as soon as possible. Like today."

Without realizing it, I'm out of my chair like a jack-in-the-box. "But I'm in the middle of covering two of the biggest stories I've had since I've been on this beat. The brutality study doesn't seem that time-sensitive. Why does it have to be done right now?''

I'm sure my reaction will be noted in my file, but I don't give a damn.

"Who will you put on the cop beat?" I splutter. "Who'll finish covering the stories I've paid dues the last five years to get?"

"R. Charles Covington."

"R. Charles??!!!" I'm getting loud now, hopping, burning mad. Cornelius has been on the job for two or three days and he's managed to push my buttons more effectively than Merriwether did in five years.

"R. Charles should be covering City Hall—aren't we in the middle of a mayoral election? How is he going to do that, goddammit, and cover my beat, too? Huh?" As I pose that question, it dawns on me that Merriwether and Cornelius have no intention of putting me back on police. This silly project is just an interim move until they determine which permanent hell best suits my uppity black ass.

Fortunately, the phone rings, because I feel like I'm about to go postal on Cornelius.

"Hello, Darryl." It's the Androgynous One, marking the first time we've talked since I chided her for wasting my time.

Pointing furiously at the phone, I plug in my microcassette player and start recording.

"Hello yourself. I see you're back, so you must want to help me put those guys behind bars. Am I right?"

"Yes," she answers without hesitation. "I want to see both of them in jail for what they've done."

Both of them? She's never given a precise indication exactly how many people were involved.

"I was hopin', prayin' the killing would stop after Blumberg. But they're both crazy. I never dreamed they would put bombs in garbage trucks and in peoples' trash. They practicing right now to blow up the NAACP. They'll do it, too, if nobody stops 'em."

"What are their names? Three people are dead; there's no reason for more to die. What are their names?" By now Cornelius, Merriwether and Walter Watkins are all arrayed around my desk. Cornelius fetches a notepad and starts writing questions for me to ask! A quick flick sends the notepad sliding across my desk and onto the floor.

"I want you to listen to me very carefully. Are you listening?"

"Yes, I am."

"I don't mean to be rude and I'm not trying to insult you. Please understand that. But we keep having these little conversations on the phone and people keep getting killed. It is time for this stuff to stop. So I have a proposition for you. Either you tell me who these maniacs are, or you agree to meet with me face-to-face, or you stop calling me. Your choice. Maybe you can live with blood on your hands. *I can't.* If a bomb goes off and kills a lot of innocent people inside the NAACP . . . let's do something to prevent that. What do you say?"

Watkins shoots me a thumbs-up.

This whole encounter has an air of unreality about it. Twenty feet away, people are chatting without a care in the world. The newsroom continues to hum along, an insular little universe lurching along to the rhythms of a daily news cycle.

Meanwhile, I'm sitting here frantically negotiating to save lives as my editors concoct ways to get me banished from the paper.

"He'll kill me if I do what you ask."

"Oh, as long as your hide is safe, to hell with everyone else. The whole city can get blown to hell as long as nothing happens to you."

For the first time, I sense anger on the other end of the phone line. "Yeah, that's easy for you to say. You'll be safe no matter what—and get a good story, too. Don't try psychology on me."

Totally exasperated, I sigh loudly.

"What's a good time to meet with you?" she asks in a little-girl voice.

"How about in an hour? At the base of the Washington Monument on Charles Street?"

"That's too open," she says with a mocking laugh. "Every cop in the city could take my picture—or take a shot at me. I'll meet you at the Peabody Conservatory, in their library. Do you know where it is?"

"I can find it."

"Darryl, if you're really interested in saving lives, don't call the cops. I can help you catch these guys, but you have to hold off on the police."

I can't commit to that in good conscience, so I say nothing. "What will you be wearing?" I ask, hoping the abrupt segue derails her train of thought. It does.

"I'll have on a tan skirt and a green blouse. And sunglasses."

"Good. And I'll be wearing—"

"I knows exactly what you look like, Darryl. See you at four o'clock." Click.

"She's going to meet me!" I shout triumphantly to no one in particular. "The anonymous caller is going to meet me!"

"Where?" Merriwether and Cornelius ask in unison. I eye them suspiciously and make a snap decision not to include them in the loop. For all I know, they may want her to meet with R. Charles, the blond-haired boy wonder. "At the Peabody," I respond, conveniently omitting the library part.

"Call Photo," Cornelius says to me, barking orders like he's Patton. "We need to have a photographer on each side of the building, including the parking garage."

"First of all, we never have that many photographers to spare," Watkins says gently.

"That's right, Cornelius," Merriwether chimes in.

"Plus, we would never risk spooking a once-in-a-lifetime source by having a bunch of photographers lurking around," Watkins continues. I listen to this with minimal interest.

Finally I'm going to meet with the person who's turned my summer, and my life to an extent, on its ear. How does she know what I look like?

I excitedly place a call to homicide detective Phil Gardner, half expecting to find him out of the office. For once he's actually in police headquarters. "Deep Throat has agreed to meet with me," I sing into the phone.

"Really! Where?"

I swivel around in my chair and see that Merriwether, Cornelius and Watkins have moved to Watkins's office and are deep in conversation.

"Before I tell you, you have to promise not to have a whole bunch of cops all over the place."

"No problem, Darryl."

"I'm meeting her at the Peabody Conservatory's library. You know where that is?"

"Sure do. What time?"

"Four o'clock."

"Great. I'll be there, sitting at a table, reading a book. I might have one other person there, no more, who will secretly be taking pictures. You won't even see him."

For me, calling Gardner served two purposes. It goes without saying that I want to help catch whoever is behind these crazy, homicidal acts. But in case the Androgynous One is trying to lure me into a trap, it will be nice to have police at the scene.

As I walk out of the newsroom, the twin-headed Tom Merriwether/Cornelius Lawrence monster—the dreaded Tomelius—glumly watches my departure. As I head to my destiny, whatever it is, there's an uncomfortable knot of tension in my stomach.

The library on the campus of the Peabody Conservatory is a place where time has ground to a halt. Visitors are uniformly awestruck by the spectacular Victorian interior architecture, skylights that soothingly illuminate a spacious central reading area filled with dark wood, beautifully bound books dating back centuries, and six tiers of cast-iron balconies that stretch to the ceiling six stories above. It's like stepping off the streets of Baltimore and traveling back to nineteenth-century Europe.

There's a reassuring sight at the first reading table: Detective Phil Gardner has on dark green shades and never looks up from a book as I walk by. He probably doesn't even know what the title is, I think as I pretend to ignore him, too. Where's his trademark shoulder harness? Must be wearing an ankle-holster handgun.

Glancing up at the balconies, I wonder where his partner is. Is he or she holding a camera? Or a gun for dealing with this woman if things get out of hand?

Damn, it's quiet in here. Colder than the North Pole, too. The air conditioner is pumping out an Arctic air mass to safeguard priceless tomes.

Walking softly in my rubber-soled shoes and listening to the sound of my fast-beating heart, I see a diminutive woman sitting at the end of the library, at the very last table. She's conspicuous by an absence of reading material—and by the way her head keeps swiveling with the regularity of a light-house beacon. She couldn't be more obvious if she tried.

This paranoid waif had me searching my apartment for bogeymen and flinching when the phone rang in my office or at home? When she sees me she starts waving madly, as if I can't see her as plain as day. She and Gardner are the only people seated inside this massive place. She crooks a bony finger in my direction, triggering irritation that yields to déjà vu. That gesture seems awfully familiar, I think as I continue walking toward her.

That thought quickly vanishes, replaced by thoughts of self-preservation. Don't get comfortable, Darryl. Don't get complacent just because you're dealing with a petite little thing. If she makes any sudden moves, if she so much as scratches her ass too fast, just dive between one of these stacks of books. Then pray that Gardner and whoever is with him can take her out before she gets to you.

Miss Vicky! That's it!

I triumphantly extend my hand and give her a firm hand-shake. This is the woman I ran into at police headquarters, the one charged with prostitution for her misdeeds with the black radio executive. This is who has been driving me mad, sending me on lengthy guilt trips and causing me more than a few sleepless nights.

"Hi, Darryl, do you remember me?" she asks, theatrically taking off her glasses to reveal the mother of all black eyes. A one-eyed jack, she peers at me out of her one good orb. The bad eye is swollen shut, so she must have taken that shot recently.

"I sure do. We met at police headquarters a few weeks ago. I didn't write about you because you were so worried about your boyfriend. Miss Vicky, right?"

"Uh-huh. Victoria Ambrose."

Reaching into my pants pocket, I pull out my microcassette recorder, which I lay gently on the table and turn on. A glowing red light signifies the machine is recording. I yank out my notepad and a pen.

Ambrose looks appreciably older than she did a few weeks ago, more haggard. Her choppers are still pretty and white, but now one of the front teeth is chipped.

The sass and spunk that sparkled from her during our first encounter are notably absent. In their place are weariness and resignation. As well as the mien of someone scared shitless. That makes two of us.

"Why did you wait so long to meet with me?"

Tears immediately well in Ambrose's eyes. Tilting her chin toward the ceiling, she sweeps her mouse-colored brown hair back with her hands in an anguished gesture. I hope she doesn't turn on the waterworks, because we have business to take care of.

"Ever get involved in sumpin' that just flew outta control, that just took off and went where you never thought it would? So fast you ain't realize what was happenin'?"

"No," I answer, handing her a folded yellow paper napkin from a fast-food restaurant. "Not really."

"You lucky, then. 'Cause I . . ." The dreaded tears start tinkling from the corners of her eyes, sparkling in the sunlight and splattering onto her blouse. Please, lady, just tell me what I need to know so I can be on my way. Slam, bam, thank you, ma'am. You should be able to appreciate that.

"Your boyfriend do this to you?" I ask, pointing toward her black eye, which she hurriedly hides behind shades. "This is who you were trying to protect?" I continue, not waiting for an answer. I'm willing to bet he's one of the bombers and she's ready to drop a dime on him after getting roughed up. Better strike now, while she's mad and still hurting.

"You ain't bring no cops, did you?" Ambrose says, halfway rising out of her chair as though preparing to bolt. A remnant of the old defiance.

"We've already been through that," I reply harshly. "And I don't have any more time for fiddle-fucking around, either." It amazes me how docile and compliant she is after that.

"One of these maniacs is your boyfriend, isn't he?"

"I wouldn't call him no mani—"

"Whatever."

"He was just a john and things grew from there. He's . . ." Ambrose rolls her head slowly from side to side, flexing her neck. "I'm not sure what Mark is to me. He ain't a bad man, really, just a little mixed up."

I can't believe Ambrose is sitting here calmly making excuses for this turd as if he's caused a minor fender-bender instead of being responsible for people's deaths.

"What was that name again?"

"Mark. Mark Dillard. He lives at 4503 Baker Street," she says, neatly anticipating my next query.

"Who's his partner?"

Gardner lets out a cough that rattles around the cavernous library. A signal of some sort?

"Bob, uh, Robert. Last name is Simmes. Dunno where he lives—it's in South Baltimore somewhere. Other guy working with 'em was Harry Boyles. But he killed himself after they put a pipe bomb in that garbage truck." All this recited in the monotone of someone going over a lunch menu.

"Which of them shot Blumberg?"

"Mark did that. He hates Jews," Ambrose says, pausing and blushing furiously. "And blacks. That's why he can't never know 'bout that trick I turned."

"And who was responsible for the garbage-can bombings?" I look down at the notes I've been scribbling. "Was that Dillard and Simmes?"

"Yeah, they was the ones."

"So let me get this straight. They've killed three people, right?"

Ambrose actually begins counting on her fingers! Out of the corner of my eye I see Gardner still hunched over his book, ostensibly as engrossed as when I walked in the door.

"Noooo. Um, it's really four. There was an undercover cop, some guy named Brown, who came over to Mark's house. They killed him in the house, then burned up his body in an incinerator."

"Lemme get this straight. Was this a Baltimore city cop? They've killed a Baltimore city cop, in addition to their other victims? How do you know all this?" A hell of a headache is starting to take root behind my left eyeball. "How have you been getting this information?"

"Mark tells me at night when he gets drunk and we fu— make love."

"Is there some way we can stop his NAACP bombing plan?"

"Nope, I don't think so; it's too late for that now." Ambrose takes off her shades again and fixes me with a spacey one-eyed stare.

"What do you mean? What the hell are you talking about? If you tell me where they're hiding and where they keep their explosives, we can stop them, can't we? What do you mean?"

Ambrose coolly slips her shades back on and reclines in her chair. Folding her arms behind her head, she then crosses her legs, causing her skirt to creep. She has a disgusted expression on her face, as though I'm a cretin for not having figured things out.

"Two days ago Mark stole three cases of dynamite from some construction sites he was workin' at," she says, looking off into space and talking in that creepy monotone. "He and

Simmes should be on their way to the NAACP right now in a stolen flower-delivery van. It's yellow.''

My chair goes bouncing across the floor as I stagger backward, bumping into the table directly behind me. Startled, Gardner jumps up from his seat at the other end of the room, tugging fiercely at his pants leg as he retrieves his handgun from its ankle holster.

"Where are they coming from?" I scream at the top of my lungs.

Ambrose shakes her head and shrugs.

"The NAACP bombing is on *RIGHT NOW,*" I yell at Gardner, who puts his fingers to his lips and emits a piercing whistle that prompts three uniformed and plainclothes officers to magically appear. So much for his "single partner" pledge.

"Oh, my God, oh, my God, oh, my God," I chant frantically as I run full speed through the lobby and burst out of the library and onto the street. Gardner is right behind me. I feel someone grab my shirt while I'm in mid-stride, then slowly wrestle me to the grass.

"THINK!" Gardner says, looking wild-eyed and hyperventilating as much as I am. "We can't afford panic. We need a plan."

"Don't you have a radio in your car?" I yell at Gardner as though he's standing in the next block. "Can't we call the bomb squad?"

"Not enough time for that," he answers, getting up quickly. "How are they going to get the bomb there?"

"They're in a yellow van," I answer breathlessly. "A stolen florist's van."

"Let's go!" Gardner says, already running full stride and motioning for me to follow. "My car is around the corner." On the way we encounter a well-dressed, middle-aged brother with a cellular phone in one hand, a briefcase in the other. Shouting "I need that!" I snatch the phone from him and send him sprawling, legs akimbo. Documents go flying everywhere.

Clutching his knee, he begins to bless me out and starts

yelling for the police. I don't hear a single word of it, nor do I remember getting to Gardner's police car and hopping in. I just know that one minute we're running, the next Gardner is driving and putting an alert on the radio for a yellow florist's van headed in the direction of downtown and the NAACP building.

"Get some traffic units down to the NAACP to block off the driveway," he shouts grimly into the radio.

As he does this, I start dialing on my newly procured cell phone. "Hello, I need the number for the NAACP. Please HURRY!"

The operator swiftly patches me through. "You have reached the national headquarters for the National Association for the Advancement of Colored People," a cheery electronic voice intones. "In order to better assist you, please choose from the following options . . ."

"Oh, shit, shit, shit!" I pound my fist furiously on Gardner's dashboard, waiting for a live person to come on the line. I'm oblivious to the fact that Gardner's dash light and siren are going like gangbusters, or that he's weaving through traffic like Mario Andretti as we wend our way toward the NAACP's national headquarters.

"Good afternoon, NAACP. Please hold."

"No, WAIT!" Muzak comes across the line.

"Merciful God in heaven, please make someone pick up this line," I plead in a quivering voice.

"NAACP. How may I direct your call?"

"You need to evacuate your building! Two terrorists are headed there right now with a truck full of dynamite, and a lot of people are going to get hurt if you don't get everybody out NOW."

"I'm going to put you through to Security. Please hold."

"NO!"

Click, click. The sound of a call being routed to a different line. Clapping my hand against my forehead, I groan and roll my eyes.

"Hello, NAACP Security." The voice of a bored-sounding brother.

"Listen carefully, man. My name is Darryl Billups and I'm a reporter with the *Baltimore Herald*. Two clowns are headed to your building to blow up a van filled with dynamite. It's a yellow van, a florist van. You need to evacuate the building right now, or a lot of people will get hurt. These are the same guys responsible for the sanitation bombings."

"What did you say your name was again?" he asks suspiciously.

"JESUS H. CHRIST! Did you hear a damn thing I said? My name is Darryl, but that's not important. A terrorist is on his way there in a van full of explosives. Start telling people to get the hell out of the building!" The last words tumble out in a hoarse rasp.

"Okay, if this is a real situation, what number are you calling from?"

Tears of frustration blur my vision "PLEASE stop asking questions and get those people out of there before they get blown to smithereens."

Click. The dumb motherfucker hangs up.

As we continue down St. Paul Street, a three-lane, one-way thoroughfare heading toward the inner harbor, Gardner narrowly misses a cabbie who must have seen our flashing light and heard our siren, but proceeds into the intersection anyway.

"If we see the van, can we at least shoot the tires out or something?"

Shaking his head vigorously, Gardner pulls around the cab, coming so close to a pedestrian that he nearly separates her from her green-and-gold shopping bag. I can almost count the freckles on her face, almost feel the horror emanating from her wide eyes.

"Against department regulations," he grunts.

"Then, goddammit, give *me* the gun so I can take a shot."

Gardner doesn't answer, but does lay his handgun between us on the seat. He pats the weapon before something in the distance catches his eye.

"What's that ahead?" he asks in a strained voice as we pull up to a traffic light. "Look up there, two stoplights ahead of us. *Please* tell me that's not a yellow Nelson's Florist van.''

Squinting hard, I look in the general area where he's pointing. It's four-thirty and rush hour is starting to rev up, so the vehicle he's talking about is partially obscured by traffic and by pedestrians crossing the street. Opening the door, I stand on the doorsill and cup my hands around my eyes.

In the left lane, three lights from the signal where you make a left to the five-story NAACP office complex looming in the distance, sits a yellow florist's van, plain as day. It's stopped in the middle of the block.

I'm trembling when I return to my seat. "It's a Nelson's van," I hear myself say in a hollow voice. "That doesn't mean that's our van, though." I add, trying to sound hopeful.

Neck veins bulging, Gardner switches off his siren and starts mashing the horn. We're stuck in the middle lane, three cars back from the light. The lead car gets the message and carefully eases out into the intersection, prompting fist shaking and horn blowing from oncoming traffic. Fortunately, the vehicles with the green light are going only about ten miles per hour, so the car makes it across safely.

But the red economy sedan directly in front of us presents a different picture. Not only won't its teenage driver move, but he flips us the finger. Growling as he scoops the gun off the seat, Gardner races out the door. Before he reaches the driver's window, the teenager squeals across the intersection, deftly weaving through vehicles like an NFL running back. As Gardner wriggles behind the wheel again, a disturbing sight unfolds in the distance.

Stretching about a mile into the distance, six traffic lights flick from red to green, a perfectly synchronized wave that begins with the light farthest away and slowly makes its way to the light nearest us.

Overhead, I hear the racket of a city police helicopter that's coming behind us at maximum speed, seemingly at rooftop level.

Turning his siren back on and blaring the horn, Gardner swings over to the left lane.

Ahead, a figure jumps out of the van, races through the surrounding sea of gridlocked cars and disappears from view.

"Suspect running south from Light Street along Pratt Street," Gardner snarls into the radio. Instantaneously, I hear a different pitch from the police helicopter as it turns to track the suspect from above. Gardner and I face each other at the same instant, thinking the selfsame thought: God, please don't let this van blow up.

I fight a strong urge to leave Gardner's car and make a dash across St. Paul Street myself. Self-preservation is a powerful instinct. But I keep my butt glued to the seat. And my eyes on the yellow van that's now a block and a half away. Out of nowhere comes a tremendous blast that causes pedestrians and motorists alike to jerk their heads toward the source.

Hearts fluttering, sphincters tight enough to bend steel bars, Gardner and I both hit our heads on the roof. But it's just a hellacious backfire from a beat-up flatbed hauling a load of scrap metal. It sure galvanizes Gardner into action.

"Listen up," he bellows, hopping out of the ear and holding up his police badge. "A vehicle ahead of us may contain a terrorist bomb. Please exit your vehicles and move back this way," he orders, pointing behind us. The request results in astonished gawking and a few motorists who point in our direction and laughingly nudge each other.

Gardner's response is to scamper onto the roof of a low-slung sports car stuck in traffic beside us, raise his gun to the sky like a starter's pistol and fire off three rounds in quick succession. Pow, pow, pow! As the last shell casing tinkles to the pavement, bedlam reigns in downtown Baltimore. Screaming and falling over cars, curbs, newspaper boxes and one another, startled commuters quickly turn an entire block of St. Paul Street into an impromptu track meet, then a vast used-car lot. A queer-sounding polyglot of music and conversation fills the air. Practically everyone who fled left his keys in the ignition, doors open and stereos on.

However, my focus is on the yellow van, still a block and a half away. As the vehicles around it start trickling forward, its brake lights suddenly flash on and a hand reaches out to shut the open driver's door.

I start galloping along the sidewalk, past scores of hastily abandoned cars until I find one with no traffic idling in front of it. The late-model Cadillac's engine is still running when I scoot behind the wheel. A half second later, Gardner comes sprawling through the passenger-side door, huffing and puffing.

The rear tires howl in protest as I gun the engine and squirt up St. Paul, flashing through the intersection toward the yellow van. Don't ask me how or why, but I notice the Cadillac is an absolute pigsty, with banana peels and other crud on the floor.

Now there's about half a block separating us and the van, which is shielded by a phalanx of cars as it inches toward the next light. The van's progress is momentarily blocked by vehicles whose drivers have inconsiderately stopped in the intersection. The logjam dissolves far too quickly and easily, though, making it possible for the florist's van and whoever's driving to creep through the intersection.

Two more to go.

Now traffic is starting to flow smoothly, without the herky-jerky stop-and-go of a few moments earlier. There's no traffic whatsoever behind me—the fleet of abandoned cars has neatly cordoned off St. Paul Street.

Directly beside the van, two rambunctious boys roughhouse in a black hatchback as they repeatedly bounce a blue Nerf ball off the windows, driving their harried mom to distraction. Jamal flashes through my mind for the briefest instant, and I'm suddenly keenly aware of how incongruously normal everything seems.

I'm operating without forethought or premeditation, just adrenaline-fueled single-mindedness. I have no time to ponder or formulate; I just have to keep the yellow truck away from the five-story brick building on the left at all costs.

And now the truck is moving through another intersection, free and easy as you please.

One more light to go.

Just when it seems the van will make the final intersection, turn left, cross the street and cruise up the NAACP's semicircle driveway unimpeded, the orange DO NOT WALK sign starts flashing in the crosswalk and the traffic light quickly flicks yellow, then red. No one follows the florist's van into the left-turn lane, allowing me to ease in right behind it.

The Cadillac's wheels haven't even stopped turning, so how is it that Gardner's sprinting up to the van's passenger window, gun drawn and shouting directives? Firecrackers pop and Gardner is moving jerkily, stumbling and falling awkwardly between a Harley-Davidson and a transit bus.

Another sound pierces my consciousness, some cursing and frantic gibberish about not being ready to die. The voice sounds remarkably like mine.

Now the van is running the red light, scattering pedestrians who were calmly walking across the street a second earlier, only to find a yellow van bearing down on them and displaying no sign of stopping. A baby carriage cartwheels lazily through the air where the van has just been, shedding baby bottles and disposable diapers. But fortunately, no infant, which was in its mother's arms.

Fishtailing and laying rubber, I follow, jockeying to get between the van and a circular driveway about fifty yards down the road and to the right. Thanks to the Cadillac's big V-8, it's not much of a drag race. I drive half on the sidewalk and half in the street before catching the van about fifteen feet in front of the driveway.

As long as I live, I'll never forget the sight of the van's driver when I finally pull alongside his vehicle. The fury and determination streaming from his pale eyes are frightening to behold. It must be the last thing homicide victims see in the eyes of their murderers. A police car, lights flashing, blocks the NAACP's driveway. An officer is crouched behind it, pointing something our way. A white splotch appears on my windshield, followed by another before I realize what's happening. I'm getting fired on!

About thirty more yards up the road are concrete barriers, a walking path for pedestrians directly behind that and the sun-speckled water of the Inner Harbor, which is filled with sailboats.

The van crunches into my left fender as its driver tries desperately to turn into the driveway. But the Cadillac's mass allows me to force the van to the left, past the driveway and the police car, across a gently sloping, landscaped hill in front of the NAACP. We're doing about forty-five miles per hour, uprooting petunias, azaleas, spruce and throwing up rooster tails of brown soil.

As we fly over a small crest, I see the harbor looming directly ahead, then a metal light pole with a concrete base right in my path. There's a tremendous jolt, the *pfffft-whoooosh!* of an air bag before the horizon goes topsy-turvy. Deposited on the ceiling of the car, I hear—no, I feel—an ungodly roar that makes my vision quake and my ears ring. Then there's a dark cloud, a brief rain shower and a sound that's alien to me: *tink . . . tink . . . tink-tink-tink-tink-tink . . . tink.* Shrapnel plummeting from the sky.

I never saw it, but I'm told the van got airborne after I hit the light pole, narrowly missing a couple strolling along the pedestrian walkway beside the harbor and holding hands. Rotating in midair, it splashed on its side into the harbor, six feet below the promenade. The cataclysmic explosion sent a cloud of black smoke and a geyser of white water towering over the harbor, and unleashed a storm of shrapnel that for a split second put white-water rapids in downtown Baltimore's Harbor.

Inverted legs pump furiously past me on both sides of the upside-down Cadillac. Wriggling out the driver's window, I run toward the harbor, where at least twelve people are lying on the promenade, all bleeding profusely. As everyone heads in the direction of the explosion, I walk the opposite way, toward the shops of HarborPlace.

There's splashing in the water that doesn't sound like water hitting a promenade mooring. Getting down on my hands and knees and peering under the side of the promenade, I see the driver of the van, frantically slapping at the water with his left arm. His right arm is missing from the elbow down, and his head and face are a mass of oozing lacerations.

Shouting "Police! Police!" I untie a line from a boat docked on the promenade, tie it around a life buoy and toss it into the water. The driver grabs it with his remaining hand and holds on as I pull him out of the water, an incredible display of strength for someone with his injuries.

Surrounded by a rapidly growing puddle of water and blood, the man pants rapidly, unable to catch his breath.

"Are you Mark Dillard?"

He nods and motions for me to come nearer, as though he has something to tell me. As Gardner sprints in our direction, I bend my head over to hear what Dillard has to say. He reaches up with his only arm, grabs my neck and starts choking me for all he's worth.

Enraged, I stand, pulling Dillard up with me, and we go crashing into a nearby flower kiosk, knocking it over. Then I just start throwing punches, hitting him repeatedly in the head and staining my hands with his blood before Gardner drags me off.

"Darryl, Darryl, stop."

Gasping, I look first at Gardner, then at Dillard, whose breathing is shallow.

"I thought you were dead," I gasp to Gardner.

"What you saw was one fast-ass brother dodging bullets," he replies, grinning. "Lemme help you up.

"Call an ambulance," he tells a uniformed cop arriving on the scene with a portable radio.

Pulling Dillard's good arm behind his back, Gardner pulls out his revolver and places it against Dillard's wet head.

When the paramedics arrive, Gardner reholsters his weapon and disgustedly wipes blood and seawater on his pants leg.

"Say, chief," he says, grinning, "ever give any thought to a law enforcement career?"

EPILOGUE

MARK DILLARD TURNED OUT TO BE ONE RESILIENT NEO-NAZI. The coward has yet to stand trial for the Inner Harbor bombing, which resulted in thirty-one people going to city hospitals. Fortunately, the most serious injuries were cuts caused by shrapnel and punctured eardrums.

With a big assist from the police helicopter, officers were able to catch Bob Simmes as he tried to blend in with rush-hour commuters on their way down to the Charles Street subway station. Simmes's trial will be separate from Dillard's.

Victoria Ambrose, on the other hand, is being held in an undisclosed federal holding facility. Emotions are still running high in Baltimore over Blumberg's death and over the sanitation bombings, so Ambrose's whereabouts are being kept secret for her own safety. Ditto Dillard and Simmes.

About fifty shops and businesses had their windows blown out by the explosion, which police say was caused by about three hundred pounds of dynamite stolen from two Harford County construction sites.

You wouldn't believe some of the phone calls I got after the botched NAACP bombing. Most good, a few sickeningly hateful.

I can hardly believe it, but I'm a big-time celeb now. Not surprisingly, the botched July seventeenth bombing attempt made international headlines. My own mother has taken to calling me Celebrity Man, with an ear-to-ear smile plastered across her saintly face. The first couple of times she did it triggered a warm, gratifying rush, but now I sort of wish she'd stop. I love making her proud, but it's getting a little embarrassing.

People I've known forever are treating me differently, even my boy Mad Dawg. Nobody's genuflecting or kissing my ring, mind you. It's more subtle than that. And maybe it's my imagination, but from some folks I detect an undercurrent of jealousy. Whatever.

Acquaintances who were never terribly friendly in high school or college or at work suddenly feel compelled to track me down and chat me up like we're long-lost friends. This celebrity business is sure some strange stuff. It felt good for about the first two or three days. But I'm starting to dislike the changes it takes other people through.

'Cause I'm still the same ol' Darryl Billups. Just a little older. And a lot wiser.

If I were the big hero, the decisive man of action so many people think I am, Sheldon Blumberg wouldn't have gotten killed. And the carnage that followed his death probably would have been nixed, too. That's what I honestly believe deep down and it bothers me.

Yolanda says I'm too hard on myself. So does Phil Gardner. I don't know, maybe it's a Catholic thing, maybe I'm always on the lookout for guilt to latch onto. I don't think so, though.

In the meantime, strangers have been approaching me in supermarkets and stores and shaking my hand. If I were to capitalize on all the free-drink offers that have come my way, I could stay blitzed twenty-four, seven, three sixty-five. And women! One came on to me that was sho' nuff Da Bomb! She pulled her brazen seductress routine right in Yolanda's face.

These ladies—these people—don't know me. They're transfixed by an image, an aura created by the media. I have a whole new respect for the power of my industry.

Thankfully, it's a fickle beast. I'm merely the flavor of the week and will get kicked to the curb in a little while, which is cool with me.

Along those lines, I called *The Washington Post* yesterday. The editor I spoke with, a self-impressed Negro if there ever was one, personally called me back. This after having sat on my résumé for three months without bothering to let me know he received it.

Everybody in America who's granted fifteen minutes of fame seems to cash in, and I hate to sound mercenary, but I have bills to pay. Hell, I'm still whittling away at student loans taken out a decade ago.

I already have one firm job offer, from a local TV station that wants to brag that Darryl Billups works there as an investigative reporter. I'm going to give it some hard thought, but I doubt that I'll accept the position. TV reporters rarely have the luxury of immersing themselves in stories the way print journalists do. Plus, I'd have to buy a whole new wardrobe, worry about getting haircuts, put on makeup . . . I don't think so.

Oh, yeah, did I mention that I quit the *Herald?* Sure did. Right after the television station's offer.

If they come back with a better offer, though, I'm all ears. Because despite the Tom Merriwethers and the Cornelius Lawrences, I really do like the newspaper business. There's something about the cut and thrust of daily journalism that gives me a rush no other profession could probably offer. Plus I still have a lot of career goals—maybe I'm a dreamer, but I still want to run a paper one day.

Right now, though, the game plan is to go somewhere that has no phones, televisions or newspapers and veg out for a week. Or two. It would be ideal if Yolanda could join me.

No two ways about it—girlfriend's got my nose open. I want her to be my lady and I want to help her raise Jamal. She may even be *the one* who finally gets me to jump the broom. We'll see.

Of this much I am certain: Whatever I wind up doing, it's been a helluva ride thus far. And I'm eagerly anticipating the future.

Read on for a brief preview of
HIDDEN IN PLAIN VIEW
Blair S. Walker's thrilling new
Darryl Billups mystery
A May 1999 Avon Books Hardcover

HIDDEN IN PLAIN VIEW

WHEN IT COMES TO SPREADING A FOG OF TEMPORARY INSANITY inside the male brain, few things rival sex. But this time it's my girlfriend's sister who's lost her mind—that's the only explanation I have for the ridiculous proposition she just whispered in my ear.

"What's the matter, Darryl Billups, you frigid? Imagine that shit, a frigid brother! Now that's got to be a damned first!" LaToya laughs easily as she tightens her grip on my tie. Her other hand has a death grip on my behind.

Smiling sweetly, LaToya pulls me toward her and smacks her lips. It's at this point I realize that this simple child might not be joking. This is my punishment for those times I've glanced at LaToya and idly wondered what her shapely pelvis would feel like wriggling under mine.

From the next room comes the sound of rustling bedsheets. LaToya's twin sister, Yolanda—my girlfriend and potential fiancé—is still asleep. In our apartment!

"Look, LaToya, this isn't funny. I don't know what you're trying to prove, but you need to chill," I say in a low voice. "I know you don't want me to call your sister!" Grabbing at her wrists, I pull her hands away and step back.

Arching her unkempt eyebrows, LaToya lets out a snorting laugh. "Go ahead, call her ass," she says with a contemptuous wave. "See if I care. Because me and Sis share *everything.*"

I'm halfway tempted to call her bluff and wake Yolanda. But nothing but major-league unpleasantness would flow from that move. And blood is still thicker than water—I don't want to stack LaToya's word against mine. Anyway, LaToya will be out of here and back in Houston in a few days.

It's amazing how two children from the same family, identical twins at that, could be so different. Yolanda has her adventuresome side, but for the most part she's prudent, sensible, responsible. I guess she has to be with a three-year-old son.

But LaToya is the original wild child, someone who dangles over the precipice regularly, just to see if she can pull herself back at the last second. Our little encounter isn't about her finding me irresistible. It's about danger. The only thing that surprises me is that she would contemplate stabbing her own flesh and blood just for an adrenaline rush.

The more I learn about you, Sistergirl, the more you scare me.

Before I'd even met LaToya I suspected she had a loose screw, just from listening to Yolanda talk about her. Now, there's no doubt in my mind.

"Don't judge me," she murmurs, reading my mind. "*Try* me!"

I find this so preposterous, so utterly outrageous that I can't help myself—I begin to laugh. Loud, too, so Yolanda will get out of bed and see what the commotion is all about.

I hear more rustling and sure enough here comes my sweetie, rounding the corner barefoot, wearing one of my T-shirts and rubbing her eyes. It always freaks me out when Yolanda and her twin are in the same room together. They make a classic before-and-after shot. Pre- and post-sanity, that is.

Yolanda is my baby, as beautiful a sister as God ever put on the planet. When you love someone they automatically become attractive to you, but Yolanda was always the epitome of fine, with her auburn cold waves, high cheekbones and awesome full lips, before I even knew her name.

LaToya looks like Yolanda, too . . . on acid. She has the same lithe, willowy frame and long legs. Even the same semi-husky voice. And Yolanda's face, only framed by platinum-blond hair about a tenth of an inch long. Fuzz, really. Each of her ears has been spindled, folded and mutilated with six earrings apiece, and a nose ring juts out of her flared left nostril.

Top that off with another one sprouting from her right eyebrow, and a third in her tongue, and you have a classic beauty—camouflaged by industrial-grade peroxide and several pounds of metal. Why, LaToya, why?

She proudly informed me and Yolanda that she even had her clitoris pierced. We'll have to take her word on that one.

"Hey baby, hey Sis. What's so funny?" Yolanda asks, frowning. She can be one evil sistah first thing in the morning. Especially when a bunch of foolishness has awakened her at 9 A.M. on her day off.

I walk over and plant a kiss on my woman's forehead, followed by a hug. I was afraid that life with her and Jamal would grow old pretty fast. But a few months into our big experiment, I'm finding that it's not such a bad arrangement, not bad at all.

"Nothing's funny. LaToya was just telling me one her little jokes before I left for work."

"Really?" Yolanda walks into the kitchen and opens the refrigerator door, yawning. "What was it?"

"Nothin'," LaToya spits out. "Just a little something about an impotent brother. But I couldn't remember the punch line."

"Oh, really?" Yolanda emerges from the refrigerator with a bottle of milk and a bemused expression. "Don't pay my sister no attention, baby," Yolanda says in a sleepy voice. "Not much she won't say or do for shock value."

"So I gathered. Well, I'm gonna leave her here to work her charm on you."

"Okay, babe. Be careful, okay?"

LaToya stands with her arms crossed, watching us disdainfully. "Excuse me while I barf. This 'Leave It to Beaver/Cosby Show" shit is a little more than I can take." She grins, rummaging through her black rupsack for a cigarette. Neither me nor Yolanda smoke, which is another reason I'll be glad to see LaToya go.

Standing on tiptoe, Yolanda snags a box of cereal from the cupboard, then comes to where I'm standing and gives me another hug. "Don't pay LaToya any attention, she's just jealous. She wants to move beyond meaningless one-night stands, but doesn't know how."

LaToya throws back her head in mock dismay. "Chile, if anybody's jealous of anybody around here, it's you," she purrs. " 'Cause my kitty is *wiiild*—it's too damn much for one man. It cannot be domesticated."

I laugh uneasily, eager to head to the *Baltimore Herald* so I can get away from Yolanda's touched-in-the-head sibling. Things are a little too intense around here for me.

"Hey, see you guys later," I say, adjusting my tie. "I'm in the wind. And, LaToya . . . why don't you tell Yolanda your joke? Maybe she can help you finish it."

Chuckling, I close the door to our apartment and walked outside to my little black Japanese coupe that's at one hundred thousand miles and counting. I shake my head all the way to work, thinking about my encounter with LaToya. Thank you, LaToya, for livening up my morning.

But your bold ass will definitely be on a plane headed to Houston come Saturday. You best believe that.

Mysteries with a touch
of the mystical
by

JAMES D. DOSS

Embarrassed

THE SHAMAN LAUGHS
72690-4/$5.99 US/$7.99 Can

THE SHAMAN SINGS
72496-0/$5.99 US/$7.99 Can

THE SHAMAN'S BONES
79029-7/$5.99 US/$7.99 Can

And in hardcover

THE SHAMAN'S GAME
97425-8/$22.00 US/$29.00 Can